The Port Fee

A
Storm Ketchum
Adventure

by

Garrett Dennis

TBD
Port
Starbird
NY
PRESS

This book is a work of fiction. Common Sense For Cape Point (CSFCP), the Kinnakeet Boatyard, HatterasMann Realty, the Sea Dog Scuba Center, the Outer Banks Monitor, Tibbleson Construction, and all named modern-day characters are fictitious. Other characters, businesses and organizations, locales, scientific and religious references, and historical figures and events are real, but may be used fictitiously.

THE PORT FEE
Storm Ketchum Adventure #3
ISBN: 978-1533281869 (1533281866)

To my daughter, still my favorite Critter.

The Outer Banks

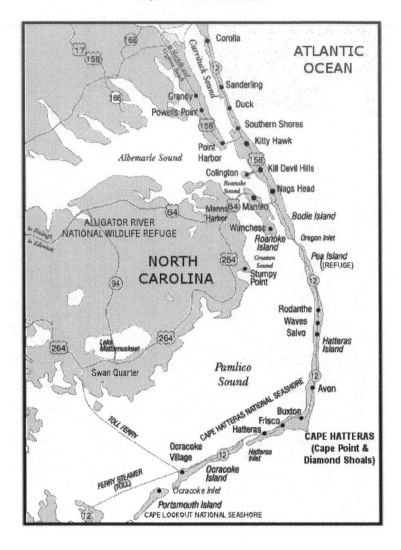

~ One ~

He was an old man who never fished alone, and he'd gone eighty-four days with no hint of trouble on the horizon.

*B*ut, once again, that was about to change. Ketch had always liked to think he wasn't the type to seek out trouble – but the fact was, it seemed to be somehow attracted to him these days more often than not, like a moth drawn to a light. Being nipped by the sleuthing bug as he'd been last summer probably didn't help. He used to be better at minding his own business before that. But then, he was no longer alone as he'd pretty much been not that long ago.

"Did you hear that?" Suzanne called to Ketch. "Did someone scream?"

"What?" Ketch, who'd been lulled by the soothing sound of the mild Atlantic breakers while packing away the drone he'd gotten for Christmas, looked up. "What's that you say?"

Suzanne stowed the keeper she'd been examining in her shell bag and briskly strode to where Ketch knelt with the drone case and his canvas backpack. "I thought I heard someone scream. It sounded like Sally. Oh, there they are," she said, swiping aside a blond lock that had blown across her face and shielding her eyes against the bright early June sun. She pointed toward two small figures racing toward them now on the hard-packed sand above the surf line. Ketch quickly finished his job, zipped the pack, and got to his feet.

"Papa, Papa!" Bean entreated as he approached. Though Ketch could see that his eyes were wide, he didn't appear to be in full panic mode. Nonetheless, the boy quickly hid himself behind Ketch's legs and grabbed on to them, seemingly for dear life.

Sally, who'd been a step or two behind him, did the same with Suzanne. Unlike Bean, she was crying. "Mama!" she sobbed.

"Sally, what on earth is the matter?" Suzanne asked, turning and kneeling before the girl. "Are you okay? Did someone get hurt?" She glanced up at Ketch, her voice pitching higher. "Is he all right?"

Ketch extricated himself from the boy's embrace and squatted before him. "Bean, what is it?" he calmly inquired.

"Zombies!" the children chorused.

"There's two zombies crawlin' in the water," Bean said, pointing to a spot somewhere farther up the beach. He said no more, apparently feeling that was adequate explanation.

"What?" Suzanne sputtered.

Ketch stood and looked, but he couldn't see anything. He and Suzanne had allowed the kids to range pretty far ahead, though, so that didn't surprise him. But the youngsters had never been out of their line of sight, and they'd had Henry to chaperone them.

"They sneaked up on us! They want to turn us into guts!" Sally cried.

"Maybe they saw some seaweed," Ketch said, "or maybe some odd-shaped pieces of driftwood."

"That's right, it was probably something like that. Kids, there are no such things as zombies. They're just make-believe," Suzanne reassured the youngsters. "Where did you hear about zombies, anyway? You don't let them watch scary shows at your place, do you?" she asked Ketch.

"Just *Scooby Doo* now and then," Ketch answered, "but that's a cartoon. Who knows what they hear in school, though?" he added, a little defensively. "Here comes Henry. Maybe he'll know what happened."

Henry, jogging as best he could while carrying the shell bags and nets the little ones had abandoned in their hasty retreat, reached them then. "I checked it out," he said, dropping his burdens onto the sand. "They saw somethin', all right. Mister Ketchum, I think you should come with me. Mama, you should stay here with Bean and Sally."

Henry was keeping his wits about him as usual, Ketch thought. And still insisting on calling him 'mister' and 'sir' despite the close friendship that had developed between them over the past year. He'd never known the boy to be disrespectful of his elders, and once again Ketch was impressed by his maturity. He was thirteen now, but strangers would think him older, especially if they dived or boated with him, or if they had occasion to avail themselves of the budding landscaping service the enterprising lad was now operating in his spare time.

Granted, he'd perhaps had to grow up a little faster than some since his largely absentee big-shot father had taken the next logical step and jettisoned the rest of the family altogether last fall, but he'd been wiser than his years even before that. Ketch hoped Bean would turn out half as well.

"You have to stay here," said youngster was now in the process of informing Henry's sister Sally. "But I'm seven, so I can go."

"I'm *almost* seven!" she protested, no longer crying.

Bean shook his head. "You're only six."

"Well, I'm fifty-nine, and I want both of you to stay here," Ketch said, inwardly amused at the difference kids thought a single year could make. But then again, he himself had undergone somewhat of a sea change in the past year, hadn't he? "Bean, since you're seven, I need you to make sure nothing happens to the ladies, okay? And watch my backpack, and please don't fool with the drone. I got some good aerial pictures today, and I don't want to lose them." Not that it would be the end of the world if he did lose them, or even if the boy broke the drone. The things of Man were less important to him now than they'd once been.

"Okay," Bean grudgingly acquiesced. Truth be told, he didn't look all that eager to return to the scene anyway, Ketch thought. He was probably just showing off for Sally.

Bean and Sally had become fast friends and they were together almost constantly in their free time, at either Suzanne's rental cottage on the canal or Ketch's nearby houseboat. Despite Bean's natural interest in the drone Ketch had been toying with, and indeed any sort of gadget in general, Ketch wasn't really surprised that beachcombing with Sally had taken precedence this afternoon.

"You might want to bring your radio," Henry suggested. Ketch raised his eyebrows, but didn't ask why. He wordlessly retrieved it from his backpack and the two of them set off, Henry leading the way.

With Ketch's close-cropped salt-and-pepper beard and sun-bleached attire, and the tarp hat he habitually wore when on the beach or at sea, the barefooted pair might have evoked thoughts of Hemingway's Old Man and his boy in a casual passerby. But there was no one else in sight in any direction along the strand this afternoon, neither on land nor on the water.

That would be unusual in most parts of North Carolina's Outer Banks, the chain of long, slender barrier islands that ran along the coast as much as thirty miles out to sea. But Portsmouth Island was no longer inhabited and could only be reached by boat, and the ATV tours run by the Austins out of Ocracoke typically didn't extend this far south – if there'd even been any tours today. It was still early in the season and it wasn't a weekend. Ketch knew there were a few surf fishermen and campers around somewhere, but he hadn't seen anyone in town this morning other than a couple of the Park Service folks quietly going about their business.

"See that driftwood stickin' up over there?" Henry said. "I put that there to mark the spot."

Now that they were close to the marker, Ketch could see what the problem was, and why the young ones had gotten spooked. Bloated, discolored, and decomposing bodies, almost unidentifiable as human, could do that to you.

"Looks to me like a couple of divers musta got themselves into some kinda trouble," Henry remarked.

"Yes, and it didn't just happen today," Ketch observed, standing before the two carcasses slowly washing back and forth in the shallow surge below the water's edge. Though their wetsuits were torn and tattered in places, they were still recognizable as such, and one was still wearing a frazzled buoyancy compensator. It looked like an obsolete old horseshoe collar model, the kind one had to orally inflate. Ketch had used one of those when he'd gotten certified way back when, but he hadn't seen one since. Both victims were still wearing fins, but the rest of their presumed gear was missing – no masks, snorkels, tanks, gauges, or weights.

Ketch noticed it was high tide. "I should drag them out of the water so they don't go back out when the tide changes," he said. "Do you want to raise the Coast Guard?"

Henry swallowed hard and shook his head. "I'll help you, sir. They might be too heavy for one person."

Ketch nodded at the boy and said, "Here, take this." He handed Henry the bandanna he always carried in a back pocket. "Wrap it around your nose and mouth." Ketch himself had long ago become inured to the smell of death in the animal rooms at the pharmaceutical company where he'd done research before he retired. "And try not to touch any exposed skin."

They managed to relocate the bodies without further defiling them, though even Ketch's stomach did in fact lurch a bit at one point. Then Ketch tuned the handheld marine radio he'd carried with him from the boat to VHF channel 16, the general-use maritime frequency, while Henry vigorously rinsed his hands in the seawater a little farther down the beach.

Surprisingly, it was possible to get a cell signal here and there on the island, but it wasn't guaranteed to be available when and where one needed it. Also, he wanted to conserve his phone's battery since he had no way to charge it on the island, so he was glad he'd brought the radio along. He was also glad he'd opted for one with integrated GPS, since it would be hard to pinpoint the position of the bodies otherwise. The small brown mile markers posted along the shoreline might not be of much help to a ship at sea.

Now if he could reach someone... He knew the Coast Guard monitored this channel around the clock, but one disadvantage of the handheld radio was its limited range. But someone else with a radio within a few miles could relay the call if necessary. That turned out to not be a problem today, though.

"They have a cutter nearby. I gave them our position. They said they'd be here shortly," Ketch told Henry when the boy had finished washing up.

"Okay. So what should we do now, sir? Should we all stay here? I could take Bean and Sally back to our cabin if you want."

"Thank you, Henry, but the kids might enjoy seeing the Coasties in action. Let's see how long it takes for whatever they need to do. If it gets too late, you can take them back."

They left the bodies where they were and walked back down the beach to rejoin Suzanne and the kids.

"Are they zombies?" Bean called out as they approached. "Did you get bited?" Ketch thought the boy looked genuinely worried.

"They're not zombies, and no one got *bitten*," Ketch said. "There are no such things, remember?

They're just some unlucky people."

"They don't look like people," Sally said.

"Are they dead?" Bean asked, his voice on the shrill side. "Is that what dead people look like?"

"It's a couple of drowned divers," Ketch said in answer to a quizzical look from Suzanne. Bean hadn't been the one who'd found his mother and Ketch knew he hadn't been allowed to attend the funeral, so the boy's question was probably a legitimate one. But he figured it was best to table it for the time being. "I called the Coast Guard."

"Wow!" Bean exclaimed. "Will they have choppers?" he asked, probably recalling scenes of derring-do from some TV show or other. Better if he focuses on that than on what dead people look like, Ketch thought.

"No, they're coming in a boat. Let's go sit by that dune and get out of some of this wind, and I'll tell you the whole story."

When they were settled on their towels, Suzanne gave the kids each a snack from her bag. Ketch did most of the talking, with Suzanne interjecting a kid-friendly explanation now and then. Probably to prevent him from getting too graphic, Ketch assumed – which he might have tended to do, having a scientific bent as he did.

Henry's backpack was insulated and held the water bottles. He opened it and gave everyone one. As they were drinking, a small Coast Guard cutter steamed into view, 'small' being a relative term. Thanks to the Captain, Ketch knew a Coast Guard cutter was at least sixty-five feet long by definition. It looked like they were readying an inflatable to come ashore in. Ketch stood up and started waving.

"I'd better go show them where to land," he said. "Henry, you can come with me. The rest of you stay here for now."

"Can I go too?" Bean asked. Suzanne tried to take hold of his arm when he started to get up, but he shook her off. "I wanna go!"

The inflatable was being lowered into the water now. Ketch could see the boy was enthralled by the activity, but he didn't want the little fellow getting underfoot.

"Not right now, Bean. You can see fine from here. Sit down and stay put."

The boy did as he was told and sat back down, but Ketch could tell he wasn't happy about it. Ketch felt bad about that, but he didn't relent. Though he didn't deny the boy much, this was a case of better safe than sorry.

Ketch and Henry walked back up to where they'd dragged the bodies. Ketch directed the Coasties in and summarized the situation for them after they'd disembarked. There wasn't that much to explain, really. As the men from the ship began bagging the bodies, Ketch felt a tug on his sleeve from behind.

"Uh, Mister Ketchum," Henry said.

When Ketch turned around, there was Bean. And farther back came Suzanne as well, sandals in hand and struggling to catch up as she simultaneously tried to run in the soft, shifting sand and discipline Sally, who trailed closely behind her.

"You turn around right now, young lady, and get back to that dune! I mean it!" Ketch heard Suzanne say. "I'm sorry, Ketch," she called. "He was too quick for me."

Ketch's first impulse was to berate the boy as well, and perhaps punish him somehow, but he held himself in check. His orphaned grandson was his only remaining link to his former family, and there was guilt as well as joy in that association. The boy had only been with Ketch for a few months, and Ketch hadn't even known he existed before that. He just needed some time.

He gazed sternly down at the now-apprehensive child, and then drew him closer and hugged him, to the boy's obvious surprise. "I love you, Benjamin," Ketch said, using the boy's given name for added effect, "but when I tell you to do something, you must obey me. I want you to be safe. If you disobey, you might not be safe. Do you understand?"

"Yes, Papa," Bean said. "I'm sorry, Papa."

"I know you are." Ketch gave him a couple of pats on the back and released him. "You go back to the dune with Sally and wait for us there. If you want to get a better look at what's going on, you can use the binoculars from my backpack."

The boy took off then. Ketch watched for a

moment to make sure he was headed in the right direction. Bean shortly caught up with Sally, and Ketch saw him begin to talk and gesticulate animatedly – about what he didn't know, as he couldn't make out the words over the wind and waves. The dead divers maybe, the Coasties, the binoculars, or something completely unrelated. It could be anything that came into their heads with kids that age.

"I'm sorry," Suzanne said again, standing beside Ketch now. "I should have paid more attention."

"That's okay. They can be slippery little devils when they want to be. No harm done."

Ketch, Suzanne, and Henry lingered a little while longer, watching the Coasties secure their gruesome cargo. Ketch looked back once and saw that Bean and Sally were where they were supposed to be, passing something back and forth between them. He couldn't tell what it was from here. When the inflatable had made it back through the surf, the three of them started heading back to their makeshift base at the dune.

"Oh shoot!" Suzanne exclaimed along the way. "I forgot my sandals." She stopped and looked back.

"I'll get them, you keep on," Ketch said. "We've left those two rascals alone long enough."

Ketch shuffled back up the beach. It didn't take him long to locate the sandals, but as he turned to go back a glint of light caught his eye. The tide was indeed starting to go out now, and a small object in the sand was reflecting a sunbeam as the water receded.

He went to the water's edge to investigate and saw that it was a coin. It looked like it could be gold. He knelt and dug it out, rinsed it in the water, and tried unsuccessfully to read its eroded inscriptions. Not only did it appear to be a foreign language from what he could discern, the portions of the engravings that were visible were almost obliterated in some places, and there were some encrustations as well that resisted his attempts to scratch them away. But yes, it did seem to be a gold coin from what he could see of it, and perhaps an old one at that.

He pocketed the coin and dug some more sand from his hole. There was nothing there, but when he looked up and carefully scanned the area around him, he spotted a couple more coins nearby.

"Mister Ketchum?" Henry called as he approached. "What are you doin'? Mama sent me back to see if you were okay."

Ketch could see Suzanne standing farther down the beach, shading her eyes and looking in his direction. He stood up and waved to indicate she should continue on to the dune.

"I found a coin," he said to Henry. "There are some more over there. Can you see them?"

They spent the next few minutes searching the area where Ketch had found the first coin – which coincidentally happened to be on the path along which they'd dragged the bodies from the water earlier. They ended up with a total of six coins.

"I think that's all we're going to find," Ketch said. "We'd better head back."

"Where do you think they came from, sir? The coins, I mean," Henry asked as they walked.

"I think where they came from today is, they were either caught in the fabric of a wetsuit or one of the divers had a handful of coins, and we dislodged them when we moved the bodies. Where they came from before that, I don't know."

It was Henry's turn to grow wide-eyed. "Do you think they found an old shipwreck out there?"

Ketch thought for a moment. "I've read a couple of books on the shipwrecks of the Graveyard. There have been wrecks all along this coast, but I don't recall any right around here that date back to the pirate era. One of the Coasties said they found an abandoned skiff yesterday anchored offshore not too far from here. If that boat belonged to our guys, maybe they did discover something, who knows? Those coins had to come from somewhere."

"How many wrecks have there been in the Graveyard?"

"Oh, thousands since Europeans first started coming here five hundred years ago. And before that, who knows? That's why our coast is called the Graveyard of the Atlantic. It doesn't happen much anymore, but in the old days, before modern navigation and weather forecasting, there were a lot of accidents in these waters, even though the captains knew about the conditions here. This is where the Gulf Stream comes up from the south and meets the Labrador Current coming down from the north. The result is sudden storms and turbulent seas with shifting sandbars."

"Right, like the Diamond Shoals off Cape Point. But if they knew it was dangerous, why did so many ships come here?"

"They didn't really have much choice. Especially in the era of sail, if they were transporting cargo between the northern and southern markets, including the Caribbean and South America, they had to sail past here along the way, and they could save time and money by riding the currents. And even if they were traveling between the Americas and Europe or Africa, they'd go out of their way to ride the currents and then turn east at Cape Hatteras to cross the Atlantic. They thought the benefits were worth the risk."

"Huh," Henry said. "I guess so, long as you didn't wreck and drown. Well, maybe this is a wreck nobody knows about yet."

"That's always possible around these parts."

"Say, how come those guys didn't get all chewed up by sharks? 'Specially if they were floatin' around out there for a while?"

"Sharks don't generally like to eat people," Ketch replied. "They prefer fish, and it didn't look like those divers had any bloody wounds..."

When Ketch and Henry finally made it back to the dune, Suzanne wanted to know what they'd been up to. Ketch briefly explained and passed the coins around so everyone could have a look at them.

"Are they pirate coins?" Bean asked.

"I don't know yet," Ketch answered. "I don't know where they came from, or exactly how old they are." If there were dates on the coins, they were illegible at the moment. He'd have to research how to clean them up online when they got back to civilization.

"The Sea Hag said it's Peter Piper's treasure," Sally casually remarked, playing with what looked like a primitive rag doll that Ketch didn't recall having seen before.

"Painter!" Bean said, looking exasperated. "She means Peter Painter."

Ketch was taken aback. "What?" he said. "How do you know about Peter Painter? And the Sea Hag?"

"Well," Suzanne said, "it seems we have a little story of our own to tell. Bean?"

"We saw the Sea Hag!" Bean proudly announced.

"And she gave us this doll," Sally said. "It's magic!"

"Just so you know, I already spoke to them again about talking to strangers," Suzanne said to Ketch.

"We didn't talk to her!" Bean insisted, shaking

his head. "No, no. She talked to *us*, and we didn't go by her. She stayed right there," he said, pointing to a depression between their dune and the next one.

"What did she look like?" Ketch asked.

"She was old," Bean answered, and Sally added, "Really, *really* old!" Meaning even older than he himself was, Ketch presumed.

"And she had old, torn-up clothes," Bean went on, "and she talked funny. She said 'Oi'm the Sea Hag', and then she said the jail birds were takin' Peter Painter's treasure and they didn't pay the fee. She said people who take stuff from here have to pay the fee."

"The port fee," Sally clarified. "Or else the ghosts get mad."

Had Bean said 'jailbirds'? And where had the kids learned about port fees, Ketch wondered? And why would anyone have to pay a port fee nowadays, when there was no longer a port here?

The town of Portsmouth had been a thriving shipping port at one time, before events had conspired to take the wind out of her sails. It was a 'lightering' port, where cargo from larger ships was transferred to shallow-draft vessels that could safely traverse the sounds. In Portsmouth's heyday, the ocean-going ships would be charged a port fee for docking, and for the use of the port's facilities and services. But all that was irrelevant now.

The decline began after the opening of Hatteras

Inlet and Oregon Inlet to the north, both during the storm of 1846. That, combined with increased shoaling in Ocracoke Inlet adjacent to the town, caused merchant ships to start diverting away from Portsmouth. And then there were attacks by Union forces during the Civil War, and the islanders began to abandon ship. The rise of the railroad system, failed attempts to establish other businesses here, the eventual decommissioning of the local U.S. Lifesaving Station, and a string of devastating hurricanes finally finished the job of turning Portsmouth into a ghost town.

"The ghosts are the people that used to live here," Bean was explaining.

"And they get mad when people come and take things," Sally reiterated.

Things of value, Ketch thought she probably meant. Noncommercial items like the abundant seashells and the fish taken by recreational anglers shouldn't be of concern to ghosts or anyone else.

"But we don't have to worry," Bean said, "'cause she gived us the magic doll. She said if we have the doll, the ghosts can't do anything to us."

"She *gave* you the doll," Ketch said. "What about the jailbirds? Did she mean those people we found on the beach?" Bean and Sally both shrugged. "Okay. Well, did she say why she wanted to give you the doll? We aren't taking anything important from the island." Ah, but then again maybe they were, if the coins counted.

"She said we're dingbatters, but we're just kids

and don't know better," Bean answered.

"What are dingbatters?" Henry asked.

"A dingbatter is an outsider, someone who doesn't live here. It sounds like this woman might be a Hoi Toider," Ketch mused. "That's interesting..."

"And what, pray tell, is *that*?" Suzanne inquired.

"It's a person who speaks with a certain accent that was common around here at one time, an Elizabethan English brogue of sorts that the original colonists developed. Like this – 'it'll be a hoigh toide on the saoundsoide tonoight, Oi reckon'."

"That's how she talked!" Bean exclaimed.

"Isn't that how Crocodile Dundee talked in the movies?" Suzanne asked.

"Ah, you've seen those? Yes, sort of," Ketch said. "Which isn't surprising, since the English colonized Australia. The people here also had some unusual words for things, like 'dingbatter'. I hear that accent in Ocracoke now and then, but hardly ever any farther north than that nowadays." Ketch thought for a moment, then changed tack. "If you didn't go near her, how did she give you the doll?"

"She throwed it," Bean said. "And then she was gone!"

"She *threw* it. Gone how? Did she run away?"

Bean shrugged again. "She was just gone. And then I goed to get the doll, 'cause she didn't throw it far enough."

"You *went* to get the doll," Ketch said.

"I checked the doll," Suzanne said. "It's just old rags." Ketch peered more closely at the doll Sally still held. It looked like someone had made a jellybomb-like shape from a single rag tied off with a piece of twine at one point. The head, which he guessed was stuffed with another rag, had two buttons for eyes and a crudely stitched mouth. There were no arms or legs, but the trailing part of the rag below the head was suggestive of a dress.

Henry had already climbed to the top of the dune with Ketch's binoculars and started to pan what he could see of the island behind it. "Nothin' movin' out there," he called, then came back down. "If there really was an old lady, I don't know where she went."

"Well, there had to be someone, right?" Suzanne said. "Otherwise, where did that doll come from? I know the kids didn't have it before. Unless they just found it and then made up a story about it?"

"It's not a story," Bean said. "It's true!"

"I believe you," Ketch said to him. "Suzanne, I don't think they could make up a story like that. They wouldn't know what a port fee is, and I've never told them about Peter Painter or the Sea Hag. I doubt they learned about them in school this past year. I'm sure I would have heard about it."

"Well, I certainly didn't tell them either,"

Suzanne said. "I've never heard of them before. So they're real?"

"Yes on one, 'sort of' on the other. Bean, did she say anything else?"

"The sand pirates," Sally said.

"Yeah," Bean corroborated, "she said the sand pirates are gonna get in trouble too, 'cause they didn't pay the fee."

"What are sand pirates?" Henry asked.

"I don't know," Ketch replied. "Are you sure she said 'sand' pirates, like the sand here on the beach?" The kids nodded. "Well, I'll have to look that one up. But I can tell you about Peter Painter and the Sea Hag."

"Peter Painter was a pirate captain who lived right here on this island, in the town of Portsmouth, where we went this morning," he began. Sally gasped. "That was a long time ago, in the early seventeen hundreds. He was supposedly very successful, but there's no record of what happened to his ship, nor any rumors about any treasure he might have had. He may have worked with Blackbeard for a while. But most pirates didn't really have treasure chests full of coins and jewels, you know – they sold the cargoes of the ships they captured to merchants, like the ones in Portsmouth, and that's how they got money to live on."

"So those coins aren't really from Peter Painter's treasure?" Bean asked, sounding disappointed.

"Probably not. But they might be. I'll try to find out later."

"What about the Sea Hag?" Henry said. He sounded eager. Though he was considerably older than the two younger children, he was generally just as fascinated as they were by Ketch's tales and today was no exception.

"I read a story about her some time ago, in one of Judge Whedbee's books," Ketch said. "He wrote about the legends and folklore of the Outer Banks. Some people say the Sea Hag of Portsmouth was a bad witch who lived in the southern forest on this island, not too far from where we are right now. They say she was hundreds of years old, and she rode on a steering oar from a whaling ship she'd sunk, instead of a broomstick. A girl named Veronica was sent by her stepmother to find the Sea Hag one day to ask a favor. But really, the stepmother hoped the Sea Hag would get rid of the girl."

"Why did she want to get rid of Veronica?" Bean asked.

"She was tired of taking care of her. Veronica's father was away, working at sea. But her father had given her a magic doll made by another witch, a good one, to protect her while he was gone. She took the doll with her when she went to find the Sea Hag, so the Sea Hag wouldn't eat her."

"Ketch..." Suzanne started to warn.

"What? It's no worse than most other fairy tales," Ketch protested. But he decided to dial it down and cut it short. "Well anyway, the magic doll worked, the Sea Hag helped the girl, and the girl made it back home safe and sound." With a red-eyed skull on a stick given to her by the Sea Hag that burned her evil stepmother and her two equally evil stepsisters to small piles of ash, he refrained from adding.

"Well, that was an interesting story. You certainly do know a lot about the history of these islands," Suzanne complimented Ketch. He wondered if she was being facetious, but the smile she gave him then appeared genuine. He thought he could also detect a 'thank-you' in her eyes.

"Do you have that book, sir?" Henry inquired. "I wouldn't mind readin' it sometime."

"I do, and you're welcome to borrow it whenever you like," Ketch said.

"Did the Sea Hag take the magic doll away from the girl?" Sally asked. "Yeah," Bean said, "is that why she had the doll? 'Cause she gived it to me and Sally."

"She *gave* it to you," Ketch said. "I don't know. That was just a story from a long time ago."

"A long, *long* time? So she's not real? The Sea Hag?" Bean asked. He was at an age where he was concerned about distinguishing between what was real and what wasn't, and he again looked worried.

"Yes, a very long time. So she might have been real then, but she's not real now," Ketch reassured him. Timelines, especially when outside the scales of their own short lives, were also a difficult concept for kids that age.

And then, in a burst of logic and empathy, both of which impressed Ketch, Bean said, "Maybe the Sea Hag was real, but she wasn't really a witch, but nobody liked her and they made up stories about her."

"You might be right about that," Ketch agreed. "But there's no way to know for sure. It was a long time ago," he repeated for the umpteenth time. Or maybe she'd been a witch, he thought, but of the ersatz Wiccan variety like the ones he'd encountered last fall, who weren't capable of performing any truly magical feats other than convincing gullible acolytes to believe in them. And maybe she hadn't done a very good job of that or had been a loner, and had been shunned and discredited by the superstitious old-time islanders.

"And now she's dead," Bean said. "But why did that lady say she's the Sea Hag?" he persisted.

"That lady you kids saw is probably just confused," Suzanne said. "Sometimes people get confused when they get very old. Ketch, do you think that woman really believes she's the Sea Hag of Portsmouth Island? Do you think she lives here?"

"I don't know about her mental state, but it would be tough to try to live on this island nowadays. No one else does anymore, according to everything I've read, not since 1971 when the last two residents left. There's no electricity and no place to shop, so you'd have to sail to the mainland for supplies. There aren't many edible plants that would grow here and there's no potable water anywhere, though I suppose she could collect rainwater. And I know there are some small animals, which could be trapped or hunted. And fish, of course, and turtles."

"But where could she live?" Henry wondered.

"That's a good question – and where could she live without being noticed, since I've never heard anything about her before? Not in any of the remaining buildings in the main village, because she wouldn't be able to avoid the Park Service workers who maintain them. There were two satellite communities below the village along Straight Road, separated by creeks and marsh – but there are some archaeologists studying the Middle Community ruins, and there's nothing habitable left either there or at Sheep Island. I suppose one could cobble together some kind of shelter in what's left of the forest, but there are campers and hikers, especially in summertime..."

"Maybe she's a ghost," Bean matter-of-factly suggested.

"No, I don't think so," Suzanne asserted. "There are no such things as ghosts, either."

Although Ketch considered himself above baseless superstition, he wasn't entirely sure about that last statement. But Suzanne was right, there was no sense stirring up more discussion along those lines. He guessed they'd be lucky if the kids didn't have nightmares tonight as it was, after what they'd seen. Maybe he shouldn't have told the Sea Hag story... So he wouldn't contradict her, then. At least she knew better than to tell the kids there were no such things as witches – there were indeed, as history has recorded and as Ketch well knew from his own misadventures in the fall.

"Well, how about if we start heading back?" he said. "It's getting late, and I imagine we'll be wanting some supper before too long." Ketch figured he'd fire up the grill first thing when they got back to the cabins, so he could get dinner started as soon as possible. Tired and hungry children were often not happy campers.

"Yes, let's," Suzanne said. "It's been a long and eventful day."

So they packed up their gear – and their trash, of course, as there'd be no one to pick it up for them later. It would be highly disrespectful to sully this pristine place, not to mention illegal as well.

While they walked, he made a mental list of the things he'd need to do when they got home. Let's see, there was cleaning the coins, learning what sand pirates might be, perhaps a little more research on local shipwrecks... Oh, and finding out who those divers were, if possible. He didn't know what to think or do about the woman who'd claimed to be the Sea Hag, but he'd add her to the list as well.

So then, five items to remember. As was his custom, he'd file that number away in the back of his mind instead of writing anything down, and trust his memory to supply the details later. He found it amusing to think that this was always how he'd grocery-shopped, and now it was also how he solved mysteries – another one of which seemed to be developing here.

~ T w o ~

He opened his eyes and came back from a long way away.

*K*etch hadn't realized how tired he'd been. He'd replenished their ice stores at the camp office and then whipped up a fine dinner for them all, consisting of crab-stuffed flounder, Caesar salad, artisanal bread, wine, and soft drinks he'd packed in his cooler for the occasion – all of which had been served by candlelight. Though their unit was wired for electricity, you had to bring your own generator, which he'd decided against doing. There'd also been a small and miraculously un-squashed cake for dessert, and Suzanne had remarked that he'd turned the Spartan cabin into a fancy restaurant. He'd replied that it was really more of a supper club, a movie reference that Kari would have gotten but Suzanne did not.

Afterward, Suzanne had taken all of the kids to the campground showers in exchange for Ketch cleaning up from dinner, an offer he couldn't refuse. It wasn't quite full dark just yet, but Bean and Sally were already sacked out after another pirate story and Henry was in bed reading with a flashlight. Ketch had brought his small traveling guitar (a Martin Backpacker) with him, but the younger ones especially had been way too tired for any further activities. Suzanne had gone back to get a shower of her own, and Ketch had dozed off in a chair on the deck. Not for that long, he didn't think, but long enough to dream.

His dreams didn't usually stay with him for more than a few seconds on awakening, if at all, but he vaguely recalled being out at sea on the Captain's boat. The two of them had been engaged in dumping fifty-gallon drums full of body parts into the ocean, assisted by a naked witch and a street urchin he recalled from an atypically vivid dream from much earlier, back when he'd been drinking too much. Weird and grisly, yes, but he knew where all of it had originated, so he didn't find the dream disturbing.

Until Bean had arrived on the scene a few months back, he'd hardly ever dreamt about his long-estranged ex-wife and son (that he could recall) in the four years he'd been living in Avon since his early retirement. Lately, dealing with Bean had caused some of those older memories, good and bad, to occasionally resurface in his dreams, but thankfully not this time. Those dreams *did* sometimes disturb him.

He stretched his legs out, clasped his hands together behind his head, and yawned. It had indeed been a long day. Starting from Avon on Hatteras Island at the crack of dawn, they'd towed the *TBD* south to Hatteras village with his truck, taken the free ferry across Hatteras Inlet to Ocracoke Island, and then departed for

Portsmouth Island from the public launch at Silver Lake, the village of Ocracoke's sheltered bay, on his reliable old seventeen-foot Whaler Montauk. Though it wasn't a flat-bottomed boat, it had a shallow draft and they'd managed to cross Ocracoke Inlet without mishap.

They'd docked at the north end of Portsmouth Island and taken a self-guided walking tour of the main village, then sailed to the south end and checked in at the Long Point Cabin Camp. After unloading their supplies and eating a simple lunch at the campground, they'd hiked quite a ways up the thirteen-mile-long beach on the Atlantic shore of the island in the afternoon.

Though his new Tundra had the double cab and the *TBD* could carry seven people, it had been a cramped journey with the five of them and their gear. If Kari and the dogs had been able to come with them as originally planned, they would have needed two vehicles and he would have made two trips with the *TBD*. Getting here meant a long time on a crooked road (another film reference Kari would have understood) – but the soul-cleansing quiet of this wild, beautiful, and gloriously deserted place made it all worthwhile, at least for him.

Ah, the poor old *TBD*... Not a very distinguished name for a boat, but he'd been unable to come up with a more meaningful one when he'd bought and registered her a couple of years ago (or was it three years now?), so he'd written 'TBD' in for the name. He'd later learned it was considered bad luck to change the name of a boat without changing ownership – which meant nothing to him, of course, since he wasn't superstitious. Though he'd somehow not gotten around to renaming her yet, he was sure he would one of these days.

He decided to get up from the chair. He'd only Navy-showered before in his cabin and was due for a full one as well at some point before bed, but the power nap had reinvigorated him and he thought he'd take a walk first. Though there'd only be a sliver of a crescent moon tonight, he wondered if he might still be able to take some nighttime aerial shots with his drone. It was technically illegal to fly a drone over National Park Service lands, but they were pretty isolated here on Portsmouth and he figured no one important would notice or care.

He went inside to get it and his backpack and let Henry know what he was up to. He left his hat behind, since the sun was down.

When he came out again, Suzanne was returning from the showers. "That felt good," she said. "Your turn now."

"I know, but I thought I'd take a walk first and see if I can get some more pictures with the drone. I still have a set of batteries I haven't used yet."

"Oh. Well, do you mind if I come along? I'll just duck in quick to drop off my stuff and tell Henry," she decided before he could answer. But he didn't mind.

"I turned the lantern off. You have your key, right?" she said on her way back out. He nodded. It was always a sensible precaution to lock up, though Henry would be there and Ketch knew only two of the other units were occupied tonight.

From his backpack, he fished out a small tied bundle of red myrtle cuttings he'd made and gave it to her, then took another one for himself. The plant was first and foremost a natural insect repellent, but when all else failed the bundles could double as flyswatters.

"I know we didn't need these this afternoon, and it's still windy, but the bugs might be worse now that it's dark," he warned.

Modern-day Portsmouth Island was notorious for its hordes of voracious mosquitoes and biting flies. It hadn't always been that way, but deforestation and other ill-advised terraforming on the part of the island's former inhabitants had caused the marshes to expand over time, and since the island was now uninhabited there was no spraying program here like there was on the other islands.

But conditions had favored the humans so far on this trip. The bugs were less numerous overall in spring and fall, and less so on the ocean side of the island where they'd been spending most of their time, even in season. Plus there'd been a strong and steady breeze all day and so far tonight as well, which always helped. They'd all carried the myrtle bundles with them in town this morning, but the bugs hadn't been too bad there.

"Thanks," Suzanne said. "What else do you need the backpack for?"

"I also have some Skin So Soft, in case the myrtle isn't enough. I have a lot of useful things in here that I like to keep handy just in case." He very much doubted he'd need certain things tonight, like the lock pick set he'd bought to replace the one that had ironically been stolen from him, and the Mason jar-slash-urinal for stakeouts. But there were other potentially more useful items as well. One never knew what might come up.

"What a wonderful trip this has turned out to be!" Suzanne gushed as they started walking. "I must admit, I had my doubts when you first suggested it. But this place is delightful!"

"I'm glad to hear you say that," Ketch replied. He'd had his doubts as well, specifically about inviting her. A successful artist who'd recently relocated to Avon, she hadn't seemed to him like the type who'd enjoy roughing it. "I think boardwalks and amusement parks are highly overrated," he said. "I much prefer a quiet, natural place like this. I think it's a better quality experience for kids, too."

It was indeed 'natural'. Visitors were allowed to tent camp (no RVs) anywhere on the island except in the main village, and those who elected to ferry four-wheel-drive vehicles to the island often took advantage of that option – but that was *really* roughing it. For those a little less rustic, the campground, which was run by the National Park Service, provided at least some basic amenities.

Each of the twenty units in the ten duplex cabins was a combined eating and sleeping area with six bunk beds, private bath, propane stove, sink, table and chairs, and drinking water. There was also a propane heater for the shoulder seasons, and a ceiling fan and air conditioning in some units (again, if you brought a generator). Community showers, grills, ice, and gas were available on site. Anything else you might need, such as bedding (sleeping bags in their case, to keep things simple), you had to bring yourself.

That was why he'd feared this trip might not be her cup of tea. But he'd wanted to do something special with the kids to celebrate the recent end of their first year of school in their new home, and he'd known Suzanne wouldn't let Henry and Sally come without her. Kids always appreciated new adventures (at least, these kids did), but he hadn't known what to expect from Suzanne. Luckily, it all seemed to be working out – except for that unfortunate scene the kids had witnessed on the beach. Although that, too, had been an adventure they'd probably be talking about for quite some time.

"The kids do seem to be enjoying it, and it's certainly quiet here," Suzanne agreed. "Except for an occasional visit from the Sea Hag, and the odd body washing up on the beach," she then remarked with a twinkle in her eye. "It's too bad the kids had to see that, though."

"Yes. But that's a part of life, too. There's no telling what could be coming around the bend, and everything isn't always perfect. They need to start learning that at some point along the way."

"I suppose so. Anyway, you handled it well. You were good with Bean this afternoon, too. I wish I had that much patience." She frowned momentarily, then brightened back up. "Thank you for taking us on that tour of the town this morning. It was fascinating! It made me wish I'd been able to bring my paints. But I should be able to paint from our photos later."

"If we ever come here again, maybe we could bring more with us and stay longer, if we plan well."

She nodded agreement. "But it was also kind of sad – and a little eerie, for me anyway. Everything looked so tidy and orderly, even the picket fences and all. I kept expecting to see people any minute going in and out of the buildings – the post office, the general store, the church, the schoolhouse, the lifesaving station, the houses – and doing things. But there was no one there. It was a little spooky."

"Well, it *is* a ghost town," Ketch smiled. Even on a busy day in season, he'd heard there were never more than thirty people out and about on the entire twenty-two mile long island (not counting the biennial Homecoming gatherings sponsored by the Friends of Portsmouth Island). Although there'd been only about a dozen restorable structures left when Portsmouth became part of the Cape Lookout National Seashore, it was enough to provide a sense of what it must have been like to live here in the old days and fish, lighter, salvage wrecks, rescue mariners, or trade for a living – despite the absence of the saloons, warehouses, shops, fish houses, and so on that had existed in the port's prime. Those were unfortunately all gone for good.

"And we didn't even need a tour guide! How did you learn so much about all this?"

"Well, I've spent more time in the region than you have," he said. He'd lived in Avon longer than she had, and before that he'd taken numerous vacations on the Banks over the years. "And I read a lot."

"I guess you must. Oh, I wanted to ask you, is it really true that the wild horses that used to live here helped the lifesavers, like you told the children?"

"Yes, that's what I was told. The old-time islanders had a special relationship with the horses, which probably came here on Spanish ships originally. No one 'owned' any of the horses in the traditional sense. When they needed a horse for something, they just borrowed one from the herd. And when the surfmen were out rescuing people from a shipwreck, supposedly some of the horses would show up and help bring the people in."

"And they're all gone now, too..."

They walked in silence for a bit, and then Suzanne said, "It's too bad Kari couldn't come with us. Has she ever been here before?"

"She visited the village once, before I met her. I've been to the village a couple of times before, but this is my first time at this end of the island."

"What do you think will happen to that employee of hers?"

"I don't know. Getting busted with a few joints isn't so bad these days, but he had quite a lot of it. I think it was probably his second job."

Doug, one of the two divemasters who worked part-time at the Sea Dog Scuba Center in Avon, was currently in the Dare County jail. And Stuart, the other one, was out of town this week, so there'd been no one available to cover the shop. Since, after years of scraping to get by, Kari's business had finally started picking up after Ketch's timely investment, she'd been reluctant to close the shop and had decided to opt out of the Portsmouth trip.

She'd kept the dogs with her as well, as they'd agreed that might have been too much for Ketch to manage on his own with Bean and everything else. He missed those two goofballs almost as much as he missed Kari, but he'd be seeing them all again soon enough.

Ketch and Suzanne walked on in another companionable silence a while longer, and then he said, "Let's stop here, if you don't mind. I'd like to get the drone out." He knelt on the sand and popped the drone case open.

"Okay," she said, and found a place to sit nearby. "Wow, look at that sky," she intoned, gazing upward into the now-black night. "I don't think I've ever seen this many stars before." Another gift from the island, Ketch thought – no light pollution.

It didn't take him long to switch out the batteries. "Well, you're about to see one more. She's ready to fly."

"What's that?" she asked, pointing out to sea. "Is that a ship out there?"

He looked in the direction she was indicating, and his eyes found the dark object she was referring to. "Yes, I think so. It looks like some kind of small barge, I think – well, small for a barge – but I can barely make it out. I wonder why it isn't showing any lights?"

"Could it be a shipwreck?"

"I doubt it. But I'm surprised a ship like that could be that close to shore. I guess it must have a shallower draft than the bigger barges. I hope so, because the water isn't that deep around here until you get farther out." Reading nautical charts while serving as mate on the Captain's fishing charters had taught him that. "I'll take a closer look." He got his binoculars out of the backpack and trained them on the ship.

He eventually spotted a couple of minute shadowy figures moving around on the deck. "I see some people. They don't seem to moving too fast, so I doubt they're in trouble." He panned the length of the ship with the binoculars, and found he could discern some complicated-looking machinery in the pale moonlight. "It looks like they might be dredging – though I can't imagine why, in that particular spot and at this time of day." He put the binoculars aside, picked up the drone transmitter, and stood up.

"What are you doing?" Suzanne inquired, rising to stand alongside him.

"I'd like to get a closer look at that ship," he said. "I think it might be within range, and this transmitter has a built-in monitor. I can see whatever the camera is pointing at, with the real-time video feed."

He was glad he'd had the foresight to bring three sets of batteries. Although they were rechargeable, he couldn't recharge them here on the island. He'd used two sets during the day, and with the one he had left he should be able to get up to twenty-five minutes of flight time if he needed it – but maybe less depending on how hard the drone had to fight against the sea breeze.

Ketch had been able to spend some time honing his piloting skills since Christmas, which was fortunate as he could tell right off that he'd need some skill out there over the water. He had to wrestle with it some, but he finally managed to get the drone close enough to the ship to see some more detail. It should be easier coming back with the breeze at its tail, but he decided not to press his luck with the flight time. Starting from the stern, he began moving the drone steadily along the length of the ship. He'd make just one pass and then fly her back.

The video was good quality, but a little shaky due to the wind. Still, he could see now that there was definitely some kind of dredging operation in progress, as indicated by a large pile of sand on the deck. Was this a sand barge, then? It was unusual for one of those to be out in the open ocean. The feed was also good enough for him to catch one of the figures he'd seen earlier raise what looked like a shotgun and aim it at the drone. Before he could process that or react to it, there was a flash and the screen on his monitor went black.

"What happened?" Suzanne said, watching over his shoulder.

"Hit the deck!" Ketch commanded, bellyflopping onto the sand. To her credit, she immediately followed suit without comment. Other women he'd known would have questioned and contested his order, often angrily, if he'd dared to try to tell them to do something without fully explaining himself beforehand. They'd be the first ones to buy the farm in an emergency situation, but that hadn't ever seemed to bother them, if they even thought about it.

"Storm Ketchum! I just took a shower!" Suzanne half-laughed lying next to him. When she saw that he wasn't smiling, she nervously asked, "Why are we doing this? Is the drone out of control?"

Ketch had already mashed the transmitter's automatic return-to-home button three times. This model also featured a fail-safe return function in case of signal loss, but nothing was happening either way. He couldn't see or hear the drone and his screen was still dark. But the transmitter seemed to be functioning otherwise, and he now noticed it was in fact indicating a loss of signal.

"I think they shot it down," he said.

"*What?* Really?"

"I saw someone point a gun at it, and then I lost contact."

Suzanne thought about that for a moment, then quietly said, "And you thought they might start shooting at us next?"

"I did, yes. But now that I think about it, they're too far out to shoot at us. And if they're doing something they shouldn't be doing, they're probably wondering if there's another boat around somewhere spying on them, like maybe the Coast Guard. So that would most likely be their first concern."

"Okay... and when they find out there are no other boats around, then what?"

"Then they might try to see if there's someone on the beach – or not. Maybe they're not worried about being spied on, and they're just people who find drones annoying." Though in that case, they probably wouldn't have guns and be running without lights, he didn't add. "Either way, we're probably safe."

"Probably?" she said. "Well, don't you think we should at least try to get behind a dune or something? Or try to get back to the cabins?"

She started fidgeting next to him, and Ketch realized she might be getting panicky. He'd felt a little of that himself initially, but he'd known he needed to stay calm and rational. And think before acting, as he and Kari constantly reminded her scuba classes.

"There's not much moonlight tonight," he said in as calming a tone as he could muster. "If we stay down and stay still, they shouldn't be able to spot us. I don't think we should be getting up and moving around just yet."

"Okay, if you say so, Doctor Ketchum," she relented, though she didn't sound fully convinced. Ketch noticed that her right hand was tightly clasping his left.

It occurred to him that a little levity could often help defuse a tense situation. "I forgive you, by the way," he said. He noticed his binoculars were within reach, so he casually retrieved them, discreetly freeing his hand in the process.

"You forgive me? For what?"

"For calling me 'Storm'. You know I hate that name." Though he was only mentioning it now to distract Suzanne, he really did hate it. It had been an embarrassment when he was a child and it still was now. He knew why his parents had named him that, but he couldn't forgive them for it. He could respect them, however, which was why he'd never legally changed it even though they were both gone now.

Today the name was at least good for eliciting a small giggle, albeit a nervous one. But it was an improvement. "I know. I won't do it again, I promise," she said.

Ketch brought the binoculars up and trained them on the ship. One possibility she hadn't thought of yet, and which he wouldn't mention, was they could come ashore in an inflatable. They could also shine a searchlight at the beach, if they had one. But maybe he was just being paranoid. Besides, he had a feeling they might not want to attract that much attention, and he wasn't seeing any signs of either activity so far.

"Sand pirates," Suzanne mumbled.

"What?" Ketch said.

She cleared her throat. "Sand pirates. Isn't that what that old woman said, that there were sand pirates here? I had this picture in my head of Blackbeard peeking out from behind the dunes, which is silly. But maybe those people out there on that ship are stealing something – like sand. Could that be possible?"

Ketch thought about it. "I suppose so," he said. "I did see a pile of sand on the deck. I'd wonder why they'd have to be sneaky about harvesting sand when there's so much of it around, but then I imagine maritime laws and environmental restrictions could play into it. Following rules and regulations usually costs money, so you can save money by not following them." That had been the motivation behind the illegal ocean dumping scheme Ketch had uncovered last summer – well, one of them, anyway, the other being considerably more sinister as it had turned out. "I'll look into it when we get back home."

"Okay." She was starting to fidget again. "Are you sure we shouldn't get away from here?"

He noticed something then through the binoculars that should settle her down. "It looks like they're hauling anchor now," he said.

"Really?"

"Yes." He continued watching a little while longer, and then the faint sound of engines ramping reached them on the breeze. "The ship is starting to move. They're sailing away."

"Well!" She exhaled loudly and visibly relaxed. "That's a relief! So we're safe now?"

"Yes, I'd say so." Ketch lowered the binoculars, took a deep breath, and ran a hand through his hair. How did he get himself into these situations, he wondered?

But he knew the answer to that – he'd lately fallen out of his old habit of sticking his head in the sand, as it were, and simply hoping for the best. The old Ketch wouldn't have tried to spy on that ship, for example. But the old Ketch also wouldn't have stood up for himself and followed through when the going had gotten rough, and then where would he be today?

He thought this was mostly a good development, but he also knew this new and supposedly improved attitude of his had pulled others into conflicts more than once. Maybe he needed to work on finding some kind of middle ground, especially now that he had Bean to consider.

Something to think about... Meanwhile, they could get up now, he thought, and he was mildly surprised that Suzanne hadn't yet done so herself. But before he could move, she took his hand again, gently this time, and wiggled closer to him. Their shoulders were touching.

"What a relief!" she repeated. "That was scary." She squeezed his hand. "So, now that we won't be getting chased or shot at..." She leaned in a little more. "Tell me, Ketch, do you believe in *curpe diem*? You know, seizing the day, making the most of every moment?"

Ketch considered before replying. "I guess, for me, it would depend on the moment," he said, not moving a muscle.

"I see... Well, what about this moment right now?" she pressed, lightly stroking the back of his hand. "The two of us here all alone, on this beautiful, deserted beach... It's perfect, don't you think? And neither of us are married." When he didn't respond right away, she joked, "What's the matter, am I too old for you?"

That *was* funny, but he didn't laugh. She was only a little older than Kari. If anything, some might say they were both too young for him.

"No," he said. "But I'm afraid this isn't the kind of moment I can seize, Suzanne. I like you, and I find you attractive, but it wouldn't be right. I'm sorry."

"Oh," she said, sounding disappointed. "Well, that's okay, I understand." She let go of his hand and raised herself to a kneeling position. "Actually, I'm kind of glad to hear *you* say *that*. It shows you're a good man, Charlie Brown."

Ketch knelt as well and started brushing the sand from his shirt. "So, was that just a test, then?" he asked, smiling benignly.

"No! I just thought... I know Kari wouldn't like it, but she isn't here and she'd never have to know." She paused. "But you'd know, right?"

"Right."

"I get that," she said. "Really, I do."

"Thank you."

"No, I probably owe *you* an apology." She shook some sand out of her blouse, unintentionally (he hoped) giving him an unfettered glimpse. "I'm not usually that forward, and I'd never have even asked if we were both married. I guess that business with the ship shook me up, when I thought we were about to be shot at. But still, I know..." She smiled wanly back at him. "I guess sometimes I'm just not as good a person as I should be."

"Well, you're not the only one. I hope I haven't made you feel bad."

"No, please, I'm fine," she demurred. "Well, maybe a little embarrassed. Are we still friends?"

"Of course. It's no big deal, really," he said, packing up what remained of his gear. And he meant it. It was just another body to bury, as in that saying where a true friend helps you bury the body and says no more about it. He stood and extended a hand to help her up, and she took it.

"I'm sorry about your drone, too," she said when they began walking back down the beach.

"So am I. But oh well, easy come, easy go." He knew it was illegal to shoot down a drone, but he couldn't very well lodge a formal complaint since he'd been flying it illegally in the first place.

"Kari got that for you, didn't she?"

"Yes, and I know how much it cost her. It wasn't just one of those cheap toys." He let out a rueful chuckle. "That's probably going to upset her more than you would have."

Suzanne laughed at that. "How's the adoption going?" she asked.

"Oh, it's taking forever, of course, as these things usually do. Bean's mother is deceased, and my son had no problem signing off on it, so you'd think it'd just be a formality, but still..." He shook his head. "They'd think nothing of sticking him with foster parents, who are often just in it for the money and don't give a hoot about the kids – and of course if you're rich and famous, there's no problem. I know of an old rock musician who's single and was allowed to adopt a six-year-old boy even though he'd been in and out of mental institutions much of his adult life. But they make people like me jump through hoops."

"But you think it'll go through, right?"

"Yes, I think so. They're not pleased that Kari and I aren't married, but I'm told that's less of a stumbling block these days. They don't like us living on a houseboat, though. That's one reason I decided to rebuild my house."

That would be the original *Port Starbird*, the aged but comfortable soundfront cottage in Avon that he'd managed to save from a predatory developer, only to see it subsequently damaged beyond repair by a hurricane. He'd bought the houseboat after that (and named it *Port Starbird* as well), and had considered selling the house lot to Suzanne to build on. Now she was looking to buy a place somewhere else in Avon.

"Speaking of houses, how's your house-hunting going?" he asked.

"Not that well. I'm fussy, and my commissions are keeping me too busy to spend a lot of time on it. I have a lot of painting to do this summer."

"Well, my new house will be larger than the old one was." Thanks to the psychotic witch he'd tangled with, and not that pain-in-the-ass insurance company. Those outfits were just a bunch of legalized con artists, all of them. He reminded himself to check in with his lawyer again to see how the out-of-court settlement negotiations were proceeding. "Maybe we could all move in there together."

Suzanne laughed again. "Oh, sure! And then we could have our own reality show on TV."

"No, I don't mean like *that*," Ketch said with a smile.

"Why not? It's been done before."

"Yes, but never well, from what I've heard." He wasn't sure if he should, but then he asked, "Are you seeing anyone yet?"

"No, I don't have time for that either right now. I have the kids too, you know. And besides, at my age all the good ones are already taken." She looked up at him. "Like you."

"Oh, I'm not that good," he said – and he meant that as well. He'd gotten involved in some things over the past year that had made him somewhat of an outlaw. But not a true criminal, at least not to his way of thinking. He firmly believed there was a distinction between the two.

Nevertheless, he knew he could be considered an accessory to murder, or at least involuntary manslaughter, though he'd never personally committed such an act. And then there were the funds he'd appropriated (that sounded better than 'stolen') from that nefarious witch's ill-gotten stash – never mind that she'd deserved everything that had happened to her and more besides. Oh, and some technically illegal methods he'd employed in his amateur investigations. But Suzanne knew little of these things.

Speaking of investigations, Ketch now had a

sixth item to add to his mental to-do list, namely finding out more about that ship. Maybe the Captain would be able to help with that.

Meanwhile, first things first. A shower for him (if he still had enough energy), and then it would be time to call it a day and hit the hay. Tomorrow morning they'd pack up their stuff, and he'd load the *TBD* for the return trip while the kids waded and played on the beach that was less than a stone's throw from the cabins. They'd be back in Ocracoke in time for lunch at the Jolly Roger marina pub, another of Ketch's favorite places, and then they'd head on home.

The campground was quiet and there were no lights showing when they got back to their cabins. Henry must be asleep now, too. Ketch had rented both of the units in their duplex, which consisted of two octagonal cabins on stilts with a common landing and stairs connecting the outdoor decks. It was supposed to have been him and his entourage on one side, and Suzanne and her kids on the other. But the kids had all wanted to sleep together tonight, so she had them all and he had his unit to himself.

When they reached the top of the steps, Suzanne gave him a questioning look, then silently pecked him on the cheek and turned left. He turned right and didn't look back, and that was that.

~ **T h r e e** ~

The many times he'd proven himself meant nothing.

She still felt it was her duty to zing him at almost every opportunity – to keep him on his toes, Ketch supposed. Some things never change, as they say, but then he didn't really want them to in this particular case.

"Huh! Look what done slunk in – my man, the one that was out with another woman all night long," Kari laughed when he walked through the front door of the dive shop. "Boys, he's back!" she called.

She knew enough now to stay out of the way. Jack, the beagle-lab mix Ketch had rescued from a shelter just before he'd settled in Avon, was the first one through the doorway that led to the back rooms of the shop. The dogs had apparently been napping back there somewhere. Right on his heels, though, was Chuck, the goofy shepherd-corgi Kari had decided to take in after he'd been displaced by the hurricane last summer. Even though Chuck was technically her dog, they both would have bowled her over to get to Ketch. He knelt and braced himself as they came at him skidding and scrabbling across the waxed plank floor, tails wagging furiously.

"Hi, guys!" he said, enveloping them both in a

big bear hug. "I'm glad to see you, I missed you!" After enduring an abundance of slobbery kisses and murmuring some more endearments to them, he was finally able to disengage. Only then did Kari dare to approach him.

He stood up, quickly wiped his face with his bandanna, and attempted to swipe away the dog hair from his shirt.

"Oh, forget it, it's a losin' battle," she said. Though the dogs were brushed daily and Ketch furminated them once a week, dog hair was an integral part of their lives and no outfit was complete without it. "Let me hug your neck."

And that she did, and more. She wrapped a leg around him, pushed him back against the wall, and expertly fit herself into his embrace in a way that could have gotten them cited for public lewdness if they'd been outdoors. He opened his eyes during the kiss and glanced around the interior of the shop. Fortunately, there was no one else there.

"I missed you," she breathed in her seductive Carolinian way. "You missed me too, huh? I can tell."

Yes, he had missed her, he thought as he looked down into her deep green eyes. He once again felt like a schoolboy with a crush, as he often did whenever they'd been apart for any length of time. And the new haircut, punk-ish though it was, made her even more alluring. She'd seen it on a rock singer on TV, and now her auburn hair was shorter and kind of, well, spiky. But it looked good on her.

It amazed him that they could both still feel this way after being together for a year now, and in close quarters much of the time to boot. They'd crashed at her tiny Buxton apartment for a while after the hurricane, until Ketch had bought the houseboat. The houseboat was roomier than the apartment, and was larger and more luxurious, by marine live-aboard standards, than any of the other floating dwellings docked at the boatyard. But it wasn't as spacious as his new house would be, and meanwhile Bean had come along. So there were three of them now, plus the two dogs.

"Kari? Could you come here, please?" someone called from the back of the shop.

"Just a sec!" Kari answered.

"Your mother's back there?" Ketch asked. "It's a good thing she hasn't come out here."

"Yeah, well just you wait 'til later, mister. You ain't seen nothin' yet! Unless you're too tired?" Her eyes narrowed. "I bet you and her snuck off somewhere last night after you put the kids to bed, didn't you?" she teased.

"You know I wouldn't do that."

"I do know," she said, looking him in the eye. "But seriously, I see how she looks at you sometimes, don't think I don't. So you just be careful, at least 'til you don't want to be anymore." She flashed him a sad little smile and pulled away then, but not before giving him another suggestive bump. "Where's Bean?" she asked before he could remind her one more time that she had nothing to worry about.

She'd told him early on that she expected he'd tire of her eventually, as everyone else always had – but he wasn't like everyone else. He himself wasn't concerned about such things. What will be, will be, was his attitude these days. He knew he at least didn't have to worry about her previous boyfriend, since that abusive scoundrel was now at the bottom of the ocean.

"Bean's back at her place with Sally and Henry. We're supposed to go there for supper. I ordered pizzas to be delivered and Suzanne's making salad. Oh, and I also called the Captain. He's bringing drinks."

"Okay. So how was the trip? Did you get some good pictures with your new toy?"

"I think we all enjoyed it, for the most part. And I did get some good photos, but I lost them." She raised an eyebrow at him. "I'll tell you all about it at dinner."

"Kari Gellhorn! Y'all really ought to get on back here," Pauline called again.

"Just a sec, I'm lockin' the door!" Kari called back.

He'd made it in just before closing time, which was later than he'd hoped. It could take as little as fifteen minutes for the ferry to cross the inlet between Hatteras Island and Ocracoke Island in good conditions, but it was currently taking about an hour. The shoaling in Hatteras Inlet had gotten bad enough to force the fleet of deep-draft vessels to take a more circuitous route to avoid running aground, and funding for more dredging hadn't come through yet. He'd known this and planned ahead, but this afternoon there'd also been an hour-long line of other vehicles waiting at the Ocracoke ferry landing. He hadn't expected that to happen until suppertime.

"What are you two looking at?" he said to the dogs, who were sitting side-by-side nearby. They were both grinning at him in their doggy way and swishing their tales back and forth. It looked like they were hoping for something.

"Oh, they're gonna try and tell you they hadn't been anywhere for a run. But I took 'em to the beach yesterday and again this mornin' before I opened up, so don't let 'em con you." She took his arm and steered him toward the back of the shop. "Come on, we better get in there before Mama busts a gut."

"Hello, Pauline," Ketch said. "Good to see you." The dogs followed them in to what served as Kari's in-shop classroom and resumed their former positions.

"Hey, Ketch," Pauline said as she gave him a quick hug – not the kind Kari had given him, though he imagined she was capable of that as well. This mother and daughter were very much alike, at times disquietingly so. If he'd met Pauline before he'd met Kari, things might have turned out differently. And that wasn't just his ego talking – Pauline had told him that herself.

"A news bulletin came on the TV that I thought you should see," she said. "I rewound and paused it while y'all were busy gettin' busy out there."

Ketch's face flushed a bit at that. "See, it's a good thing you got the DVR with your digital package," he said to Kari, trying to change the subject. Pauline pressed the play button on the remote, and they all gathered beneath the bar-mounted flat-screen.

There was no footage, just the face of a newscaster with a banner headline running across the screen. The two convicts who'd had everyone in a tizzy after escaping from Central Prison, a maximum-security facility in Raleigh, had been found – but not alive. Their bodies had been recovered by the Coast Guard from a beach on Portsmouth Island, where they'd washed up.

Well, how about that, Ketch thought. There was one thing he could check off on his to-do list – he now knew who the dead divers were.

The bodies were discovered by a family group who'd been beachcombing on the island yesterday afternoon. The convicts were apparently victims of a scuba diving accident. An abandoned boat that had been reported stolen had been found by the Coast Guard a day earlier off the island. Whether or not the convicts had stolen the boat, what they might have been diving for, and the identities of the beachcombers were unknown at this time.

"And you hope it stays that way – right, Ketch?" Pauline drily remarked.

"*What*?" Kari exclaimed. "Was that you? Lordy, were you the one that found those bodies?"

"How did you know?" Ketch asked Pauline.

"I know you," she smiled. "And it just figured, that's all."

"Well, I do hope it stays that way," he said. "We don't need to be hounded by reporters."

"I'll say!" Kari cut in.

"Oh, I don't know, maybe it'd be good for your business," Pauline said.

"Wonder what they were doin' around Portsmouth Island," Kari mused.

"I don't know exactly what they were up to, but I might know what they were hoping to find," Ketch said. "I don't think the Coast Guard does, though."

"You do? All right, mister, spill it! I want details!" Kari demanded.

"Patience," he said. "You know I don't like to have to repeat myself. I'll tell you all about it at dinner, so the Captain can hear it, too. But I can show you these for now." He fished the coins from his pocket and spread them out on a nearby tabletop.

Kari and Pauline looked them over. "Are these gold coins?" Kari asked. "Did those convicts find a new shipwreck? And why do you have 'em? Why didn't the Coasties take 'em?"

"We didn't find the coins until after they'd left

with the bodies. I think they must have fallen out of someone's hand while Henry and I were dragging the bodies out of the water."

"You and Henry drug 'em out of the water?" Kari parroted in disbelief.

"We had to, or they would have gone back out with the tide."

"My goodness!" Pauline chuckled. "This just gets better'n better!"

Kari thought for a moment. "What about Bean and Sally? Did they see the bodies?"

"Yes, unfortunately. They were the ones who saw them first." Ketch became sober. "I'm sorry that happened, but I think they're okay. Look, we can talk more about all this at dinner." Ketch started leashing the dogs. "Oh, Pauline, you should join us. We're having pizza at Suzanne's."

"Are you sure? I don't want to impose."

"I'm sure it'll be fine with her. I ordered too much food, like I always do." The dogs strained at their leashes. Ketch didn't ordinarily leash them on the beach and the back streets, as they were both well-behaved and obedient, but he chose not to trust them on Route 12 where the shop was located. No sense asking for trouble – there was usually enough of that as it was, in one form or another. "We should get going," he declared.

The women agreed, though reluctantly on Kari's part. Ketch knew waiting wasn't one of her favorite things, but unlike the Captain, he truly didn't enjoy having to retell his stories. He wondered what that old salt would make of all this, and if parts of it might find their way into one of his tall tales somewhere down the road.

Ketch and Kari decided to drive to the boatyard and feed the dogs, then leave the vehicles and walk to Suzanne's. It wasn't far, and he figured the dogs would enjoy the walk since they would not in fact be going to the beach tonight. Pauline would drive straight to Suzanne's.

He again brought his backpacker guitar along, in case Henry wanted another impromptu lesson. He'd started teaching the boy, at the lad's request, a few months ago. He left everything else in the back of his otherwise unpacked truck.

Except for the bottle of Kari's favorite wine that he'd put in one of the coolers and forgotten to remove when she'd backed out of the trip. There was room for it in the outside pocket of the guitar bag, so he stuck it in there. It would be a pleasant surprise for her when they got to Suzanne's. It was expensive, and that had hurt a little at first, but he'd always kept some handy despite that ever since their first night. And now it didn't hurt anymore. Some things do occasionally turn out right, he thought.

The Captain, wearing his old skipper's cap as always but looking spiffy otherwise, was just getting out of his truck when they arrived at Suzanne's. His spanking-new, tricked-out F-150, that is. Ketch had been pleased that none of them had balked at his offers of largesse, even though they'd all known where the money was coming from. In fact, far from balking, the Captain (a fellow outlaw from way back) had responded in his trademark pragmatic manner. 'Hell, most a the money in the world's tainted, you know – taint yours, and taint mine,' was what he'd said with a sly grin.

But it hadn't really surprised Ketch all that much – after all, that witch had owed all of them to varying degrees. So in addition to the Captain's F-150, Kari had her new Outback, and Pauline a new Cadillac and a bit of home remodeling necessitated by the witch's antics. Len, a boatyard denizen who was independently wealthy despite outward appearances, had declined Ketch's similar offer, but not on moral grounds. Ketch had only just met Suzanne at the time, and she hadn't been involved in that little escapade.

"Ahoy there, maties!" the Captain's booming voice reverberated over the canal. A pelican squawked and flew off in alarm.

"Hello, Captain," Ketch said. "Hey, Don," Kari said, and the dogs greeted him in their typically joyous manner.

Though some probably found his voice and manner grating, Ketch had no complaints. The Captain was the best friend he'd ever had, and he was the kind of friend who actually would help you move the body. Though others called him 'Don', 'Captain Don', or 'Captain Manolin', Ketch just called him 'Captain'.

"Hey, gimme a hand with these drinks, will ya?" he said to Ketch.

"I'll take the boys inside," Kari said. "Y'all come on now, hear?" She started up the front steps of Suzanne's cottage and the dogs dutifully trailed behind her.

"So how was your trip?" the Captain said.

Ketch allowed as it'd been fine, and had turned out to include some unexpected new adventures.

"Do tell! Like what? Did you tap that?" the Captain leered, tipping his head toward the house. "You dawg!"

"No, I didn't 'tap' her!" Ketch protested. "Why is everyone asking me that?"

"I don't know, but I sure woulda! Guess that's why I could never stay married."

"'That would be one reason, yes."

"So you really behaved yourself then? Well, good for you." The Captain started hauling twelve-packs out from the back of his truck. "I always behave too, you know, just not always well!" he cackled.

"How much are we going to drink tonight?" Ketch inquired with a box in each hand. It appeared the Captain had also picked up two bottles of wine and a bottle of tequila, plus a jug of pop for the kids.

"Nobody knows!" the Captain declared. "I'll take home whatever we don't use, then I won't have to shop again for a while. Got no one to drink with now, though, at least not a the female persuasion."

"Joette's gone already?" Ketch had never fully understood the attraction there – in fact, it seemed downright unnatural to him – but he'd never hassled the Captain about it. The two of them had hooked up last summer during a party at the old *Port Starbird* house and then intermittently kept on with it. Though the Captain was only a little older than Ketch, he'd been ridiculously old for Joette, and probably scandalously so to some folks.

In addition to the Captain no longer having her to 'tap', they'd now lost their eyes and ears at HatterasMann Realty, the disrespectfully named agency that had been run by Bob Ingram, who'd been Ketch's local nemesis until he'd finally been jailed for racketeering. The true Hatterasman was the legendary embodiment of Hatteras Island spirit and endurance, a Paul Bunyan-like symbol of the hardy and resourceful early settlers of the island. 'Mann' was the maiden name of the wife Ingram had inherited the agency from, possibly after killing her (though that had never been proven). Well, at least the scoundrel would no longer be trying to condemn and seize his property, so Ketch guessed they didn't really need their agency spy anymore anyway.

"Yeah, she got her new job and done up'n moved, three days ago. She's probly partyin' down to Hotlanta by now – the bitch!" the Captain laughed. "But what the hell, it was fun while it lasted."

"Three days ago? And you still haven't found a replacement?" Ketch jibed.

"I thought I might could have me one the other night at Pangea, over by the Avon fishin' pier."

"Really? Isn't that place a little hoity-toity for you?" They had great food and a good selection of craft brews, but it was a bit on the fancy side. "So what happened?"

"Well, turned out she had a magnetic personality – attractive from behind and repulsive from the front. She had a laugh that sounded like a dog that's fixin' to throw up. And when she sang karaoke, she sounded like a sea lion givin' birth to a tool shed. Why, when she –"

"All right, that's enough, Rodney!" It was Ketch's turn to laugh. "That's too bad. Well, let's go in. I've got a tale to tell *you* for a change."

They entered to what some might have termed a cacophony. The women were jabbering in the kitchen while they got the table ready (the pizzas had already arrived), Bean and Sally were shrieking as Henry chased them around the house pretending to be a monster, the dogs were barking at Henry, and on the stereo Jimmy Buffett was singing about boat drinks in the background. But oddly enough considering his solitary nature, Ketch found the scene comforting. It was nice to have a family of sorts again after his years alone.

He remembered to retrieve Kari's special wine from his gig bag, to her great delight, and they eventually managed to settle everyone down enough to eat. The dogs alighted in strategic spots around the table – that is to say, near the kids – so they'd be available to dispose of any extra pizza crusts in an environmentally friendly way.

The first thing Kari, Pauline, and the Captain wanted to hear about was what had happened on the Portsmouth trip. Ketch spun a sanitized version of the yarn, with the kids chiming in to elaborate on the parts that were important to them. And while he passed around his coins again, Sally introduced everyone to her new doll, which was now named Veronica.

Then, when Bean and Sally were finished eating, Ketch and Suzanne sent them off to play so the adults could talk. Henry elected to stay at the table, and Suzanne allowed him to.

"So, y'all found the dead crooks washin' up on the beach, and then the gold coins, and the kids met the ghost a the Sea Hag, and then sand pirates – lordy, what'll they think of next? – they blew away your fancy Christmas toy," the Captain recapped. "Well hell, that's just a day at the beach, compared to some things I seen in *my* time! Why, I remember once when I was stationed down in Florida..."

"Boo!" Kari and Suzanne said almost simultaneously. "Not the right time, Don," Pauline admonished, but with a kindly smile. "And that part about the drone isn't funny," Kari sulkily remarked. "That wasn't money well-spent, that's for sure."

"All right, all right!" the Captain said, throwing up his hands. "I get the pitcher. So what's it all mean, Sherlock?" he said to Ketch.

"I'm not a detective," Ketch insisted, as he had in the past. "Not a licensed one, at any rate. But I think it all centers on that old woman. We've agreed that the kids couldn't have made all that up, and according to what they said, it seems she knew about pretty much everything that was happening on the island. Which also implies that she wasn't just a day visitor."

"But how could she be livin' on that island without anybody knowin' it? And how would she be able to survive there?" Kari objected.

"I don't know," Ketch said. "But I suppose just because we've never heard of her, that doesn't mean no one has. Maybe I could go back there and ask the Park Service volunteers if they know anything about her. I'd like to find her and see what else she might know."

"Accordin' to the old woman, those convicts were divin' on a shipwreck," Pauline said. "I wonder how they knew where to find it, and if it was some kind of treasure ship? A pirate ship like she said, or maybe one of those Spanish galleons. That's not English on those coins."

"I can't see what that sand barge has to do with anythin'," the Captain said. "And why the hell did they have guns?"

"I have some homework to do," Ketch said. "I

need to find out how to clean up those coins, and then maybe we'll be able to tell how old they are and where they came from. And I should research whether there might be any shipwrecks in that area. And then –"

"Aren't you gonna turn those coins in?" the Captain interrupted.

"Not just yet. I want to see if I can get some answers to our questions first."

"Yeah, I figgered that," the Captain said. "Anythin' I can do to help?"

"Maybe, now that you mention it. Do you still have contacts in the Coast Guard?"

"I got a couple buddies I could call on."

"Do you think you could find out if they know of any legitimate dredging operations going on around the island? Also, I wonder if they could get you the coordinates where that stolen boat was found?"

"Sure, I'll see what I can do. Tomorrow's Saturday, but that shouldn't make a difference. I'll start callin' 'round first thing in the mornin'."

"Sounds like you're fixin' to go back to Portsmouth," Kari said, giving Ketch a knowing look.

Ketch sat back in his chair. "Maybe," he said. "But just a day trip this time. Are you doing anything on Sunday?"

"You mean besides checkin' in rentals in the mornin', and then takin' care of Bean and the boys the rest of the time?" she replied. "We can't just run off on the spur of the moment these days, in case you forgot."

"They could stay with me for the day," Suzanne said. "I could even keep Bean overnight tomorrow, if that would help. The kids would keep each other occupied, and Henry and I could take turns walking the dogs."

"You'd do that?" Kari said. "Well, that's right nice of you. And you too, Henry. Though nobody asked you first, huh?"

"That's okay. I don't mind, Miss Gellhorn."

"Well then, thank you kindly, young man." She turned to Ketch. "Well, Stuart's comin' back to work tomorrow, and I might could get him to cover the shop. He'd only have to be there 'til noon at the latest, since it's Sunday."

"Maybe I should go along with y'all," Henry piped up. "If you both dive, you'll be needin' a tender topside."

"No way," Suzanne said. "It might be dangerous. You can help by staying here and walking the dogs like you just said you would."

"Well, I can't do it," the Captain said. "I got a half-day charter on Sunday – and now it looks like I got no mate." He winked at Henry.

"Could I mate for Captain Manolin on Sunday then?" Henry asked.

"He's qualified to do it, in case you're wondering," Ketch told Suzanne. Henry had been serving as second mate under Ketch on the semi-retired Captain's occasional fishing and diving charters, and Ketch knew he could handle the first mate's duties, at least on that particular boat.

"Maybe. We'll talk about it later," Suzanne told him.

"I can't be away from the shop this comin' week," Kari said. "I've got an Open Water class startin' on Monday, and I need to find somebody to replace Doug."

"She's the only instructor we have," Ketch said, thinking they should try to line up another one sometime. He and Stuart were divemasters, a certification level below instructor. They could serve as assistant instructors, but they weren't certified to teach without an instructor present. "So it would have to be Sunday, or next weekend. I know Sunday's a rush and we have some details to iron out, the biggest one being whether or not the Captain can get us those coordinates in the morning. But I have a feeling we shouldn't wait until next weekend."

"It seems like you'd have a lot of preparations to get through between now and Sunday," Suzanne said. "And Ketch, don't forget you have that meeting tomorrow," she reminded him.

"You've got a meeting?" Kari said. "With those pipin' plover people again?" Ketch nodded. "How come I didn't know about that?"

"I forgot to tell you," Ketch said, "and I mentioned it to Suzanne earlier. But I think we'll still have time to prepare. It's just a lunch."

"So, you two are really gonna try to find that

shipwreck," Pauline flatly stated.

"Yes, if there is one," Ketch said. "And hopefully talk to someone in the village about that Sea Hag woman while we're there."

"Well..." She hesitated, then decided to forge ahead. "Are you sure you've really thought this through? Suzanne might be right about it bein' dangerous. We don't know exactly what kind of divin' accident those convicts had. What if there *is* some kind of treasure wreck, and what if they weren't the only ones who knew about it? I've heard of things gettin' nasty between competing treasure divers before. Maybe those people on the barge – you know, the ones with the guns - weren't just collectin' sand, maybe they were dredgin' around the wreck. What if they killed those divers?"

The Captain chuckled. "Sounds like maybe you been readin' too many Clive Cussler books," he said.

"Oh?" Pauline retorted. "And what kind of book was it at that witch church last fall? And right in my house, too!"

"She's right," Ketch said. "Anything's possible. Captain, could you ask your contacts to find out if there were any indications of foul play with those divers? I guess I could call Dan, too, and see if he knows anything." Dan was with the SBI, the State Bureau of Investigation, and Ketch had worked with him in the fall. So, back up to six items on his list now. "Pauline, would you mind if I called him?"

"No, but I still think you ought to turn those coins in and let the authorities handle things."

"Oh, Mama," Kari said, rolling her eyes.

"Don't 'oh Mama' me, young lady. You've always had this fantasy about bein' a treasure hunter, and maybe even a pirate, ever since you were little – and probably him, too, I wouldn't be surprised," Pauline said, indicating Ketch. "But real life isn't like children's stories, you know."

"Okay," Kari said. "I admit, it's exciting to think we could discover a new wreck, and maybe even an old one with some treasure on it. But I hardly ever get to go divin' just for fun anymore, and it could be great for the shop. The Sea Dog could be famous and I could get more business."

"Yes," Pauline acknowledged, "if nothin' bad happens." She shook her head. "I'm sorry, but I think y'all might be takin' too many chances. Ketch, you do remember what happened the last time you did that, right?"

"Mama!" Kari scolded. Suzanne and Henry looked confusedly at Ketch, who said nothing. He felt like he'd been slapped across the face. Of course he remembered. How could he forget? And hadn't he been thinking just the other day that maybe he should start being more careful, since he was responsible for Bean now? But the lure of discovering a shipwreck, and possibly sunken treasure – and yes, the thrill of another chase – those were temptations that were hard for him to shake off.

"I'm sorry, but it's true," Pauline said, sticking to her guns.

Ketch came to a decision. "Pauline, I understand your concerns, and I thank you for caring. If I find out that the deaths of those divers are being treated as a homicide, I'll call the whole thing off and do just as you said. Otherwise, I want to go ahead with it. I don't know how many more adventures there will be in my life, and I don't want to pass this one up. Is that good enough?"

"It's good enough for me," Kari said.

"Raisin' your grandson isn't enough adventure for you?" Pauline sighed. "Well, I guess it'll have to do. Knowin' you two, especially my daughter, it's probably as good as I'm gonna get." She paused. "I can talk to Dan tonight, Ketch, so you don't have to call him. I'm gonna invite him over when I get back to Manteo."

"Won't it be a little late for a date night?" Kari asked. "It'll take you an hour to drive back up there."

True, but if it were Ketch driving, he knew the time would fly by quickly. The scenery along the lone two-lane road on that largely unspoiled stretch of the Cape Hatteras National Seashore, with the Atlantic to his right and Pamlico Sound on his left, never failed to calm whatever metaphysical savage beast might be lurking in him at the time, and he invariably found the transit across the Bonner Bridge over Oregon Inlet downright heavenly. And though he was, well, in love with Avon and Hatteras Island, one might as well say, he also liked Roanoke Island and its towns of Manteo and Wanchese. Granted there were some bad memories associated with those places for him, but there were good ones as well.

"It's not a date night. I just need to answer a question he asked me a while back. I've been thinkin' on it, and I decided I'm gonna say 'yes'."

Kari was the first one to get it. "You're gettin' married?" she squealed. "Aw, good for you, Mama!"

"So you approve?"

"'Course I do! It's not for me to say anyhow, and it's been way long enough since Daddy passed. So don't you worry about me. Dan's a good guy, I like him."

"Congratulations, Pauline," Ketch said, and the others at the table echoed the sentiment. Ketch knew Dan and Pauline had been seeing each other for at least a year. They were about the same age – as were all three of them, actually. It was a little strange to think that if he and Kari ever married, Pauline would be his mother-in-law.

"Well," Suzanne said when the hubbub had finally died down, "it's getting late for the kids, and I need to get Sally in the tub before bed."

"Ahem, was that there a hint?" the Captain teased.

"You go on ahead and take care of Sally," Kari said. "We'll clean up in here before we go. Except you, Mama, you just go on. You've probably been makin' that poor man wait long enough already. And thanks again for helpin' out at the shop, I really appreciate that."

"You're welcome. Ketch, I'll give you a call in the mornin' after I talk to Dan."

"Same here, soon's I know somethin'," the Captain promised. He collected a stack of paper plates from the table and passed them to Ketch. "Here you go! You scrape and I'll erase."

Though it was early for the adults, Ketch welcomed the opportunity to get home and start whittling away at his to-do list – which was now back down to five items, since he didn't have to call Dan. But there was still a lot to be done before Sunday. His only regret was he hadn't gotten to spend any time with Henry, and his poor guitar had gone un-played again.

"Goodnight, sir," Henry said to him. "I'm goin' on up to help Mama. Maybe we'll get a chance to play some other time."

"You read my mind," Ketch said. "Yes, definitely another time, as soon as possible."

When they were finished at Suzanne's, Ketch, Kari, Bean, and the dogs walked back to the boatyard. If one could still call it that, Ketch thought. The closest thing to a slum in Avon, nothing much got built, repaired, or even dry-docked at the Kinnakeet Boatyard these days. It was more like a floating trailer park, with numerous houseboats, mostly rentals, that never went anywhere and only a handful of more mobile vessels that did. Most serious boaters and fishermen sailed out of Hatteras village at the southern end of the island. But some interesting people lived at the boatyard, and Ketch liked the Bohemian atmosphere of the place.

And the name was right. 'Kinnakeet' had been the original name of the town of Avon, back before the government had established postal service there in the late eighteen hundreds and arbitrarily changed the name. The original name meant something like 'land of the mixed' in the Algonquin dialect of Chief Manteo's tribe, and had referred to the town's eventual mixed population of Indigenous Americans and English colonists. The current name, on the other hand, didn't mean anything to Ketch. And they'd done the same thing with other towns on Hatteras Island – Chicamacomico had become Rodanthe, Clarks was now Salvo, Cape was now Buxton, and Trent was now Frisco. It verged on sacrilege in Ketch's opinion, but there was nothing he could do about it.

The Captain's *My Minnow*, an older but meticulously maintained thirty-five-foot Bertram Fly-Bridge, was one of the boatyard's mobile vessels, but she was dark tonight as the Captain had decided to drive back to his Hatteras condo. That was just as well. Though Ketch enjoyed his company and often found him helpful, he had work to do tonight.

Bean was on his last legs by the time they reached the *Port Starbird*, but Kari insisted on a shower before they tucked him into bed. Ketch needed one himself, so he took the boy into the shower with him. He'd been quite the little trooper the last couple of days, but the poor kid was exhausted now, so Ketch made it a quick one. He'd let him sleep in tomorrow as late as he liked.

Before Bean nodded off, though, he managed to thank Ketch again and tell him he was glad they'd 'goed' to Portsmouth. Ketch didn't correct his grammar this time.

Kari decided to shower after that, so Ketch booted up his laptop at the galley table. It was dark out now, but he didn't bother turning on any lights. Jack and Chuck curled up on either side of his chair and went to sleep. Kari joined him at the table when she got out of the shower.

"Hard at work already, huh?" she said, dropping into another chair.

"Yes, I'm trying to find out how to clean those coins. The experts say non-experts should never clean coins, because they'll get damaged and have less value to collectors. I don't care too much about that right now, but I also don't want to obliterate anything. So okay, no acids, and acetone is iffy, and no chlorinated water... Ah, distilled water doesn't hurt gold. I have an old Waterpik somewhere, but it might be in the storage unit..."

"Did you notice nobody asks us when we're gettin' married anymore?" Kari cut in. "I guess we've put 'em off enough so they figure we're a lost cause. But I'm happy for Mama."

"Why did she come down today? I meant to ask before."

"It was inventory time, and she offered to help since all my other helpers were either on vacation, in jail, or off chasin' after floozies."

Ketch chose to pass on the bait this time. "I'm sorry I wasn't here. But it was too late to cancel the reservations, and the kids would have been disappointed."

"I know, it's okay," she said. "I still don't want to anyway, you know. Get married, I mean."

"Nor do I," Ketch said, looking up from the laptop. "I'm glad we still agree on that." Never been in her case, been there and done that in his. He liked to think he was capable of learning from his mistakes, and he didn't intend to make that one again.

"But you know what that means, right?" she said with mischief in her eyes. Ketch was pretty sure he did, since he knew that look. "Without that piece of paper, you've got to work harder to keep me." She leaned back in her seat and began unbuttoning the dress shirt of his that she'd put on after her shower. It was her only garment, he noticed. "So you better shut that thing down, mister, and start workin' hard on *this*," she concluded.

Well, so much for his plans with the laptop for tonight, he guessed. But he'd be up at the crack of dawn as always, so he could resume his research then. Besides, she was always the number-one item on his everlasting to-do list, even if he usually left it unspoken. So he turned off the laptop, went over to her, and got to work.

~ **F o u r** ~

True nobility arises from being better than one's former self.

*A*s opposed to being better than other people, that is. Ketch had read something to that effect somewhere a while back and it had resonated with him. Could he himself be considered noble in that sense, he wondered?

He was more outgoing and resourceful now than he'd ever been before, he'd largely gotten over the 'depression' he liked to think he'd suffered from (as opposed to a nervous breakdown, which he chose not to acknowledge), and he'd left behind that brief phase of drinking way too heavily. He also thought he was kinder now, and more like his parents had hoped he'd be with his recent sleuthing avocation, and he was trying to make amends for his past failures with his son by taking on Bean.

But wasn't humility a component of nobility? Whether it was considered so or not, he thought it should be, so he decided to stop patting himself on the back. Instead he patted Jack, who'd joined him out on the deck to watch the sun come up (Chuck liked to sleep in).

Good old Jack... Ketch thought he was probably the smartest dog he'd ever had, not to mention being a literal lifesaver on at least two occasions –

one being during that violent confrontation on the Captain's boat a year ago, and before that helping Ketch rise up out of his smoldering funk much more effectively than any human therapist had been able to.

How the mind can wander this early in the morning, he thought. Well, his mind anyway. He ruffled Jack's fur and rose from his chair. It was time to go inside and get back to work – on his laptop, this time. There was no telling what could happen when Kari and her libido awoke on any given day, and then there'd be Bean and the dogs to take care of, but he could at least get started. After he fired up the coffeemaker, that is.

He began by putting his personal online investigative team to work on researching sand pirates. And through those good folks at Google, he learned that there was indeed such a thing as sand piracy.

There was a huge demand for sand all around the world. Various types of sand were used as abrasives in manufacturing, for making concrete, in hydrocarbon extraction, for improving driving conditions on icy roads in winter, for beach replenishment, and as a source of industrially useful minerals and elements. The sand could be mined from beaches, dunes, and inland pits, and could be dredged from riverbeds and the ocean floor.

Where the piracy element came into play was in places where there was a lot of building and development going on. Because the cost of transporting such voluminous and heavy cargo could quickly become prohibitive as the distance increased, most of the time the sand was mined as close as possible to where it was needed. And in at least some instances, if mining that nearby sand wasn't permitted, it was mined illegally.

This had happened sporadically on every continent except Antarctica at one time or another, and even right here in the U.S.A. There was currently a 'sand mafia' in India, where illegal sand mining was endemic around the growing cities. Criminal organizations there laid claim to mining sites and defended them against competitors, government regulators, and anti-mining activists, going so far as to resort to assassination when necessary. An entire man-made beach in Hungary was stolen a few years back, and at around the same time the equivalent of five hundred truckloads of sand were pirated from the Coral Springs beach in Jamaica. Entrepreneurs hoping to find valuable gems had looted the diamond sands along the coast of Namibia, sometimes stripping beaches down to the bedrock. The loss of the beaches had led to habitat destruction, coastal erosion, and flooding.

Ketch sat back and thought. There were beach replenishment projects now and then along the Outer Banks due to the periodic lashings the islands took from hurricanes and nor'easters, and dredging operations to keep the inlets passable, but as far as he knew they were on the up-and-up. But what about private development initiatives? The only one he could think of on Hatteras Island or Ocracoke Island that might need significant amounts of sand at this time was the new condominium complex whose construction was underway near Cape Point in Buxton.

There'd been some shadiness going on with that one, he knew – or at least, that was what he'd been told by some of the folks from the CSFCP, the new organization he'd joined over the winter. And he knew the developers were trying to add building substrate at that location. He'd ask his new friends, Bob and RAM, later if they'd heard where the sand for that was coming from, as they were supposed to be attending today's CSFCP lunch at Pangea. If there was any more monkey business going on there, they'd be bound to either know about it or have a theory.

Though if that sand barge was working for those developers, it would probably have to make quite a few trips to meet their needs. That didn't seem practical at first glance – but if it was being done illegally, practicality might not be their main concern.

If his friends didn't have the answer, maybe he could at least take Bob aside and have him solve another mystery, that being RAM's full name. It seemed to be a 'thing' in these parts for people to sometimes be addressed by their initials, and he couldn't for the life of him recall what R.A.M.

stood for. 'Robert' something, probably, but he was lost after that.

He heard Jack's tail thump out on the couch where he'd settled. "Good mornin', y'all," Kari softly called. She patted Jack, then came up behind Ketch and gave him a quick shoulder massage. His mind went blissfully blank for a few moments, and then he noticed she was fully dressed. That was fine with him this particular morning.

"You wore me out last night," she said, "and that's sayin' somethin'! I guess you really did miss me, huh?" Without waiting for an answer, she went over to the counter and popped a bagel in the toaster. "I'm goin' in to the shop early today. It'll just be me 'til Stuart gets in, and I want to make sure I have all the tanks filled so I won't have to mess with 'em later. I want to try and set up a couple interviews, too, to replace Doug."

"Okay," Ketch absently responded. He was searching for shipwrecks now.

"I see you already got the coffee goin'," she said. "Thank you! You're a good man, Charlie Brown."

Ketch cringed a little, even though she used that expression periodically. Suzanne had said the exact same thing to him the night before last in a less innocent context, and he found that vaguely unsettling for some reason. He got up and fished a Diet Pepsi out of the fridge. He didn't drink coffee himself. As for food, he thought he'd wait for Bean.

"When Bean gets up, I think we'll walk the dogs

over to the lot and check on the new house," he said. He hadn't stopped by there since before the Portsmouth trip, and he wanted to see how it was coming along. It might also be time to give the builder some more money, so he could check on that as well, and the dogs could take a dip in the sound if they liked. "Then I think I'll put him to work on those coins while I do some more research. I think he'll enjoy that, if I can find that Waterpik. I know I have a couple of jugs of distilled water."

"Oh, I forgot to tell you, I saw it under some other stuff in the back of my closet just now when I was gettin' dressed. I don't know how it ended up there, but that's where it is."

She sat down at the table with her buttered bagel and a cup of coffee. Chuck, lured by the scent of wild dough, moseyed in and joined Jack next to her chair. They were a couple of moochers like most dogs, but at least they were polite about it.

"That's good, thanks. Now I won't have to go to the storage unit." Ketch squinted at an almost unreadably comprehensive map of all known North Carolina shipwrecks he'd found, then tapped on the screen to zoom the image. "I was right, there aren't any known pirate ships, or treasure ships of any kind, around the south end of Portsmouth Island. There are wrecks, but they're all more recent than that. There was a Spanish galleon that sank up around Ocracoke Inlet in 1750, the *Nuestra Senora de Guadalupe*. But that's miles away from where that stolen boat was found, and she was carrying silver, not gold."

"Well, there must be some kinda old wreck around there. Do tell me what you find out later, so I can throw some gear together for tomorrow if it turns out we're goin'." She finished her coffee and slid her plate over to him. "Here, I don't want this last piece. You can feed it to the wolves if you want. Hey, remember that funny poster we saw one time? 'Once we were wolves, wild and wary, and then we noticed you had sofas'." She laughed. "Well anyway, I've got to get goin'." Ketch broke the remaining piece in half and the dogs scrambled to rearrange themselves on either side of his chair.

"Oh hey, good mornin', Bean!" she said as she got up from the table. The boy shuffled over to her, and she gave him a hug. "I have to go to work, so I'll see you later, okay?" He nodded and then slumped into the chair she'd vacated. "You're gonna leave him off at the shop before your meeting, right?" she said to Ketch. "Okay. Bye, guys!" she said to the dogs, giving each one a quick rub on the head.

"You're up earlier than I'd expected," Ketch said to Bean after she'd left. "Are you sure you don't want to sleep some more?" Bean shook his head, which was now resting on his arms on the table. "It looks like you're not really awake yet. Should I take you out on deck and hose you down?" That got the boy's attention. He picked his head up and blearily grinned at Ketch. "Okay then, how about some breakfast? And then we'll take the dogs for a walk."

After a quick breakfast, Ketch got Bean washed and dressed. Then they all headed over to the soundfront lot where Ketch's old house had once stood. The new one looked to be coming along nicely, and he was lucky enough to catch the general contractor on site. Ketch gave Jack's frisbee and Chuck's ball to Bean and sent them all down to play at the water's edge so he could talk with the contractor. He got an update from the man and wrote him another check.

Although it was true that the new house would have triple the square footage of his old bungalow-style cottage, Ketch had an oversized lot and he'd deliberately chosen a design that wouldn't look too ostentatious. He didn't want it to stick out like a sore thumb and be out of place in his North End Road neighborhood. In fact, with the shake siding he'd selected, it would recall the look of the original *Port Starbird*.

There'd be no mortgage on this house. Ketch was paying as he went, using funds from the witch's bitcoin stash. Her smartphone, which Kari had filched for him, had contained all of her church's financial information. The bitcoins were an investment the witch had made with some of the proceeds of her black market trading, and she'd boasted to Ketch that her digital bitcoin wallet was worth ten times what she'd paid for it due to the recent boom in the bitcoin market. That money was in addition to, and separate from, the accumulated value of the estates she'd conned her acolytes into bequeathing to her church. He'd decided to keep the bitcoins as payback for what she'd done to him – something that still rankled him from time to time, though he thought he was pretty much over it now.

He'd initially toyed with the idea of unilaterally reimbursing the families of the victims from the witch's traditional bank accounts, but the logistics had turned out to be daunting. In the end he'd decided to copy the bitcoin data he needed, delete it from the phone, and turn the phone in to Dan at the SBI and let the State handle the restitution issue. Dan had graciously accepted Ketch's dubious story of the CSI-types somehow overlooking the phone at the crime scene and him finding it later.

Handily for Ketch, bitcoins were an anonymous global Internet currency that had no ties to any banks or governments, and all he'd needed to access this digital money was the private software keys from the witch's phone. As with numbered accounts, whoever had the numbers could have the money, no questions asked. But spending a windfall like that without paying taxes on it wasn't as easy these days as pulpy novels and TV shows made it out to be.

Although he didn't really want to be a tax evader, out of curiosity Ketch had looked into moving the bitcoin money into a numbered offshore account with a bank in the Cayman Islands, a favorite literary trope of many writers. But in real life, that was no cakewalk, not for everyday people like himself, anyway. In recent years, agreements had been drawn up that allowed the U.S. government more oversight of foreign accounts in order to guard against tax evasion and other kinds of fraud, such as money laundering. And the banks, to protect their own interests, were now requiring detailed information from would-be foreign depositors, including references from domestic banks and legal verification of income.

And then, if one wanted to withdraw the money and spend it, it had to be wired from the Caymans to a domestic bank account, or one had to use a debit card from the foreign bank. Traveling to the Caymans to withdraw money in person was a major expense and inconvenience, and it wasn't safe to walk around with large amounts of cash. And unless one wanted to risk trying to smuggle it home, there'd be more bureaucratic hurdles when re-entering the U.S. with it.

The bottom line was, there'd be no hiding what he was doing, unless he wanted to learn how to create and manage something like those quasi-legal shell corporations that were also a favorite pulp device. But that would cost him money and eat up way too much of his time, and could also end up getting him in trouble if anyone decided to look more deeply into his activities. So he'd simply cashed in the bitcoins by selling them on an

Internet bitcoin exchange and having the exchange deposit U.S. dollars directly into his plain old U.S. savings account.

He'd missed the peak of the boom that had accelerated even further after he'd taken down the witch, but when he'd cashed out in January the bitcoins had still been worth over five times their value when the witch had owned them. So they'd ended up being worth fifty times what the witch had bought them for. The quarterly tax returns he'd already filed to forestall any penalties must be raising some eyebrows at the IRS, and he wouldn't be surprised if he got audited. But tax-wise there was nothing illegal in what he was doing – as far as they'd ever know, he'd just made an anonymous investment in bitcoins some time ago and decided to liquidate. So even if he was technically a thief, at least he wasn't a tax evader.

It did annoy him that he was losing almost half of the money to taxes since he couldn't document any cost basis, but it was worth it to him to be legally free and clear. And even after the money he'd spent on the new house and the gifts for his friends, he'd still be a millionaire when the dust settled. He figured the shot in the arm that was giving his retirement investment accounts should see him through the rest of his days, even if he used some of it to send Bean to college. That almost made what he'd gone through to get it seem worthwhile.

So, no worries there. And today there was

another mystery to be solved, the game was afoot, and life was good. He joined Bean and the dogs at the sound, played with them for a few minutes, and then herded them all back to the houseboat so he could get back to work.

Though it was a postcard-worthy morning at the boatyard, sunny and breezy and not unpleasantly hot, Ketch wanted Bean to clean the coins in the galley sink. It was almost sinful to stay in on a day like this, but it'd be too easy for the boy to lose the coins out on deck. He figured he should at least open windows and let the invigorating salt air in, which he did. Then he gave the dogs each a new bone to gnaw on, and retrieved the Waterpik and the jugs of distilled water from their hiding places.

He set Bean up on a stepstool in front of the sink, showed him how to use the Waterpik, and gave him a brief demonstration on the first of the coins with the machine and an old toothbrush. The boy was delighted by the activity and Ketch doubted he'd be able to sandblast the coins into oblivion, as the Waterpik wasn't as powerful as a pressure washer, so he shouldn't have to watch him like a hawk. In fact, it looked to Ketch like it might take a good while to remove the encrustations, if this method even worked. But it would keep the lad entertained and busy for the time being.

The strains of *Enter Sandman* began emanating from Ketch's cell phone as soon as he'd sat back down at the table with his laptop. That had been Mariano Rivera's iconic walk-on music until the end of his final season with the Yankees the previous year. And now it was the last time around for Derek Jeter, the sole remnant of the core of Ketch's old home team. He reminded himself to check the TV schedule sometime soon, as he wanted to try to catch a few more of the games than he'd managed to last year.

"Hey, Ketch," Dan said in Ketch's ear. "Long time no see. Everything good on your end?"

"Yes, thank you, no complaints here. I heard you got some good news last night. Congratulations!" Ketch winced after he'd said that. What if Pauline hadn't told him yet, or had changed her mind on her way home?

"Yeah, how about that? I was kinda surprised – but in a good way, of course. She's one headstrong lady, isn't she? Anyway, I told her I'd give you a call this morning."

"Thanks, I appreciate it. So what's the story?"

"Well, you're in luck. There was some question of who should have jurisdiction over those bodies you found. The Coast Guard picked them up, but Portsmouth's in Carteret County, but it's not a real town anymore, and those convicts escaped from Raleigh – anyway, the punchline is they ended up here at the SBI. Now the autopsy reports haven't come in yet, but I can tell you there were no external injuries. But the coroner said their eardrums were ruptured and he saw signs of internal bleeding. So the working theory is, they might have gotten caught in an underwater explosion of some kind. In that kinda situation, it's the pressure wave that gets you, not shrapnel or whatever – you know, like fishing with dynamite. So that could explain what happened to them."

Ketch knew about this. On land, the air absorbs some of the energy of an explosion. Water, on the other hand, moves with the explosion instead of absorbing it. This increases the destructive range of the explosion, and when the pressure wave hits you, it compresses air-filled pockets throughout your body and causes internal damage. If you stood just outside the range of an explosion on land, you'd be unharmed – but at the same distance underwater, the pressure wave would kill you. Maybe that could explain why those divers were missing most of their gear, he thought.

"I see," Ketch said. "Does Pauline know all this?"

"She does indeed, and she's not keen on you and Kari diving wherever those convicts were, I can tell you that, too. I might have to agree with her on that. Sounds to me like maybe they found some old wreck from the war with some live ordnance on it. Might not be safe to go messing around with something like that, even if there's some kind of booty there."

"Thanks, Dan. I'll pass all this along to Kari and see what she thinks. The question might be moot anyway, since I haven't heard back from the

Captain yet. He was supposed to contact someone he knows in the Coast Guard and try to get the coordinates of that stolen boat."

"Well, if he does, and you do decide to go on ahead with your plan, I hope y'all will be extra careful. And if you see any evidence of a crime down there, please be careful to not do anything that could mess up a police investigation. I'm already sticking my neck out by not ordering you to stay away from there."

Ketch promised they'd be careful on both counts, and he thanked Dan again before hanging up. Bean was still hard at work at the sink, so he decided to look up images of gold coins on his laptop. He hadn't gotten very far when his phone rang again.

"Ahoy, it's your Skipper callin'!" the Captain's gravelly voice rang out. Ketch held the phone farther away from his ear and hoped the salty dog would watch his language. Bean would be able to hear him even though he wasn't on speaker.

"I know, I have caller ID," Ketch said. "Where are you?"

"Well, I ain't wherever you're at, else I'd just a-come a-callin'."

Ketch figured he was probably still down at his condo. "Right. Bean is here with me, just so you know. Were you able to find out anything?"

"Gotcha, no cursin'," the Captain said. "Well, I found out the Coast Guard didn't know nothin' 'bout any night-time dredgin', nor daytime neither, goin' on around Portsmouth this week. Which is strange, 'cause they're supposed to know 'bout stuff like that. So you started somethin' there. They're gonna look into it."

"Yes, that's odd." Ketch wondered if he should call Dan back with that information. "Did you ask if they had any idea what might have killed those convicts?"

"Nah, I did, but they turned that over to the civvies. But I did find out where that ole boat was found. You got a pen and paper?"

"Yes, go ahead," Ketch fibbed. He'd just type the information into the notepad on his computer for now. When the Captain had finished, Ketch said, "Got it, thanks. By the way, I knew the SBI had taken over. I talked with Dan just before you called. They have the bodies, and he said they think they might have been killed by an underwater explosion."

"Do tell! Well, that's interestin'. What kinda explosion, I wonder?"

"They don't know. Dan thought they might have been diving on some old wreck from the war, and maybe some ammunition exploded. They might know more later, when the autopsy reports come in."

"Are you guys still gonna go there and find out for your own selves?"

"Maybe. I haven't told Kari about any of this yet. I'd like to, though."

"Well, I don't know..." the Captain mused.

"Maybe y'all ought to sit this one out, like Pauline said. We could put the Coasties on it." When Ketch didn't answer right away, he continued, "But you ain't gonna do that, right? Well then, you better not touch nothin', and don't go inside if there's a wreck. I won't be there to bail your sorry ass out a trouble this time, like I done before. Uh-oh, sorry 'bout that, Bean. Anyways, maybe just take some pitchers, hear?"

"I'll do that. Don't worry, if we go, we'll be careful. Kari's a stickler for safety."

"Huh," the Captain grunted. "Well, I guess that's a good thing, 'cause you sure as hell ain't! Dang, sorry 'bout that!"

Ketch chuckled. "It's okay, I'm sure those aren't the worst words he's ever heard. Right, Bean?" The boy flashed him a guilty smile and continued his scrubbing. He'd turned off the Waterpik and was now working with the toothbrush. "Well, I'd better get going. Will you be around later?"

"Yeah, I got to get the *Minnow* ready for that charter."

"Okay, see you later," Ketch said and hung up.

"Alligator," Bean said.

"What?"

"See you later, alligator," Bean explained, and then added the corollary, "In a while, crocodile."

"Gotta go, buffalo. Out the door, dinosaur," Ketch responded. He suddenly realized those were the first words the boy had spoken the whole time he'd been on the phone. That was impressive for a seven-year-old. More often than not, kids that age hadn't quite gotten the hang yet of not interrupting.

"Do you know how to tell an alligator from a crocodile?" Ketch asked him. Bean shook his head. "It's easy. One of them will see you later, and the other one will see you in a while."

Bean's brow furrowed at that, and then his face lit up in a big grin. He put the toothbrush aside and hopped down from the stepstool. "Papa, look!" he said. He joined Ketch at the table and held a coin out for him to inspect.

"Well, look at that," Ketch said. "Good job, Bean!" The boy had managed to get one coin fairly clean, enough to see most of the detailing now.

Not that it helped all that much. There was no date and Ketch still didn't recognize the language of the coin's inscriptions, if it was indeed a language. It could just be symbols. He was no linguist and he wouldn't be able to translate much, but he thought he'd know most of the European languages if he saw them. So the coin probably wasn't European in origin. He could also tell it wasn't Chinese or Japanese, and the symbols didn't look like Egyptian hieroglyphics he'd seen. And it was obvious now that it was very old. On a hunch he started an online search for Aztec currency.

"Now that we can see more of this coin, let's see if we can figure out what kind of coin it is," he said, directing Bean to sit beside him. "It's old and I don't know what kind of writing that is, so I'm thinking it might be Aztec. The Aztecs were people who lived in Mexico a long time ago, and they had gold."

Bean peered intently at the screen along with him, but Ketch could tell he was mostly looking at the images. Since he was just starting to learn to read, Ketch summarized for him.

"But it says here the Aztecs mostly traded for things they needed. They didn't use much money, and their money wasn't made of gold. Guess what was one thing they used for money?"

"What?"

"Chocolate." Bean made a disbelieving face at him. "Well, actually the cocoa beans that chocolate is made from. They also used copper sometimes, but they didn't make coins. Their copper money was shaped like boat anchors. See this picture here? They were called 'tajaderas'. So if this coin was made by the Aztecs, it's probably a piece of jewelry or religious art, not a coin. Do you see this hole here?" Now that the encrustations had been mostly removed, a hole near the edge of the coin was discernable. "This coin, and maybe the others, might have been part of a necklace or medallion."

"Did the pirates steal gold from those people?" Bean asked.

"Not that I know of. It was mostly the Spanish navy that stole gold from the Aztecs. But then the pirates stole the gold from the Spanish ships sometimes."

"Did Peter Painter steal gold from those ships?"

"I don't know. He might have. Here, let's look up the Incas now... Okay, here we go. The Incas were people who lived in South America a long time ago. The Spanish stole gold from them, too. Hmm... Well, it says here that some of the Incas used money, but most of them didn't. They had more gold than the Aztecs, and they also made things out of it, but they didn't use gold for money."

"But look at all those coins." Bean pointed to an image. Some of the pictures on the screen did show gold coins, sometimes piles of them.

"Those coins you're seeing in those pictures were made after the Spanish conquered the Aztecs and the Incas. The Spanish forced them to mine the gold and they made coins from some of it. Those coins have years and Spanish words on them. Our coin doesn't."

Bean appeared to be lost in thought. Ketch stopped talking, to give him a chance to process what he'd been hearing. It was a lot for a kid to take in. He'd let him ask some more questions if he needed to before trying to give the boy more information.

"Did those people at the beach get blowed up?" he finally asked.

Not a question he was expecting, Ketch thought – but he reminded himself that he shouldn't be surprised. Although Bean hadn't spoken during the phone calls, that didn't mean he hadn't been listening.

"*Blown* up? Maybe," he said. "We don't know for sure yet."

Bean just nodded and moved on. "Maybe this is Peter Painter's coin. The Sea Hag said it was his. You said some pirates didn't have treasure chests. But maybe Peter Painter had one."

"Well, if he did, he might have gotten it from some old pirate, or maybe he dug it up somewhere. If that coin came from the Aztecs or the Incas, it's even older than Peter Painter."

"Maybe he had a treasure map!"

"Maybe he did," Ketch said. "But I don't think we'll ever know."

Bean shrugged. "Maybe you can find it if you go there again."

"Yes, who knows?"

"Do I have to wash more coins?"

"No, that's hard work and I think you've done enough for now. You did a good job, and you were very helpful. Even though we still don't know exactly where this coin came from, your work tells us this must be a very old shipwreck. So thank you for that." Ketch checked the time. "I have to go to my meeting soon, so we'd better get ready to take you over to the shop. I forgot to ask if there'd be lunch for you there, so maybe we should stop at Subway −" Ketch cut himself short when he realized someone was tapping on the cabin door.

The dogs both got up off the floor and growled. Through the glass, Ketch saw there was a pretty young woman he didn't know at the door. Her short blond hairdo was reminiscent of Kari's new style.

"Jack and Chuck – stay!" he commanded the dogs. "Bean, please use the bathroom and then put your sneakers on." He opened the door and stepped out, forcing the girl to back away. "Hello," he said, shutting the door behind him. "Can I help you with something?"

"Hi, my name's Cheryl. I'm with the *Outer Banks Monitor*," she cheerily replied. "Are you Storm Ketchum?"

"Yes. Are you a reporter?"

"Yes, sir, I am. If you have a few minutes, would you mind if I interviewed you for my newspaper?"

"Why would you want to interview me?"

"Well, Mister Ketchum, I heard it was you that found those convicts down on Portsmouth, and I thought I might could ask you just a few quick questions about that, if you don't mind?"

So much for keeping a low profile. He hadn't really expected it to stay a secret forever, but he'd thought he'd be granted more of a reprieve than this. "Where did you hear it was me?" he asked.

"Uh, well... I have a friend in the Coast Guard."

"I see." Ketch thought for a moment. "Does everyone know? Has it been on TV?"

"Oh no, sir. I'm the only one who knows so far, I think." She looked up at him sheepishly. "I'm new at the paper, and I need to, um, start makin' my mark, you know? So I hadn't told anybody else."

"So you tracked me down in hopes of an exclusive interview," Ketch said. "Well, I don't blame you, but I'm afraid I'm too busy right now, and I probably will be for some time."

"Oh! Well then, I'm truly sorry to be botherin' you, sir. Thank you for talkin' with me," she said and turned to go.

That's strange, Ketch thought. Reporters were generally more persistent than that, weren't they? But then, this one was new, she'd said.

"Wait a minute." She stopped and looked back at him. "Cheryl, was it? Well, Cheryl, I don't have time right now, and I can't say when I will. But if you give me your card, I'll call you when I do have time." She brightened noticeably at that. "And if you can keep this to yourself, I promise I'll talk to you first. And by then I might have more to tell than you were expecting."

"I can surely do that," she said. "Thank you so much, Mister Ketchum! I'll look forward to hearin' from you!" She passed him her business card with a big smile and took her leave.

And almost bumped into Suzanne and Sally, who were making their way along the dock toward the houseboat. "Oh, excuse me! I'm sorry," Cheryl apologized as she rushed past them. Bean opened the door and came out then.

"Hi, Ketch," Suzanne said as they boarded. "And hi, Bean." The dogs, figuring the coast was clear now, wandered out as well and watched to make sure the stranger actually got in her car and left. "Who was that?"

"A reporter. She found out I was the one who called the Coast Guard about those divers, and she wanted an interview. I told her maybe later sometime."

"Oh. Well, that didn't take long, did it? It looks like you're about to become famous again."

Ketch knew she was referring to the time he'd been on the news after exposing the illegal ocean dumping by Tibbleson Construction up in Wanchese, another company run by the jailed Bob Ingram as it had turned out – and then of course there'd been that other business with the witch and her coven in Manteo, which had also made the papers.

"Well, I'd rather not be," he said. "So what brings you around?"

"Oh, Henry's off doing some mowing and Sally got bored, so I thought we'd walk over here. I thought maybe I could pick Bean up now instead of later, if you'd like me to. He'll be staying over tonight anyway if you're going back to Portsmouth, and I figured you probably have a lot to do today, if you're doing that. Are you?"

"Yes, I think so. I haven't told Kari yet, though. I'll stop at the shop after my meeting, and then – you're right, I will indeed have a lot to do."

"Well then, why don't we just throw a few things in a bag for him quick, and you can go do what you have to do?"

"That sounds good, Suzanne. Thank you. I really appreciate you doing this. Oh, should I drop the dogs off tonight? If I do it in the morning, it'll be pretty early."

"In the morning will be all right. I'm not sure I should have, but I told Henry he could go with Don on his charter. I guess he knows what he's doing, according to you and Don, but I'll still worry. Anyway, I'll be up early with him in the morning."

"Okay then, that's what I'll do. Don't worry too much about Henry. He may be thirteen, but out there he's thirteen going on thirty, and I'm sure he'll be all right."

Ketch turned then to speak to Bean, but he was gone. He'd been about to belatedly ask the boy if the new plan was okay with him, but then he saw that Bean and Sally were already absorbed in something on Bean's tablet computer back in the cabin. Though he guessed Bean probably wouldn't mind spending the afternoon with his best friend, before the boy left with Suzanne he'd thank him again for helping out this morning, explain the situation, and make sure he knew he'd be missed. And hug him.

All things he should have done more of many years ago with his son. That was another mistake he wouldn't be making again, if he could possibly help it.

~ **F i v e** ~

He sailed his course and took what came along the way.

*T*he first thing Ketch did after Suzanne departed with the kids was complete his phone business, which he accomplished while following the dogs around the boatyard property as they caught up on their own business. He'd always been good at multitasking.

When he called Kari to let her in on the new arrangements and sound her out on tomorrow's trip, he didn't have to work at all to convince her to go. She still wanted to, and it would take more than a theory about an explosion to dissuade her. He knew she wouldn't do anything stupid when they were down below, and neither would he – especially not with her watching him. Since she was an instructor and he was just a divemaster, she was the boss when they were in the water (and probably when they were out of it as well, if he wanted to be honest about it).

Her sole concern was, they still needed a third person to stay behind on the boat while the two of them dived. She wouldn't leave the boat untended while they were in the water, and there'd be no solo diving on her watch. She felt it was unsafe to do that when wreck diving to begin with, and she reminded him that he still hadn't taken that solo diving course he'd paid her for in advance last summer.

And he probably never would, as he saw little value in it, though he wouldn't tell her that. Paying for that class had just been a pretext to help her out of a financial jam she'd been in early on in their relationship.

He also called Dan back and told him what he'd heard from the Captain regarding the Coast Guard being unaware of the activities of the Portsmouth sand barge. Dan said he didn't see how there could be a connection between that and the convicts, but then said that might just be because they hadn't turned over enough rocks yet – like the good detective that Ketch knew him to be.

After that he tried to focus on thinking of someone who might be both available and willing to spend an entire day serving as his boat tender. It had been at the back of his mind since he awoke this morning, but he still hadn't come up with anyone. He briefly wondered again whether Len might be back in town, and again dismissed the thought. He hadn't seen him around the boatyard, plus Len hadn't been too thrilled at the way their shared adventure at the witch's church had turned out last fall. But he couldn't think of anyone else. Maybe he should give him a call after all, he thought. It wouldn't hurt to ask...

And then, in one of those cosmic coincidences that make one go 'hmm', a pickup pulled into the boatyard lot and Ketch was startled to hear the familiar Tar Heel twang of the devil himself coming from its open window – as in 'speaking of', that is.

"Well hey, Ketch, long time no see!" Len hopped down from the truck and walked over to Ketch with a typically goofy grin on his face.

"Hello, Len," Ketch said, shaking the outstretched hand of his sometime friend. "I was just thinking about you and wondering if you were back yet."

"Yep, I'm back, bigger'n better'n ever! I was just gonna stop on by your boat – and here y'all are! And here's Jack'n Chuck! How you boys doin'?" The dogs, obviously remembering who he was, swarmed around him and jockeyed for his attention. He squatted momentarily to satisfy them.

"So whatcha been up to, good buddy? How's Kari?"

"Oh, the usual, and Kari's fine. Are you back for a while? I haven't seen you around."

"I'm stayin' with a friend 'til somethin' opens up here at the boatyard. I gave up my rental when I went home. I'll be stayin' the summer at least."

"Well, come aboard and have a beer."

"Why thank you, don't mind if I do!"

Ketch herded Jack and Chuck back onto the houseboat. While Len settled into one of the plastic deck chairs and put his feet up, Ketch went inside for the beers and a couple of dog treats.

"So you just came here to see me?" Ketch asked

when he came back out.

"Well, no. I came for you, too, but I must confess, I thought maybe Diana might still be around. She used to stay just 'round the corner from here. But she ain't around, so I guess I'll have to find me somebody new."

"Well, you just missed a good one. A reporter came by here looking for me a little while ago. She was quite attractive. I think you would've liked her." Though in truth, it seemed to him it would be an odd match. Despite the enviable financial situation he was in for someone who was only in his late twenties, with his straw hat and ZZ Top beard Len looked like a refugee from *The Beverly Hillbillies* most of the time, and talked like one, too. But stranger things had certainly happened.

"Do tell! Is she comin' back?"

"Not until I call her, which won't be for a few days at least."

"Aw, that's too bad." Len twisted the cap off of his bottle and held it up. "Here's to it bein' five o'clock somewhere! Hey, hang on a minute – how come some reporter's after you? Whatcha gone'n done now?"

Ketch told him about the trip that he, Suzanne, and the kids had taken to Portsmouth Island. He filled him in on pretty much everything that had happened, except for conveniently forgetting to mention the part about the drone.

"Man! That's some story. And no kiddin', you're the one that found them escaped convicts? I heard 'bout that on the news. Figgers it'd be you, I swear!" Len laughed. "So that's why that reporter come lookin' for you?"

"Yes." Ketch took another drink and thought, then decided to go for it. "Kari and I want to go back down there and see if we can find where those coins came from."

"Oh yeah? When y'all goin'?"

"Well, the only day we can do it this coming week is tomorrow, but we haven't been able to find someone to tend the boat for us while we dive."

"Tomorrow? Well heck, I ain't doin' nothin'. I could do it."

"Really? You'd do that?"

"What, go on a real live treasure hunt? Hell yeah! I always wanted to be a pirate. Will there be beer?"

"There could be, yes."

"Well then, count me in! What time y'all leavin'?"

"Early in the morning." Given what had happened in the fall, Ketch thought he'd better level with him. "You know, those convicts might not have been the only ones looking for that treasure. The people on the barge might be involved, too. We don't know yet," he said, and then he fessed up about his drone.

"Huh," Len said. "Well hell, we'll just have to keep our eyes open then – meanin' me, when you guys are on the bottom. I can do that."

Ketch didn't know what to say at first. This was

a pleasant surprise. "Are you sure? If you are, it'd certainly be a big help to us. I could pay you for your time, if you like."

"Naw, you know me, I don't need no money. You just buy the beer an' I'll be happy. Can I do somethin' this afternoon to help y'all get ready?"

When Ketch finally remembered to check the time, he realized he was going to be late for that Pangea lunch – not that it probably mattered, as most of the others were usually late as well. He guessed they were all on island time these days. It would only take him a few minutes to get there and all he'd likely miss would be some preliminary small talk. Lining Len up for tomorrow's trip was certainly worth that.

He took advantage of Len's generous offer and shooed him off with some cash and the fuel containers from the *TBD*. Len would also pick up food and drinks for tomorrow, and Ketch would gas up his own truck after lunch. Then all they'd have to do in the morning would be to get some ice along the way. He turned on the air conditioning for the dogs, filled their water bowl, locked the houseboat, and took off for Pangea.

He didn't stay a minute longer than absolutely necessary, and he didn't volunteer for any new tasks. There wasn't much he could realistically do, anyway. The lawsuit was still in limbo, and he didn't want to take the time to get hands-on with their latest documentary film right now with everything else he had going on. He'd donated some money to help produce the thing and contributed to the legal fund as well, so that would have to suffice for now.

It occurred to him that, depending on how engaging his Portsmouth story eventually turned out to be, he might be able to parlay it into more exposure for CSFCP. The mass media hadn't paid much attention to them to date – but if that reporter from the *Monitor* wanted an exclusive from him, maybe he could get them some column space in return. Something to think about...

Unfortunately, he'd been in too much of a hurry to learn RAM's real name, he realized. Ah well, one mystery at a time. Meanwhile, he needed to gas up and get back to work at the boatyard. He called Kari on the way back to let her know they were on for tomorrow, thanks to Len – hands-free via Bluetooth, of course, since he didn't believe in using his cell phone while driving even though the law here still allowed it.

He let the dogs out when he returned to the boatyard and then unloaded his truck from his first Portsmouth trip of the week, which he hadn't gotten around to doing yet. And then he reloaded it for the second trip, which was a little less involved since this one wouldn't be an overnighter. But he also had to pack and load his and Kari's dive gear this time, so he guessed it was a wash. He considered putting everything directly aboard the *TBD* to save time in the morning, but decided it would be too risky since he wouldn't be able to lock it all up overnight. He didn't think any of the boatyard denizens would steal from him, but it was probably wise to not tempt anyone.

By the time he was finished, he was a sweaty mess. Though he'd walked them this morning and allowed them to roam the boatyard again while he worked, the dogs had started to harass him about going to the beach. It wouldn't make sense to shower just yet, so he decided to satisfy them and run them over to their special spot just beyond the northern edge of town. There'd be no beach for them tomorrow, which he felt guilty about, and he could cool down and rinse off in the surf in the bargain. If he made it a shorter outing than usual, he should be back by the time he'd asked Len to return.

It all worked out as he'd hoped, and Ketch had just enough time to change into dry clothes before Len rolled in. Ketch stowed the perishables Len had bought, and then the Captain sauntered over from the *Minnow*. The dogs met him halfway, tails wagging.

"Hey Jack, hey Chuck," he said. "Why, I thought that was you!" he thundered at Len, who was now getting the fuel containers from his truck. "How the hell ya doin', you ole dawg?" A flock of small birds rose en masse from the nearby marsh and flew off.

"Oh, same ole, same ole," Len said.

"What're you doin' there?" the Captain asked as he eyeballed the containers. "Did he go and pull you into his mess?"

"Yep, I'm goin' on a treasure hunt."

The Captain shook his head. "Well, y'all better be careful, the both of ya, that's all I got to say. And I done said it enough, so how's about a beer? I could use a break." He cocked a thumb back at his boat. "Gettin' her ready for a charter."

"I want to trailer the *TBD* before I knock off," Ketch said, "but you go ahead. You know your way around the galley."

"Well now, hang on there, Ketch," Len said. "You're lookin' kinda whipped. Gimme your keys, I'll do it."

"I'll lend a hand," the Captain said. "I ain't wore out, I was just lookin' for some excuse to drink a beer."

Ketch had given up being too proud to accept help some time ago. "Thanks, guys, I appreciate it. I'll bring some beers up to the party deck."

The *TBD* was moored next to the houseboat. Len hitched the trailer to Ketch's truck and guided her onto it when the Captain backed it into the water. It didn't take them long, and then they joined Ketch up top on the houseboat.

"It don't get much better," the Captain said as he settled in under the canopy.

Ketch had to agree. Especially at the end of a busy day, the sun-drenched view from up here of the shimmering sound, the salt marsh, and the entire boatyard on a breezy summer afternoon like this was pure balm for the soul.

The Captain polished off most of his bottle in one long gulp and belched. "Dang, didn't know I was so thirsty. You know," he said, pensively examining the bottle, "some folks like to jaw 'bout whether a glass is half-empty or half-full. But it don't matter, 'cause it's refillable!" He drained the rest of the bottle and reached into the bucket for another.

"Ahoy, Mister Ketchum!" Henry called from below. He parked his bicycle on the dock and stood next to it. "Permission to come aboard, sir?"

"Of course, Henry. Grab yourself a pop on your way up."

"And a couple more beers," Len called down. "Don's drinkin' up all the ones Ketch brought up."

"Hey, Len! Sure thing. Oh, Mister Ketchum, I learned a new song. You want to hear it?"

"Well, I have to pick up some tanks before Kari closes the shop. But I still have some time. Do you remember where my guitar is? Bring it up."

"How 'bout that, live entertainment too! I'm beginnin' to like this joint," the Captain quipped.

"I had a couple yards to do today, and I just got done," Henry said after his second trip up. He opened his Sprite and drank deeply. "I hope you don't mind that I stopped by, sir. I hope I'm not interruptin'."

"Not at all, Henry, you're always welcome here. So what song did you learn?"

"Well, it's one of yours. I've been practicin' the chords for that one called *Back in OBX*. I don't remember all the words, though. Would you sing along?"

"Don't think I ever heard that one," Len said.

"It's one I wrote a long time ago," Ketch explained, "back when I was a tourist. Kari thinks it's a silly song. She says we live in the Outer Banks, not 'the OBX', and she won't buy or wear anything that says 'OBX' on it. But we don't care, we like it anyway. Right, Henry?"

It was also somewhat of a sad song for Ketch despite its bouncy tune, as it harkened back to a time when he'd vacationed here with his ex-wife and son. But he'd played it for Henry, and the lad had taken a shine to it and asked about the chords.

"I'm not much of a singer, but everyone here knows that. Okay, Henry, whenever you're ready," he said. After Henry had lumbered through a reasonable facsimile of the instrumental intro, Ketch started singing. Henry joined in when he knew the words, which meant mostly in the choruses.

Another year has passed us by
Who knows where it went and who cares why
We've got beer and a beach and a big blue sky
We're back in OBX

Dirty Dick's and Froggy Dog
And the lighthouse and fishing from Oden's Dock
Put away the watches and the clocks
We're back in OBX

We're back in OBX
Time to kick back and forget the rest
The rest of the world's BS
We're going back on island time

Yeah we're back in OBX
Who knows what we'll be up to next
Give the folks back home our best
We're back in OBX

Hatteras Island is the place to be
After a nap in the hammock let's go jet ski
Who wants to bike to the pier with me
We're back in OBX

The dog likes to swim in Pamlico Sound
And chase ghost crabs on the beach when there's
no one around
There's a Food Lion at the other end of town
We're back in OBX

We're back in OBX
Time to kick back and forget the rest
The rest of the world's BS
We're going back on island time

Yeah we're back in OBX
Who knows what we'll be up to next
Give the folks back home our best
We're back in OBX

Another week will pass us by
Who knows where it will go and who can say why
But we have beer, the DQ and a big blue sky
We're back in OBX

We're back in OBX
Time to kick back and forget the rest
The rest of the world's BS
We're going back on island time

Yeah we're back in OBX
Who knows what we'll be up to next
Give the folks back home our best
We're back in OBX

We're back in OBX
We're back in OBX

"Good job, Henry," Ketch said. "I can tell you've been practicing. You're improving."

"I ain't never been able to play nothin' myself," the Captain said. "It's voodoo to me. You're a witch doctor, son!"

Len complimented Henry as well. "Hey boy, you're gettin' pretty good there. You, on the other hand," he said to Ketch with a grin, "well, let's just leave it at that. What kinda tunin' you got him in?"

"I started him out in Open D, because it's easy to learn the barre chords. But then I showed him DADGAD, which is what I mostly use, because the open chords are easier to make. You only have to change one string by a half-step to move between those tunings."

"Yeah, but the chords ain't as strong as they are in standard tunin'. You ought to teach him those chords sometime too."

"I will one day, if he keeps on with it," Ketch said. "Well, I have to get going. You can all stay here for a while if you like, but I have to feed the dogs and get over to the shop."

"I'll be goin' too," Henry said. "It's almost dinnertime for me. Thanks, Mister Ketchum. Captain Manolin, is six o'clock early enough for tomorrow?"

"That'll be fine, Henry, see you then."

"What about me, Ketch?" Len asked. "What time are y'all leavin' in the mornin'?"

"I'd like to be in Portsmouth by nine if possible, so we can have some time in the village before we go to the dive site. So let's see, a half-hour to get to the ferry in Hatteras, an hour-and-a-half to Ocracoke if we're lucky, an hour to get ice, load the boat, and get to Portsmouth... So we should be on the road by six. You should be here before that."

"Ouch! Okay, it's a early night for me then."

"Yes, for me, too. But you don't have to worry about breakfast. We'll stop at the Gingerbread House in Frisco and grab something to eat on the ferry. They open early." Ketch knew from experience that they had the best breakfast around, as well as the tastiest baked goods he knew of. Their oversized bagels and doughnuts and turnovers and such were things his doctor probably wouldn't be happy to hear about.

Ketch took his guitar and went below to see to the dogs. The others carried the bucket and bottles down for him and then dispersed. Ketch decided to take a quick shower and put on some decent clothes. Kari wouldn't mind if he was a few minutes late, once she found out where he was taking her.

"Why thank you, what a nice surprise!" she said after they'd finished loading six tanks into the back of Ketch's truck. "I love the Froggy Dog, it's my favorite restaurant!"

They'd only need four tanks at the most if they made two no-decompression dives, but redundancy was never a bad thing when one was off the grid and something went wrong. In fact, they might not need more than two, according to the online NOAA nautical chart Ketch had consulted.

If the coordinates he'd been given by the Captain were correct, they'd be diving about two miles east of the south end of the island, and even that far out the water might be only ten feet deep in places. At that depth, they'd be able to stay down for hours on just one tank each, and without having to worry about getting bent. He was still wondering how that sand barge could have come as close to the island as it had without running aground on a shoal. Maybe they dredged their own channel before them as they went, or maybe it was one of those shallow-draft material barges he'd read about online.

"How come we don't come here more often?" Kari asked after they'd been seated in the Groggy Pirate Pub section of the restaurant. "'Specially since you're rich now and all. Seems like we could come here every night if we wanted to."

Ketch wasn't as impressed with the place as he'd once been, and he had no desire to patronize it daily. But he liked the ambiance of the pub and he didn't want to spoil the experience for her.

"I'm not *that* rich," he said. "I'm hoping that money will last me for the rest of my life, and maybe yours too if you're lucky. Besides, you know what would happen if you came here every day."

"I know, I'd get sick of it," she admitted. "So we're all set for tomorrow, huh?"

"Yes. I think everything's taken care of, except for ice."

"Good. This is exciting! I can't wait to see what we'll find down there. And even if it's nothin', it'll still be fun. How did you get Len to help us out?"

"I didn't have to twist his arm. When I told him what we wanted to do, he volunteered."

"Huh. Well, it's a good thing he did, else we might not be goin'. There was nobody I could call." She held her empty wine glass out and Ketch refilled it from the bottle he'd ordered for her. He wasn't big on wine himself, so he was sipping from a mug of some kind of craft beer that had an interesting name. "So what else did you do with all your free time today, sun yourself on the party deck? I'm just kiddin'," she smiled. "I know you couldn't have had much free time with everything you did."

"Well, I did do one thing I haven't already told you about. I met a woman."

"Oh yeah? Is she younger and prettier than me?"

"Just younger. A reporter from the *Monitor* who wanted to interview me because of those dead divers. I told her I'd call her when I had time. I'm thinking of asking her to put something in the paper about CSFCP's work in return for an exclusive interview. I don't think they're getting enough recognition."

"Were there any new developments at your meeting today?"

"No, not really. No one's happy with the new NPS beach access plan. It was supposed to be an acceptable compromise, but the environmentalists still aren't satisfied and the ORV people are still trying to sue over it. Bob and RAM came to the lunch to advocate for the ORV side, and they're still as adamant as ever – but not without reason."

Surprisingly, neither of them had known anything about where the sand was coming from for that new condo development near Cape Point. But Bob had told Ketch he'd look into it and give him a call – which Ketch fully expected him to do, since he knew Bob was opposed to the development.

"Could you refresh my memory?" Kari asked. "Who's suin' who now, and why? Start at the beginning."

"Okay. Well, back in the early Seventies the President issued an executive order for all national parks to develop off-road vehicle management plans. The Cape Hatteras National Seashore never got around to putting one on the books, and a few years ago a couple of environmental groups sued the National Park Service for not doing that here. They claimed that the four-wheel-drive vehicles people here were allowed to take on some of our beaches were damaging the environment and endangering threatened wildlife. Since there was no official ORV plan, a federal judge gave them injunctive relief, and they ran with it."

"I knew about the Aububon Society, but who else sued?"

"The Defenders of Wildlife were also in on it, and they're both represented by the Southern Environmental Law Center. They were concerned about the piping plover and some other nesting shorebirds, and several species of sea turtle that nest here. And rightly so, I think – however, I also think they went too far. The ORV people thought so too, and they sued."

"Who are they again?"

"Well, there are quite a few organizations involved. There's the Outer Banks Preservation Association, the Cape Hatteras Access

Preservation Alliance, the North Carolina Beach Buggy Association, the Cape Hatteras Anglers Club... The environmentalists dictated a plan to the NPS, and the OBPA was told to sign off on it or there'd be no beach access whatsoever. After that the OPBA appealed to Washington, but the judge who'd made the initial ruling finagled it so the suit got returned to his court, and he shot it down. There were no good-faith negotiations, and some people claim the judge was corrupt."

"I know. I've heard people complainin' about that, especially down around Buxton when I lived there. That guy who owns the Red Drum would always bend my ear if I gave him half a chance."

"Well, he and others like him have reason to be upset. When the Park Service closes Cape Point, the best surf fishing spot on the island, in the height of the tourist season, bait-and-tackle businesses like his suffer. Restaurants, too, like Finnegan's across from the lighthouse. And other kinds of businesses, if they depend on tourist trade. Surf fishermen don't bring their families here to vacation if they can't fish, and ditto for beach lovers if they can't go on the beach. There have been a lot more foreclosures since the environmentalists started taking over, and some businesses have completely gone under because of all this. A lot of people who live here are angry. That's why you see those protest signs here and there, like 'Eco-terrorists' and 'Hey Aububon, identify *this* bird' and 'We the people, not we the plovers'."

"But they're keepin' most of the beaches and ORV ramps open most of the time now, right? I don't fish and I don't know the details, but that's what I heard."

"Yes, they finally came up with a plan. But it's not always the most desirable ramps, and not always at the best times for fishing – and access goes out the window if any birds or turtles get in the way, for both ORVs and pedestrians. But still, the compromise plan gives the off-roaders access to about half of the mileage of our shoreline at various times. However, it sometimes happens that a stretch of beach is open, but you can only get to it by boat due to neighboring closures. So the ORV groups are suing again." Ketch sighed and paused for a drink.

"It'll probably always be a struggle no matter what's done about it," he said. "There are extremists on both sides. There are some environmentalists who want ORVs banned completely from all beaches, and foot traffic too in many places if they could have their way. In fact, some folks think their ultimate goal is to drive everyone off of this island entirely. And then there are the hardcore ORV proponents who think they have a God-given right to drive on the beaches whenever and wherever they like and want no restrictions at all. They say they've been doing it for generations and it's a way of life here – though it's really only grown enough to become a problem in the last generation or so. And both of the extremes make more noise than the ones in between."

"Have they ever thought about just drivin' on the beaches anyway, even if they're closed? You know, like a civil disobedience kinda thing?"

"Oh, you don't want to do that. If you get a ticket from the Park Service, you have to answer to it in a federal court, and the penalties can be pretty stiff. Also, the rangers have guns."

"Okay. Well, this might be a dumb question, but then why can't they just walk like everybody else?"

"With fishing tackle and coolers?"

"Why not? I have to lug stuff when I want to go to the beach."

"That's possible in some places, and the current management plan calls for more parking areas in certain locations for that purpose. But you wouldn't like lugging your stuff a mile or more through soft sand and tidal pools to get out to Cape Point. And there are more and more places now where they don't even want you to walk."

"Sounds like you might be sidin' with the ORV people."

"I'm not really on either side – or maybe I'm on both sides, depending on your point of view. I'm on the side of common sense, like it says in our group's name. I'm in favor of protecting the environment and I believe there have to be some conservation efforts, but I think people also have to be part of the equation. Legally speaking, this seashore is a national park, not a wildlife refuge like Pea Island. People think it's a question of preservation versus recreation, but it shouldn't be an either-or proposition. The national parks were explicitly established with both purposes in mind, and that's what I think some people are losing sight of. Like it or not, people are here to stay. This isn't just a wildlife habitat, it's also a human habitat, and we all need to coexist. That's what Common Sense For Cape Point is all about."

Kari shook her head at Ketch and smiled.

"What? Did I say something funny?" he asked.

"No. It's just – well, listen to you, gettin' all worked up about all this. Wasn't that long ago you didn't want to be bothered with stuff like this. When you first moved here, there was no way you'd get involved with this kinda thing."

"Well, that was wrong. I live here now, and I care about this island and everything that lives on it."

"I know you do, and there's nothin' wrong with that."

"All of this nonsense started over just a few endangered plovers," Ketch went on, growing impassioned again, "and this year I heard only two nesting pairs have been sighted so far. Hundreds of acres of beach, closed for four birds! They're not native to this island, originally. And this isn't even their main nesting area, they mostly nest elsewhere, and the other birds they arbitrarily decided to offer the same protection aren't even endangered. It's gotten ridiculous."

"So what does your group want?"

"What we want is a common-sense plan. The Park Service and the environmentalists mismanaged the plover nesting sites based on questionable pseudo-science that's since been debunked. For example, they designated buffer zones for unfledged plover chicks with a radius equivalent to the length of three football fields, which is ludicrous. Buffers for other birds, and the sea turtles, are smaller, but still excessive. By cordoning off such large areas against all traffic, motorized or not, they allowed dunes to form and vegetation to grow on them, which made those areas unsuitable for nesting, and that forced the birds closer to the ocean where they were more vulnerable to predators. So then they started shooting and trapping the predators, the foxes and raccoons and coyotes and such that live in the maritime forest."

"There's coyotes here now?"

"Yes, in Buxton Woods. They've expanded into every county in the state, even here. Anyway, they've killed hundreds of those animals for the sake of a few birds and turtles. They're completely disrupting the ecosystem, and that has to stop."

"The Audubons are doin' this?"

"The Park Service is actually doing the deed, but yes, it was instigated mostly by the Audubons. You know," Ketch said, taking another quick sip of his beer, "that's actually perversely apropos in a couple of ways. John Audubon, the naturalist painter who's their namesake, killed an incredible number of birds while he was producing his masterwork, *The Birds of America*, back in the eighteen hundreds. When he wanted to study and paint a bird, he and his cohorts would go out and shoot literally dozens of specimens with light shot. He was disappointed if he didn't shoot at least a hundred birds on a hunting day. And if they were still alive, he wired them up and posed them anyway. Killing and torturing in the name of conservation, both then and now. Hey! That might be a good slogan for them."

"That's awful! How can it be stopped?"

"We want the new vegetation removed and the original nesting areas restored, smaller buffer zones, and a moratorium on killing predators. Reducing the buffer zones, along with flood mitigation and relocation of nests, all of which they've been reluctant to do so far, should also make it possible to maintain a permanent corridor to the shoreline at Cape Point that would always be open, even if everything else around it is cordoned off. And existing access ramps elsewhere should be improved, maintained, and replaced when necessary."

"Well, that should please the off-roaders. Would that be enough to handle all the ORV traffic, though?"

"Yes, because we also believe there should be

less ORV traffic. The permit system should be kept in place, and there should be some limits on the number of vehicles, and some other restrictions. People who want to fish or beachcomb or picnic with their families should be able to drive out to the Point and do their thing – but not party animals who want to have bonfires and joy-ride, drink beer, blast music, roast pigs, and so on. I haven't heard of a lot of that happening, but if it does then people like that should be banned. That's the kind of off-roader that would disturb the ecosystem. Those people can go have their tailgate parties somewhere else."

"And that might *not* please the off-roaders. Sounds like you folks are tryin' to piss everybody off," she laughed.

"No, we're trying to take care of everyone. It's a compromise solution. We don't want the people to be forced out by the wildlife, or the wildlife to be forced out by the people. Both need to be taken into account, and both need to give a little."

"And that's what your lawsuit is about?"

"Yes. And it's necessary, because although Congress passed a law requiring the NPS to periodically accept public comments and amend their plans accordingly, that system hasn't worked very well so far. The original plan has been amended somewhat, but it's still largely unacceptable. Our suit hasn't gotten anywhere yet, but a couple of our Congressional representatives have gotten interested in this issue lately, so maybe they'll be able to pressure the NPS and accomplish something."

"Huh. So there was no management plan, and the environmentalists sued, and then there was a plan, and then the ORV folks sued, and then there was another plan, and now Congress is involved and you're suin'... Do you think the environmentalists will sue again if you guys win?"

"Who knows? There are politicians on both sides, including within the environmental organizations, so anything's possible." Ketch returned to the food he'd been neglecting. "We'd better eat up, we have an early morning tomorrow." Although it was one of his favorite dishes, he was already almost too tired to enjoy it.

"That's right, and I still have one more thing to do tonight."

"Oh? What's that?"

"You! You're so smart, I just *have* to do you, I can't help myself," she laughed. Then, seeing the initial lack of amusement on his weary face, she sobered as well. "Hey, I'm just kiddin' around. No pressure, okay?"

But Ketch finally did smile. "I can think of worse ways to be pressured," he said, rebounding now. "Don't worry, I may be down but I'm not out. And it's a good way for me to get some exercise. I haven't played tennis in a while and I probably won't be able to anytime soon, so you're my new exercise program. Say, maybe we could film an infomercial and make some money from this new program while we're at it, what do you think?" His phone rang before she could respond to that. "It's Bob," he said, glancing at it. "I should take this." She busied herself with making sure the remaining wine didn't go to waste while he talked.

"Well, that's interesting," he said, putting the phone away. "Bob said he called around, and no one can say where the sand for those new condos is coming from. Or *wants* to say, at any rate, according to him. He says he got the impression that at least one person he spoke with was rather annoyed with him for asking."

"So what does that mean?"

"I'm not sure. He still thinks that development is the start of a land grab, and that the Audubons might have something to do with it. Property values have declined more than thirty percent around here over the past few years, you know, and most people think it's at least partly because of the beach access issues. That development company, which no one here had ever heard of before, got a good deal on a foreclosed property and a couple of short sales. Maybe I should go nose around there sometime."

"The Audubon Society is non-profit, right? They don't have anything to do with developin' commercial properties, do they?"

"Not directly, that I know of. I haven't looked it up yet to verify that it's true, but someone at one of our meetings told me the Audubons have sold off some land donations to developers to raise funds for themselves in the past. I do know of at least one instance where they sold a seaside tract instead of preserving it like they were supposed to. There are all sorts of theories floating around out there."

"That doesn't surprise me." Kari drained her last glass. "Well, are you ready to go?"

"Yes, I think so. I've had enough."

"Not yet, you haven't. We've got an infomercial to rehearse for," she said with a twinkle in her eye. But that was all right with him. He liked making her happy and an occasional session of bedroom acrobatics was one relatively easy way to accomplish that. Well, more than occasional with her, he supposed. But he'd be a fool to complain about that, right? And after all, there'd be plenty of time to sleep when he was dead, as the saying went.

~ S i x ~

It's always cold in the hour before daylight.

O r so it was for him, anyway. Maybe it was just his aging circulatory system trying to ramp back up after a sedentary night. But today it might also have something to do with his itinerary. He was excited about returning to Portsmouth Island and possibly discovering a historic shipwreck, but he couldn't shake a vague sense of foreboding that had started to creep up on him yesterday evening. Maybe things were just happening a little too fast.

The sky was beginning to glow to the east, but the sun wouldn't rise for a while yet. That didn't seem to be bothering Jack and Chuck much, though, now that they understood what was happening. They'd thought it strange to be fed and walked so early at first, but they were always game for an adventure. They knew they were going to Suzanne's house now, and that was fine with them.

There were lights on inside when Ketch and the dogs arrived at the elevated cottage, and Suzanne was up as promised. He could see through a window that she was in the first-floor kitchen, so they walked around to the back entrance. That meant entering through the pool area, but Ketch knew how to unlock the gate. She waved when she saw them, and they went up the steps and in without knocking.

"Good morning, Ketch. Good morning, boys," she said, pausing in her work to give the dogs each a pat. The dogs were pleased to find that she was in the process of cooking breakfast, and they were delighted when she scooped some scrambled eggs onto paper plates for them.

"Sally and Bean are still asleep," she said to Ketch, "but Henry should be down in a minute. Would you like something to eat?"

"Maybe I'll just make myself some toast if you don't mind. We'll be stopping at the Gingerbread House later." He set a canvas bag down in a corner of the kitchen. "Their leashes, dishes, food, and a couple of bones are in here."

"Good, thanks. So, are you all ready for your trip?"

"I wish I'd gotten a little more sleep – but yes, I think so. Once Len shows up, we'll be good to go. He volunteered to tend the boat for us."

"Hey, Mister Ketchum," Henry said, entering the room.

"Good morning, Henry. Or should I say, First Mate? You're being promoted today, after all. Are you nervous?"

"No, sir, I know what-all to do. Thanks to you teachin' me, I mean," he hastily added. "But still," he then admitted, "I guess maybe I *am* a little nervous."

"Well, it's just a half-day inshore charter. I'm sure you'll do fine. And don't worry about the

Captain. He may bark at times, but he doesn't bite."

Henry sat down at the table and his mother served him a tall glass of orange juice and a plate of eggs, grits, and biscuits with sausage gravy. Ketch knew she was from Michigan originally, but she'd lived in Charlotte for at least a decade before coming to Avon and she'd picked up some Southern cooking skills during that time. But not the accent, though, so far. Ketch sat across from Henry with his toast and a glass of juice.

Henry ate quickly but not hurriedly and then donned a backpack similar to the one Ketch often carried. Ketch remembered the canvas pack was one of the things Henry had been saving up for at one point. The boy was always saving up for something or other, it seemed, but he also sensibly banked most of the earnings he raked in from his odd jobs. Ketch hoped he'd get some good tips today, as the Captain didn't pay either of them a wage for crewing on his boat – which was customary in the charter business and not due to stinginess on his part. At least Henry wouldn't have to split today's tips with Ketch.

They said their goodbyes, and then Ketch walked back to the boatyard with Henry. Jack and Chuck hadn't been overly anxious or upset at his leaving, since they knew Suzanne and had stayed there before. But Ketch was disappointed he hadn't gotten to see Bean. Well, he'd see him tonight. Meanwhile, he knew Bean would enjoy a day with Sally and the dogs, and with Henry after the charter.

Kari was waiting out by Ketch's truck. Henry said 'good morning' to her, wished them both luck, and continued on to the *Minnow*.

"You hear from Len?" she asked Ketch, leaning back against the truck and crossing her arms and legs. "We're all locked up and ready to go."

Ketch noticed she was wearing the white 'Wanchese slippers' he'd given her on her fortieth birthday back in October. Combined with her new spiky hairdo and the colorful shorts and halter top she'd chosen, they made her look like a go-go dancer, or maybe one of those mod English tarts Ketch remembered seeing pictures of back in the Sixties. But they were really just an arguably more stylish variant of the fishing boots the Wanchese fishermen typically wore. He was finding the overall effect intriguing despite last night's rather strenuous 'rehearsal', but he quickly belayed the feeling. They didn't have time for that this morning.

"No, I haven't heard from Len. Maybe I should give him a call in case he overslept." Ketch got his phone out, but it rang before he could dial Len's number. "That's odd," he said. "It's Dan."

"Hey, Ketch!" Dan said. "I hope I didn't wake you. I wasn't expecting you to answer. I thought I'd be leaving you a message."

"Please leave your message after the beep," Ketch said. "Just kidding. Kari's here, so I'm going to put you on speaker if that's okay. So what's up, Dan?

"Ha! Yeah, that's okay. Well, I just wanted to let you know, we're working with CGIS now on the case of those dead divers. That's the Coast Guard Investigative Service. They're kinda like those folks on that *NCIS* show on TV with Don Johnson, except that's the Navy."

"That's not Don Johnson, it's Mark Harmon," Kari said.

"She's right," Ketch corroborated, "and I know what the CGIS does. Why are they involved now?"

"Well, that's the part I thought you might find interesting. Those two convicts that escaped from that prison? For one thing, we found out they had help from a brother-in-law. One of their inmate friends finally squealed in hopes of getting out earlier. And for another thing, we found out that brother-in-law is in the Coast Guard, and guess where he's stationed? At the District Five Sector Field Office in Atlantic Beach. And by the way, that's the office that should have known about any dredging going on down around Portsmouth Island. He's on duty there today, so they're gonna go to that SFO and question him. I'm supposed to stand by for further word."

"You're right, that *is* interesting," Ketch said. "So there might be a connection between the convicts and that sand barge after all."

"I still don't see how or why yet, but I don't believe in coincidences, at least not where criminals are involved. So I guess you might have called that one. Anyway, we'll see what happens, and I'll let you know when I hear something. Meanwhile, thanks for ruining my day off," Dan said, laughing.

"Always glad to help. Thanks, Dan, I appreciate it." Ketch saw Len's truck pull into the lot. "We're about to head down to Portsmouth, so I'd better go. Talk to you later."

"'Bout time you got here, slacker," Kari said when Len got out of his truck. But she said it with a smile.

"What? You said be here by six. Well, I still got, let's see, four minutes, so there," Len grinned back at her. "Hey, Ketch. Well all right then – come on, let's go!" They all gathered at Ketch's truck.

"Hey, Hot Stuff!" the Captain brayed to Kari from the deck of the *Minnow*. A nearby fish crow cawed loudly, apparently offended by this disturbance of the early morning calm of the boatyard. Ketch guessed the other people who lived here must be used to it, as he never heard any of them complain. "Good luck down there! Y'all be careful, and have fun!"

They silently waved back at him, climbed into the truck, and took off. Ketch was pleased to note that there was no 'red sky at morning' for sailors to take warning from. In fact, there was hardly a cloud in the brightening sky, so it looked like today's weather forecast might actually turn out to be correct for a change. He recalled reading somewhere that weather forecasters and psychics were about equally accurate, to the tune of roughly fifty-five percent. That sounded believable, in his experience.

Whatever it was he'd felt uneasy about before, his trepidation dissipated along the mostly unspoiled stretch of Highway 12 between Avon and Buxton. Other than the day-use area at the haulover near Canadian Hole, there was nothing to his left but the Atlantic dunes and only Pamlico Sound to his right. There wasn't any other vehicular traffic at this hour on a Sunday morning, and there were no kiteboarders yet at the Hole, a premier location in the sound for the wind worshippers. And somewhat sadly to his mind, there was no one hauling anything either.

It wasn't done anymore, but this area had become known as a haulover because it was one of the narrowest parts of the island and was thus a place where the Hatterasmen of old had hauled their wooden boats back and forth between the sound and the ocean when necessary. They'd fished both bodies of water as the season and the weather dictated, and in the days before internal combustion engines, sailing south to Hatteras inlet and then back north up the opposite side of the island was impractical.

It unfortunately wasn't long before the village of Buxton came into view and put an end to his reveries, despite Ketch deliberately laying off the gas pedal. Not only was he towing a boat, he'd also wanted to make this part of the trip last.

First up on their way into town was the historic Cape Hatteras lighthouse, its distinctive black-and-white spiral day marker radiant in the burgeoning sunlight. Ketch knew that each lighthouse along the Banks sported a unique pattern or coloring, so that the passing mariners of old could tell where they were during the day. The varying blinking frequencies of the Fresnel lenses were useful for that purpose in the dark, but less so in daytime. Both the day markers and the lights themselves were less essential these days, of course, in this era of satellite navigation.

The lighthouse was near Cape Point, and as they drove by Ketch decided to detour into the site of the new condo development. It was just a whim, as he didn't really have time to snoop right now, but the others didn't mind. He figured he'd take a quick look at how the construction was progressing and then drive back out to the highway.

"Well hey, look at that," Len said, pointing to the far end of the site. "Is that the barge you saw down at Portsmouth?"

Ketch stopped the truck and squinted. There was indeed a barge anchored offshore, and he could see some hard-hatted people milling around – at dawn on a Sunday morning. It was pretty early to start working on any day, and if they were union workers they were making double-time today and maybe more. That wasn't something he'd choose to do if he was paying the bills, he thought, unless he was behind schedule. Or perhaps if he wanted something done on the down low. He wondered if one of those people was the yahoo who'd shot down his drone.

"Yes, I think so. Len, pass me my backpack," he said. Ketch retrieved his binoculars from it and stepped out of the truck.

He only needed a minute to get what he wanted and jot it down in the pocket notebook he'd started carrying last summer. When he got back in the truck, he handed the binoculars and backpack to Kari to stow, put the truck in gear, and verbally commanded the dashboard nav system to dial Dan's number.

"Why are you callin' him?" Kari asked.

"I got the name of that barge. I thought it might be a useful piece of information." Dan's phone went to voice mail, so Ketch left him a message.

"Now that you have this new truck, do you miss your girlfriend?" Kari teased.

"What girlfriend?" Len said.

"You mean Adrianna?" Since Ketch's new Tundra had the built-in nav system, he was no longer using the GPS program on his smartphone, which he'd named Adrianna to keep up with the Apple folks and their Siri. He hadn't gotten around to attaching a name to the voice on the new system yet. "Yes, my life has lost all meaning since she left me," Ketch teased back. Kari lightly punched his arm, then explained for Len.

They continued on their southward trek, briefly stopping at the Gingerbread House in Frisco as planned. Ketch knew the friendly and knowledgeable proprietress of Buxton Village Books, his favorite bookstore and the only one on Hatteras Island, often breakfasted here. But it was early for her, which was too bad as she might have been able to tell him something about that Sea Hag woman. If there was anything to tell, she'd probably know about it. Maybe he'd call on her when they got back if he didn't learn anything new in Portsmouth today.

Thankfully, when they reached the ferry landing in Hatteras there wasn't much of a line. After they'd secured their vehicle, they took their food up to the enclosed passenger lounge and settled in to eat.

"It's been a long time since I seen the sun come up," Len said, biting into a breakfast sandwich. "I'm likin' it, and bein' out on the water too. Don't think I'll be makin' a habit of it any time soon, though," he laughed.

"Ketch is a morning person," Kari said. "He's almost always up at dawn."

"I don't know that I'm actually a morning person," Ketch said. "It might just be that I'm getting old. I've heard it said that old people get up early because they don't want to waste what might be their last day."

"Aw come on, you're not *that* old," Kari said. "So, you still want to go to the village before we dive?"

"Yes. I'm afraid if we dive first, we could get tied up too long and miss the Park Service people. I don't know how late they work on a Sunday."

The hour-long ferry ride passed quickly. When they were finished eating, Ketch and Kari discussed the logistics of their planned dive while Len caught some extra Z's in the corner with one side of his face plastered against a window. He woke with a start when the ferry docked at the Ocracoke landing.

"Are we there yet?" he said, grinning.

"You sound like a little kid," Kari joked. "Are you hungry, thirsty, tired, or bored? Do you have to go to the bathroom?"

"Bathroom, maybe. Can I hit the head quick?"

They were soon back on Highway 12, this time where it picked up on Ocracoke Island. It would be almost another twenty miles to Silver Lake in the village of Ocracoke. Along the way they drove past the famed pony pen, where a couple dozen or so descendants of the once-feral herd of Ocracoke horses were now managed by the Park Service.

"It's a shame them horses can't run free no more," Len remarked. "Why'd they have to go and pen 'em up like that?"

"Well, when the Park Service took over the management of the horses back in the Sixties, they didn't want the horses getting hit by cars or competing with the other native wildlife they were supposed to protect," Ketch explained. "There was a Boy Scout troop in Ocracoke in the Fifties that was the only mounted troop in the country. Each scout was assigned a horse to catch, train, and ride, just like the island children had done in the old days. The Park Service wanted to move the horses to the mainland, but the scouts petitioned to create the pen as a compromise, and the Park Service helped them raise money to fence off a large pasture for the horses."

"Do the scouts still ride the horses?" Kari asked.

"No, that died out, mostly due to the cost of the insurance that was eventually required. And they also don't have the annual Fourth of July roundup and rodeo anymore. That used to be the big event of the year here in the old days. Now the horses are just another tourist attraction with a plaque, like a lot of other things nowadays."

When they arrived in Ocracoke, their first stop was the Ocracoke Seafood Company, the waterfront fish house by the Jolly Roger marina on Silver Lake. They kept a huge freezer room open to both the fishermen and the public for anyone who needed ice, and they sold it by the shovelful on the honor system. Ketch filled their coolers and deposited the appropriate amount of money in the unlocked and unmanned wooden box that hung on the wall. Then they proceeded to the public launch and transferred their gear from the truck to the boat, and they were on their way.

The transit from Ocracoke to Portsmouth was

on the rough side due to a stiff sea breeze. The *TBD* had only a nine-inch draft and Ketch knew a safe route now, so he didn't need to watch his speed. For about twenty minutes, the boat bounced across the small wind-driven waves almost as much as a flat-bottomed skiff would. Ketch didn't mind, as the breeze would again be a good defense against the bugs in Portsmouth, but Len was glad when the somewhat wild ride was over.

"Man, my back!" he complained to a placid Kari. "How come you guys ain't hurtin' like me?"

"It's like ridin' a horse, you have to move with the boat. Don't worry," she teased, "you'll likely get some more practice at it later."

As they'd approached the small pier that was also used by the Austin ATV tours, Ketch had seen the Austin's boat on its way back out. It must have dropped off a tour group to be picked up later. They'd probably only missed one another by a few minutes, so they should be able to catch up with the group in the village. Maybe the guide would know something about the Sea Hag, Ketch hoped.

It turned out he was right on one account but out of luck on the other. After they'd tied off the *TBD* and made the short trek into the village of Portsmouth, Ketch saw the tour group coming out of the Dixon/Salter house, which he recalled had been built around 1900 in the Middle Community two miles to the south and then moved here. So they hadn't been too far ahead, fortunately.

It looked like there were five tourists plus a guide he called 'Nature Girl', though not to her face. She'd been his guide the first time he'd come here, a few years ago. She'd been around awhile even back then, and he'd run into her now and then since. She knew everything there was to know about this town and the island, as far as he could tell, including all the flora and fauna as well as the history, and she could identify every seashell on the beach. Thanking his good fortune, he left Kari and Len behind and lengthened his stride to catch up with her.

"Kelsey," he called to her when he'd gotten close enough.

When she turned around, Ketch was struck by the fact that she didn't look a day older than when he'd first met her, though she must be at least in her late twenties by now, maybe even thirty. In fact, with those freckles and her ball cap and blond ponytail, she could probably pass for a high school senior. And she was barefooted as usual.

"Well hey, Ketch. What are you doin' here today?" she coolly inquired in her typically laid-back manner. Nothing ever seemed to surprise her.

Ketch knew she didn't go in much for small talk, so he skipped that. "I'm here with a couple of friends," he said, motioning toward Kari and Len, who'd paused to examine a historic outhouse. Everything was historic here, he guessed. "We're doing some research."

She turned and waved her group on toward the post office down the way. "Go on ahead, I'll be right with y'all," she called. "So, what kind of research? For your book, or are you workin' on another case?"

"Ah, so you read the newspaper. And you remember me telling you about my book? I'm flattered. But no, I haven't fooled with that in a while." He paused for a moment to decide on how much he needed to say, while she patiently waited in her unflappable way. "I was just curious about something. I was here a few days ago with my grandson, and he had an encounter with a woman who said she was the Sea Hag of Portsmouth. I didn't see it happen, but he said she was very old and shabbily dressed and she talked like a Hoi Toider. She told him there were ghosts here, and then she disappeared. I wondered if you might have ever heard of such a person either living or visiting here?"

It seemed to Ketch that a cloud briefly flitted across her face – but if she thought either his story or his request odd, she didn't otherwise show it. "The Sea Hag? Well, that'd be some trick now, wouldn't it? She'd have to be about three hundred years old. No, wait, she was supposed to already be hundreds of years old back then, so even older than that." She stood lost in thought for a few seconds. "Nope, I haven't heard anything about a woman like that here today." She didn't ask why he was looking for the woman, and it was apparent the matter was resolved for her.

"I see. Thanks, Kelsey. Well, I'd better let you get back to your group."

She nodded. Apparently noticing that his hands were empty, she asked, "Do y'all need some myrtle in case the bugs get bad? I have some extra."

That didn't surprise Ketch, since she was the one he'd learned that hack from. "No thanks, I have some in my backpack."

"Okay, see ya." She turned and walked off, unperturbed by the fact that Ketch hadn't really answered her question about his 'research'. He knew it wasn't that she was disinterested – she just accepted whatever happened, as long as it didn't adversely impact her personally. He could think of only one occasion on which she'd overtly shown any significant emotion, and that was when she'd told him about her father passing a while back. But even then, it had hardly been noticeable. He'd sometimes wondered if she might be mildly autistic or something.

"Did she know anything?" Kari asked, coming up behind him.

"No, unfortunately. Have you seen any of the volunteer park rangers anywhere?"

"Not yet."

"There must be at least one or two around somewhere." Ketch looked back at the Dixon/Salter house, which now served as a visitor and information center. One could pick up maps and pamphlets and such there. But more importantly at the moment, it also housed the only civilized rest room at this end of the island. "I'm going to use the facilities. You and Len can go on ahead, and I'll catch up. You could tag along with the tour group if you like. Kelsey won't mind."

"All right, soon as Len comes out. He's in there now. And we'll keep an eye out for rangers."

They passed each other on the front steps of the old house. Len gave Ketch a grin accompanied by a mock military salute. "She's all yours, cap'n," he said.

Ketch took advantage of the sink to rinse the salt from his face before exiting the men's room. The house was eerily silent except for the sound of his own footfalls on the well-worn plank floor. He hadn't seen anyone else in the village this morning other than the tour group, and they'd moved on, so he had the house to himself.

Or so he thought. When he passed the doorway of a darkened back room on his way out, he caught a movement inside from the corner of his eye. Maybe there was a ranger in the house, he thought. That would be convenient. But stepping into the room to investigate, he was instead greeted by the sight of an ominous, shadowy figure sitting in a rocking chair in a far corner with a rotting wooden oar resting across her lap.

It was an old woman, and though he'd never met her she seemed familiar to him. Like Nature Girl, her feet were bare and sandy, but the resemblance ended there. Her ancient face was lined and weathered, her bone-white hair was long and scraggly, and the faded ankle-length dress and shawl she wore were dirty and tattered. The brightest part of her by far was her eyes, which were almost luminous and were now boring straight into his.

"Hello," he shakily offered. His old fight-or-flee panic reaction was threatening to kick in, but he could control it now and he stood his ground. When she didn't respond, he screwed up his courage and said, "Do you live here? Who are you?"

"Oi reckon ye know who Oi be. Set aon daown there an' bend yer ear," the woman commanded, pointing with a misshapen forefinger in the direction of a nearby bed. "This hain't moy haouse, Oi come here fer you."

He did know who she was, or rather who she thought she was – and he didn't want to sit, he wanted to walk across the room and poke her to see if she was real. Or did he? His feet felt like they were made of lead, and a sudden fatigue threatened to overcome him. But he hadn't stayed up *that* late last night. Regardless, it was far easier to just sit down as instructed, and fortunately the bed was directly behind him.

"What do you want with me?" he wheezed as he dropped onto the bed.

"Oi come to give ye fair warnin'. Yer in danger, see, on account of ye hadn't paid yer port fee."

"Yes, I heard about that," he said. Now that he

was sitting, he found he was able to catch his breath. "Why is there a port fee? There's no port anymore."

"Droime, don't tell *them* that!" the woman cackled. Her voice sounded like a scratchy record playing on an old Victrola. "They still loike their gold, see."

"Who's 'they'? And how much is the fee, and how do I pay?"

"Never moind, it's too late, yer mommucked," she said, waggling her crooked finger at him. "Hain't but one way to pay naow. Ye should of heeded yer youngun's warnin'. Naow ye need to begone, boy gum."

"Why? What do you have to do with what's been happening here?"

"Nothin'. Oi'm jest a confabbin' ole busybody, is all. Tweren't me made the rules. It's them that was, done that."

'Them that was'? She must be talking about the ghosts Bean and Sally had been told of. "Well, how can they expect a dingbatter like me to know the rules? And why am I getting another warning if I'm such a bother?"

"Aye an' yer a dizzy dit-dot, all roight, but yer unloike them others. Yer worthy of it."

"What others?"

"All them that's pantin' after Peter Painter's gold."

"What do you know about that?" His voice was weakening again, and he could feel himself beginning to nod off – which was bizarre considering he was in a room with what might be some kind of *memento mori*. His guard should be up, if anything. Now there was a bit of Latin he hadn't even remembered he knew, he giddily thought. He struggled to keep his attention on what she was saying.

"Oi know more'n you, an' Oi know ye need to git from this oisland naow. Won't be slick cam for ye here if ye don't, mark moy words. Git aon home an' boy some milk an' look after yer youngun."

Go home, buy milk, look after... Okay, three things to remember. Why milk? He was too tired to ask. No matter, yes ma'am, he thought as his eyes closed. He eased back onto the historically accurate feather-stuffed bolster and drifted off to sleep.

When he woke some time later, it took him a moment to remember where he was. Then it came back to him and he sat straight up.

Disoriented at first, he stayed put and scanned the room. Yes, there was the rocking chair in the corner – but it was empty now. Had it been all along? It was a bright sunny day outside and the room was filled with light, with no shadows anywhere. Had he fainted for some reason and then dreamed?

He'd never fainted before in his life. But he'd been close to doing so on more than one occasion, he remembered now, back when he'd been less capable of managing stress and confrontation.

Was it possible to have flashbacks from any of the drugs the witch had forced on him last fall, the way he'd heard some people did after taking hallucinogens like LSD? Either way, fainting or flashback, the thought was disturbing. But the other possibility – that the encounter had been real – was even more disconcerting.

His memory of the episode was already fading, as his dreams always did, and that bit about buying milk was just downright weird and made no sense. So he decided it must have been either a dream or a hallucination. The fact that Bean and Sally claimed to have seen this woman on Thursday was just fodder for his overactive imagination.

Right now his main concern should be catching up with Kari and Len. Who knows where they might have gotten to after all this time? He'd give the whole Sea Hag business some more thought later on. He briefly wondered why no one had come looking for him as he went out the front door of the house and down the steps.

Kari, Len, and the tour group were just coming out of the old post office a short way down the path, as it turned out. They hadn't gotten any farther than that? That was odd.

"Ketch," Kari called to him. She and Len started walking toward him, while the tour group continued on in the opposite direction. "I spoke with a ranger," she said when they'd met. "He was workin' in the post office. He said he's never heard of any old lady livin' here on the island, and surely not one who says she's the Sea Hag."

"Oh, thank you for doing that." He pulled his phone from his backpack to check the time. According to the phone, he couldn't have been in the house very long. "How long was I gone?"

"Not too long, maybe a few minutes. Why?"

He continued to pointlessly play with the phone while he internally debated whether to tell her about his experience in the house. If he told her he'd dreamed or hallucinated a conversation with the Sea Hag, she might think he had a screw loose or was coming down with something and then she'd cancel the dive. And justifiably so, because if there was indeed something wrong with him, it wouldn't be good to risk endangering both himself and her in case it happened again down below and she had to try to rescue him. But although he wasn't sure exactly what had happened to him, he felt great now, hearty and hale and refreshed, as if he'd had a good long nap.

He decided not to tell her just yet. "No reason," he said, putting his phone away. "Well, I guess we should get going."

"Already?" Len protested. "This here's a right cool place, and my back ain't recovered yet from that last boat ride."

"You don't want to talk to anybody else?" Kari asked. "There might be more rangers around."

"No, I think I've learned all I'm going to learn today about the Sea Hag." He again considered telling her about his encounter, but not right now he again decided. There'd be time later. "But it's still pretty early, so we can walk around the village some more if you want to. I think you'll especially like the lifesaving station, so let's go there. If we run into anyone who might know something, that'll be a bonus."

Thus Ketch again served as an impromptu guide on his second walking tour of the village this week. This one was shorter though than the last, as he was anxious to get to the dive site. Still, they managed to cover the lifesaving station, the Methodist church, the schoolhouse, and a couple of the historic residences before heading back to the boat. They didn't see any more Park Service volunteers.

They walked back to the dock, cast off, and got underway. This time Ketch made an effort to slow down some and provide a smoother ride than before, in deference to Len and his aching back. Their course was taking them farther down the length of the island on the Atlantic side, almost to where he and Suzanne had ended up with the kids, but two miles and change out to sea.

If the weather had been at all questionable, he wouldn't have risked running the *TBD* out that far. But the wind was dropping off, and the closer they got to their destination the smoother the sea became. Despite what the old woman had said back at the village, it might well turn out to be 'slick cam' over the dive site, as the old O'cockers used to say – and as some still did, Ketch thought, including her. If she'd been something other than a figment of his imagination, that is.

So he knew she'd been wrong about that, at least if she'd meant it literally. But he should have known that one shouldn't always take things literally, and he wouldn't know until later that they'd have been better off if a sudden squall had rolled in right then and chased them back to Ocracoke.

~ S e v e n ~

They were never lonely or fearful when they were together.

*I*t indeed doesn't get better than this, as the Captain was fond of saying. What could be better, Ketch thought, than being at the helm of your boat on a cerulean sea with the summer sun warming your skin and the salt-tinged air whipping past your face? And with a chin strap on your tarp hat, of course. But seriously, he didn't think there was anyplace he'd rather be than right here, right now, helping the world learn more of its history – if they got lucky and found a previously unknown shipwreck, that is.

He realized he hadn't thought about the earworm he'd just paraphrased in years, though it was a song he admired and one he wished he'd written himself. He resolved to spend more time with his guitar when this was all over, and to teach Henry some more tricks of the trade. And Bean, too, if he was interested enough. Maybe they could all write a new song together.

But right here, right now, it was hopefully time for him and Kari to unearth another hidden nugget from this island's nautical past. He didn't care as much about treasure as he did about that. Contrary to what Pauline had said, he had no real desire to be a pirate, not even if he could have lived the romanticized, fanciful version of what had actually been a dishearteningly hard and often short life. Instead, he might have taken up underwater archeology as a profession if he'd known himself better at an earlier age. But such is life, and he was here now.

When the GPS said they'd reached the coordinates Ketch had gotten from the Captain, they first cruised around the area to see if they could spot anything below from the surface. The coordinates were in degrees, minutes, and seconds instead of just degrees and minutes, which was fortunate. Ketch knew that seconds of latitude were about a hundred feet apart and seconds of longitude at this latitude were probably around seventy-five feet apart. So the resulting target area, though not perfectly precise, was manageable. If they'd only been able to narrow the location down to the nearest minute, they might have had to search at least a square mile of seafloor.

As it was, it was still unlikely they'd land on the wreck right off. And if it was a wooden ship from Peter Painter's era there probably wouldn't be much of it left, for another thing. So the first dive would be for reconnaissance. Once they found what they were looking for, they could move the boat closer to it if necessary – assuming they did find something, Ketch reminded himself. They still didn't definitively know if the abandoned boat found by the Coast Guard had been used by the convicts, nor if it had been anchored over a wreck site for that matter.

Though the surface was glassy and there didn't seem to be much current, it turned out the visibility wasn't good enough for them to see anything on the bottom from the boat. But that was neither surprising nor discouraging. From past experience, they knew the viz didn't start to approach travel brochure quality until one went farther out on the continental shelf.

They picked a spot, dropped anchor, cut the engine, and got to work. The depth finder showed they were in about thirty-five feet of water here. If they ended up diving at that depth, they wouldn't have to worry much about decompression limits. Consulting his dive tables, Ketch saw that their time limit for the first dive would be over three hours at thirty-five feet, and still more than two hours if they rounded up to forty feet. Their dive computers might never even raise an eyebrow at them today, and they shouldn't be in any danger of developing decompression sickness, or 'the bends'. But it was a good thing they'd brought multiple tanks, since they'd use more air the deeper they went due to the increase in ambient pressure.

They were both advanced, competent divers and they worked well and smoothly together – as they also did in other facets of their lives, Ketch reflected. He was certainly a lucky guy. They geared up efficiently, each drawing their items from the gear bags Ketch had methodically packed in the order in which the items would be needed.

He worked from a written checklist when he packed, as well as from a mental one that derived from visualizing the full dive sequence from start to finish, and every electronic item had fresh batteries. Kari didn't remark on his packing job or compliment him on it. Its thoroughness and correctness were expected and assumed.

Len had already put up the red-and-white dive flag and set out the ladder, and was now winching the boat to the anchor. "Hey, this anchor's really stuck on somethin'," he called. "I guess that's a good thing, but I hope we can work it loose later."

"We'll check on it when we go down," Ketch said. He'd decided to use his Danforth fluke, since he'd figured they'd be anchoring in sand. Maybe it had snagged on a rocky outcrop or some kind of debris. There were no coral reefs around here that he knew of.

"Well, I got the rope tight as it can be," Len declared, fishing a beer from their cooler.

"There's no rope on a boat," Kari chided him. "That's the anchor line, or *rode*."

"Oh – well, ex-*cuse* me!" Len replied with a grin. "Y'all 'bout ready there?"

"Yes, I think so," Ketch said. Eyeing Len's beer, he added, "Would you mind topping off the fuel tank before you get too comfortable?" Len said he wouldn't mind at all.

The divers were wearing light but full wetsuits with gloves and booties today, even though the water temperature at the surface had to be around eighty. But it would be cooler at depth, and prolonged immersion in any water that was below body temperature could lead to hypothermia. Their coverings would also provide protection against abrasions.

They each also wore a buoyancy control device, an inflatable vest with an integrated weight system and D-rings from which hung their dive lights and other ancillary gear, including a small underwater digital camera for him and a reel and buoy for her. Their tanks were harnessed on the backs of their BCDs, and a dangling regulator, octopus, and gauge console with dive computer, compass, and air gauge were connected to each tank. There were always newer and fancier equipment options coming onto the market, but they were both somewhat old school in that regard. They each sported a bottom timer and depth gauge on their wrists as well, though the dive computers made them redundant (in a perfect world), and they each had a knife strapped to a leg.

After performing a final gear check on each other to make sure everything was on and functioning, they rose from their seated positions on the boat's transom with mask, snorkel, and fins in hand and carefully moved to opposite gunwales with Len's assistance. Though the tanks would feel weightless in the water, they each weighed about forty pounds full on land, so the divers were top-heavy at the moment. They slipped their fins on, then spit in their masks and rinsed them in the water to prevent fogging. With masks and regulators in place and a hand over both, they half-inflated their BCDs, did backward rolls into the water, and swam to the anchor line.

"Everybody okay?" Len called to them from topside. "All's well up here, 'cept you almost made me spill my beer rockin' the boat like that!" They gave him the hand-on-head 'okay' sign, deflated their BCDs, and began to descend.

They'd decided that Ketch would go first. He forced himself to slowly follow the anchor line down, pausing every few feet to clear his ears. He was eager to get to the bottom, but he didn't want to risk an inner ear injury. It was important to always keep one's head when beneath the surface, in what was truly an alien environment – one which, though it held much beauty and many wonders, could turn hostile in a heartbeat.

It looked like they might only have a few feet of visibility. He hadn't expected great viz, but this was abnormally subpar. He wondered why the water was so turbid down here when there was hardly any current. The tides shouldn't be causing this much disturbance at this distance from shore.

He pressed the button on his inflator and squirted some air into his BCD to maintain neutral buoyancy when his computer indicated he should be approaching the bottom, though he couldn't see it yet. Kari was right behind him. He turned to check on her and they signed 'okay' to each other.

They reached the anchor before they hit

bottom. Ketch could see that it was indeed hooked on something – and that 'something' was man-made. He hovered around the object, taking care to keep his fins well away from both it and the bottom to avoid stirring up more sediment, and turned his dive light on. Kari did the same. The lights helped about as much in the silt-laden water as high-beam headlights did when driving a car through fog, so they turned them off.

The object in question was encrusted with a thick blueish-green growth. The lights had briefly shown some hints of red and orange, but those colors weren't visible now. Ketch knew that due to the way water absorbs and reflects light, the 'R' and then the 'O' wavelengths in the ROYGBIV spectrum of visible light (red, orange, yellow, green, blue, indigo, violet) were the first to be lost as one's depth increased. The red component of the sunlight penetrating below the surface of the water was completely absorbed by thirty feet. Orange and yellow usually hung around longer, but apparently not today because of the turbidity.

Although whatever had been mounted on the object was now missing, it was obvious that the object was some kind of a mount. It looked like it was canted at about a forty-five degree angle. There was sand piled up behind it, but there was a growth-encrusted metal surface extending the remaining distance to the sandy bottom on its near side. When he turned left and moved a little farther on, that surface continued.

This was part of the deck and hull of a metal ship, not a pirate ship. He motioned to Kari to follow him, and a little farther down they came to another tilted protrusion, a larger one this time. When Ketch examined it more closely, he saw that there was an open hatch at the top of it. They slowly continued on, observing other smaller bumps along the surface, another coverless hatch, and what appeared to be a collapsed deck rail.

They eventually reached the stern of the ship, where they found a propeller half-buried in the sandy bottom and what looked to Ketch like a diving plane. When he saw a smooth round hole in the hull as well, he knew. That *was* a diving plane, and the hole was a stern torpedo loading hatch. The largest of the protrusions they'd seen back a ways, the one with the opening at the top, was what remained of the conning tower. It had seemed too short at first, but the outer casing of the ship had probably rusted away and what they were seeing now was the inside pressure hull. This was a submarine.

Ketch suddenly realized he'd been too absorbed in exploring to take any pictures. He activated his camera, framed a shot of the stern, and signed to Kari that he was turning around to head back. The pictures wouldn't be much good in this water, but he wanted to at least get shots of the conning tower and the mount for documentation and then continue on to the bow.

He saw that Kari was flashing him the 'stop'

sign, so he hovered in place and waited to see what she wanted. She positioned herself near the stern propeller and somehow, without touching the sandy bottom or the ship itself, managed to strike what looked to him like a provocative World War II pinup girl pose while she neutrally hovered.

She wanted a selfie. Ketch grinned around his regulator and took the shot, and then she followed him back up the length of the ship – which would turn out to be considerable, as Ketch knew the sub had to be at least two hundred feet long. He'd earlier been pessimistic about hitting their target right off, but in reality it might have been harder to *not* hit this one.

They paused for more photos, this time *sans* histrionics, at the conning tower and again at what Ketch now knew had been the deck gun mount. There were no identifying marks on the conning tower. When they approached the bow, they found another torpedo loading hatch – and more interestingly, a large and jagged hole in the hull.

Ketch knew better than to enter, as of course did Kari as well. Penetrating a wreck like this one was fraught with dangers. More preparation than they were equipped for today would be needed if they wanted to explore its interior.

He wondered if this hole had been made by a depth charge, and if the sub's crew had been able to evacuate. Was this sub a U-boat? If so, had it accidentally run aground while trying to dodge an aerial attack, or had they deliberately scuttled the sub after sustaining damage in a battle with an Allied cruiser? Anything was possible.

Though an exploration of the sub's interior would be fascinating, one thing he wouldn't enjoy finding in there would be the skeletal remains of the crew – which he wouldn't disturb if he did. He recalled that a North Carolina dive shop years ago had sparked an international incident with the German government when they'd prominently displayed in their shop a skull salvaged from a newly discovered U-boat wreck.

So he settled for shining his dive light into the interior through the hole, and Kari did the same beside him. They saw that sand now carpeted the floor of the compartment, or rather some of the floor and some of the wall since it was tilted. Sand, and something shiny atop it in a far dark corner under some rusty, mangled equipment.

The reds and oranges were gone from the ambient light, and the yellows were struggling as well in there. But the powerful white beams from the dive lights hadn't had to travel through thirty-some feet of murky water to get inside this compartment, and they easily illuminated all the colors of the spectrum – including the quite recognizable gold of a disorderly pile of ingots in that corner.

A sudden profusion of bubbles from their regulators indicated that both divers had spotted the gold bars. They had to be bars of pure gold, Ketch realized. He knew that gold was one of the least reactive of the chemical elements and didn't combine easily with oxygen, so it didn't rust or tarnish. Those bars looked brand-new. And since there were no encrustations on the bars, they must have only recently been removed from some kind of storage deeper inside the sub.

This must be what those convicts had been after. But how had they learned where to find this wreck? Ketch found it hard to believe that people like that would have had access to historic documents like government and military dispatches and such in a prison library, and there was no known submarine wreck on the charts anywhere near here. And why hadn't it ever been found before, since it was in such shallow water?

He saw that there were a few smaller objects on the sand at one end of the pile. They weren't as shiny as the gold bars, and unlike them they were showing some encrustation. They could very well be more gold coins like the ones he'd found on the beach, he thought. But the coins he'd found definitely predated this sub. Maybe the convicts had stumbled across someone's coin collection in there, too.

He toyed with the idea of quickly ducking inside to retrieve a few of the bars – mainly for evidence, but maybe also for souvenirs. But then he remembered the dangers of penetrating a wreck without a plan and the necessary gear. This compartment was sizeable and full of corroded pipes, cables, instruments, and other equipment.

He might accidentally stir up more silt, which could instantaneously reduce his visibility to zero and obscure the way out. And then he'd also expose himself to the risks of getting cut or injured and possibly causing a cave-in if his tank snagged on something or bumped into anything.

The convicts must have done it, though, and more, but they may have been better prepared. And even if they hadn't been, they likely weren't as risk-averse or safety-conscious as he was. Maybe they'd paid for that insouciance, Ketch thought. He remembered what Dan had said about the possibility they'd been caught in an explosion. So there was another thing to consider – he didn't know how close they were to the torpedoes, if any remained. Maybe the convicts had set one off somehow, though if that had happened it seemed like there should have been more damage here.

For now, he'd just take another picture or two. He had a gaff (which he'd never used, since oddly enough he didn't fish) back on the *TBD* if they wanted to try to extract some of the bars from outside the compartment on their next dive. He'd also brought a lift bag and a small net, which could come in handy since gold was heavy.

He directed Kari to shine her light on the pile and snapped a shot of it, then focused on one bar at the near end of the haphazard pile. He thought he could discern a stamp of some kind on its face, so he zoomed in on that. The image was fuzzy through the particle-laden water, but now that the bar was enlarged he could make out the Nazi eagle symbol, an eagle clutching a swastika in its talons. So yes, this must be a U-boat. He showed the view to Kari.

When he was finished shooting, he turned to Kari and jerked a thumb up to indicate he thought they should ascend. She nodded in agreement, and they finned back down the hull to the anchor line at the gun mount.

They ascended slowly, gradually adjusting the air in their BCDs as they went, and swam to the stern of the *TBD*. They skipped the safety stop at fifteen feet this time because they hadn't gotten anywhere close to maxing out their bottom time, so there wasn't enough residual nitrogen in their blood to be a concern. They'd have to do something truly stupid to get the bends today. Ketch floated at the surface while Kari doffed her BCD, tank, and fins. She handed them up to Len and used the ladder to board, and then he followed suit.

"So, did y'all have any luck? What'd you find down there?" Len asked.

"We're on top of a U-boat," Ketch said. "The anchor's hooked on the deck gun mount."

"A U-boat? No shit!"

"Yeah," Kari said. Peeling her wetsuit off, she nonchalantly added, "And there's a pile of gold bars down there, too, that somebody dragged out from inside the wreck. And probably more still inside."

"Get outta town! What's a Nazi sub doin' with gold? I thought they just come skulkin' 'round Torpedo Junction to sink our ships."

That, and alternatively Torpedo Alley, were more nicknames the Outer Banks had earned during World War II, Ketch remembered. Nazi U-boats targeting Allied shipping had torpedoed over eighty ships between Cape Hatteras and Cape Lookout, mostly in 1942, before a system of military escorts and patrols had become well enough established to curtail what had essentially been a turkey shoot for the German sailors.

"Well, I'm just guessing here," Ketch said, "but it could have been the private stash of some high-ranking Nazi official trying to escape to someplace like South America toward the end of the war. The Nazis had a lot of gold. They stole it from the countries they occupied, and they confiscated the belongings of the Jews they rounded up for their concentration camps and melted down the gold for bullion."

"I heard they even took their gold teeth and fillings," Kari commented with a grimace.

"So that's what them jailbirds was after," Len said. "Since they're outta the picture now, are we gonna be rich'n famous?"

"I'd rather not be famous," Ketch retorted, working his wetsuit off. He was glad he'd packed their travel cyclone jackets. Though it was a warm day, the water that had gotten inside his wetsuit had cooled and he was a bit chilled at the moment.

"I don't think we'll be getting rich, either. We're not in international waters, and under the Abandoned Shipwreck Act our government would likely take ownership of the sub and its contents, especially since it's a historic wreck. And the German government might get in on the act as well, so any time and money we invested in salvaging that wreck would probably be wasted."

"Well, what if we take the gold first and then report the wreck? Or don't even report it?"

"That'd be dishonest," Kari said. "And it'd be dangerous, even if we had the tools and the trainin', which we don't. We're not qualified to salvage that gold on our own, if there's more of it inside the sub somewhere. "

"Yeah, I guess you're right," Len said. "Well then, maybe we might could just take a few bars from that pile y'all saw while we're here, if you can reach 'em. You know, for souvenirs. Who'd miss a few? Were they standard reserve?"

"No, they're just bricks," Ketch said.

"Too bad. With the price of gold, one of them big ones would be worth almost half a million. But even one of them little kilobar's worth about forty grand right now."

"Holy moley!" Kari exclaimed. "For one gold bar? How can that be?"

"Well, I know a gram's been goin' for around forty bucks most days lately," Len said, "and that adds up to forty grand for a kilogram."

"He should know," Ketch said. "He's an expert

at trading commodities." He knew that was how Len had accumulated his substantial nest egg, under the tutelage of his mega-farmer father.

"Yeah, and this kinda gold might be even better'n pirate gold. Easier to sell anyway, I bet."

"Maybe not, with swastikas stamped on them," Ketch pointed out. "I could see where some folks might get upset about that, and maybe even demand that it be seized for restitution."

Len shrugged. "I don't see why it should make a difference. I could just say my grandpappy brung it back from the war'n give it to me before he passed. It ain't illegal no more for citizens to own bullion."

"That used to be illegal?" Kari asked.

"Yep, 'til the Seventies," Len answered. "Before my time, lucky for me. So what do y'all think, is that doable? Could we just take a little?"

"I suppose we could try dragging a few out of the compartment with my gaff," Ketch said. "And I brought a lift bag. Kari?"

"Huh. Well okay, I guess so. But no goin' in there. If the gaff doesn't work, we leave it be." She unhooked the reel and buoy she'd been toting on her BCD. "It's probably best we don't mark this site for everybody else to find, right? So I can carry somethin' else down next time."

"Wonder why nobody ever found that ole U-boat before?" Len mused. "It ain't in deep water, nor that far from shore."

"I was thinking about that earlier," Ketch said,

"and I have a theory. Or rather a hypothesis, since I have no real evidence. I noticed the sand on the other side of the sub goes right up to the conning tower, but on the side where we found the hole the sub is almost completely uncovered. It's as though the sub is leaning against a sand cliff. So I'm thinking maybe the sub got shoaled over during a storm after it sank, and then that sand barge siphoned the sand away in front of it. That could explain why the water's so turbid here, too. And maybe the people on the barge were the ones who found the wreck."

"But what would they have to do with those convicts?" Kari asked.

"I don't know. Maybe that Coastie who's being questioned today connects the two somehow, but that's just a wild guess."

"Huh," Len grunted. "Well, one thing we know is it ain't no pirate ship. But there's still gold, so that's cool."

"Right, and that's another thing the Sea Hag was wrong about," Ketch remarked, busying himself with the cooler. All the fresh air, not to mention the diving, had made him famished and lunch was overdue. He set the Subway subs Len had picked up for them, along with squirt containers of mayo and sub sauce, on the bow locker, then started passing around water bottles. "I saw a few gold coins like the ones we found on Thursday in that pile, too. So it's all Nazi treasure, not pirate treasure like she claimed."

"What else was that Sea Hag woman wrong about besides the pirate treasure?" Kari broke in, mayo in hand. She and Len had quickly claimed their subs as soon as he'd set them out, so they were apparently hungry as well. "You said there was another thing she was wrong about."

Ketch sighed. He knew what was about to happen. "Well, she said we wouldn't have smooth sailing today."

"Oh yeah? When did she say that? You hadn't mentioned that before. More detail, please."

The girl was sharp, no doubt about it, and he knew that once she'd sunk her teeth into something she didn't let go of it. Deciding it would be best to come clean, he recounted what he remembered of his adventure in the Dixon/Salter house between bites of his sandwich.

"Uh-huh," Kari said when he'd finished. "And why didn't you tell me about this before? Never mind, I know why. You thought I might abort the dive, right?"

"Yes, and I apologize for that. But I felt fine right after, and I've felt fine ever since. I feel fine right now, honest."

"Oh, so now you're bein' honest?"

"Pardon me, y'all, for buttin' in on your lovers' quarrel," Len said, "but I don't think he's havin' flashbacks or whatever."

"Oh no?" Kari said. "Well then, Doctor, what do you think it might be? A mini-stroke, or maybe a brain aneurism that could blow any minute? When did you last get checked for aneurisms and such?" she asked Ketch.

"Just this past spring, at my annual physical."

Len shook his head. "I think it was a ghost," he solemnly declared.

"Oh, come on now!" Kari objected. "Really?"

"Well, think about it. This ole lady keeps poppin' up outta nowhere, she knows who he is and where he's at, she knows what he's gonna do - and she knew about them convicts and that sand barge when the kids saw her, too, and then she just vanishes into thin air..."

"Or they saw some senile old woman, and Ketch was delusional this mornin'."

"I'm tellin' ya, I seen some shit in my time," Len insisted. "You ever been to the Devil's trampin' ground? I have. It makes you feel bad just bein' there. Nothin' grows there and dogs won't go near the place, I seen that for myself. And I was at a house one time where it sounded like somebody was movin' furniture around upstairs, but there was nobody up there. And what about the *Deering*, that Diamond Shoals ghost ship, and the flamin' ship of Ocracoke, and Blackbeard's pirate lights in Pamlico Sound? There's tons of stories like that, and lotsa folks 'round these parts even nowadays seen stuff that can't be explained. There's more goin' on in the world than meets the eye, I believe that."

"You're not helpin' his case any," Kari said. "If there's somethin' wrong with him, he shouldn't be divin'. And if that Sea Hag woman *is* real and what she says is true, he still shouldn't be divin', and we shouldn't even be here."

"But it isn't all true," Ketch said. "She hasn't been right about everything. There's no pirate ship, the sea couldn't get much calmer, and nothing bad has happened to that sand barge, for starters. And I really don't think there's anything wrong with me," he insisted. But Kari didn't seem convinced. "Okay, look," he said, "I'd like to do one more dive. But if you believe we should go home, we can do that. I won't argue anymore, I won't be upset, and there won't be any recriminations later either way, I promise. So I'll leave it up to you."

Kari chewed a while in silence, and the others focused their attention on their food as well. Finally, she spoke.

"Okay," she said to Ketch. "It's against my better judgement, but I know how much it means to you – and truth be told, I wouldn't mind havin' me some of that treasure. I've learned you don't get much in life without bein' bold. So I'll do it – but like I said, no penetration."

"Sounds like what them Catholic girls used to tell me in high school," Len quipped, and they all laughed. Ketch silently thanked him for breaking the tension.

"Okay," Ketch said. "But seriously, no pressure. Are you sure?"

"Yeah, what the heck," she said. "You can probably go a little while longer down there without seein' any more ghosts, right?"

"That's the spirit!" Len joked. This time, though, the others just groaned. "Say Ketch, how come that Sea Hag was talkin' 'bout Peter Painter's treasure? I hadn't never heard of that guy before. What about Blackbeard? Everybody says he's the one done buried treasure somewhere."

"Yes, but most people think he buried it inland, if there ever was any. He supposedly had wives in Bath, Elizabeth City, and Edenton as well as Ocracoke, and he lived in Bath for a while. People have dug around all those places over the years, but if any of them ever found anything substantial, they've kept quiet about it. But according to legend, Teach's Lights can at times be seen at night in the sound near Ocracoke, and it's said that if you follow them until they stop, you'll know where the treasure's buried."

"Yeah, so what about Peter Painter?"

"I don't know. I'd never heard anything about any treasure of his before, either. He was a lesser-known pirate in these parts, and he was active a few years before Blackbeard came on the scene. He might have joined Blackbeard's crew late in his career. I've read that when Blackbeard was ambushed and killed near Ocracoke by the Royal Navy in 1718, the list of the crew that were also killed included someone named 'P. Painter'. But maybe he wasn't killed and he made off with Blackbeard's treasure, who knows?"

"Maybe. Hey, speakin' of pirates, I heard

there's gonna be another trial for Bob Ingram. That's gonna be, what, the third one now?"

Not again, Ketch thought. He wished Len hadn't brought up that particular topic at this particular time. But what's done is done, no sense trying to ignore it.

"The third one for killing his wife, yes," Ketch said. "So that's four altogether counting the one for racketeering, which is a done deal. No matter what happens, he'll be in jail for at least the next twenty years."

Kari just kept eating. She and Ketch both knew who had killed Ingram's wife, and Ketch knew it weighed heavily on her that the authorities wouldn't leave Ingram alone about it, despicable as the man was in other ways. He found it hard to understand why the District Attorney continued to pursue it, when the evidence was all circumstantial and hadn't been convincing enough to get a conviction the first two times. They didn't even have a body to prove there'd been a crime, and the man was already in prison for his other transgressions. What a waste of time and taxpayer money.

"Yeah, that guy's screwed over ever which way." Len excused himself and dropped into the water down current from the boat, presumably to use the facilities. Ketch took advantage of his absence to surreptitiously embrace Kari and kiss her.

"What was that for?" she gasped, coming up for

air.

"You know what," he said with a smile, using their private code.

"Yeah, I do," she smiled back, "and me too." Untangling herself, she said, "Okay, let's get geared up again." She went to where her BCD was racked and started switching out the used tank.

"Ain't y'all supposed to wait for an hour after eatin'?" Len asked, climbing back aboard.

"That's just an old wives' tale," Kari said. "The sooner we do this and get on outta here, the better. All that business about ghosts gave me the creeps, dang y'all."

They didn't need to wait due to eating, but they'd ordinarily have to sit out a minimum surface interval mandated by their depth and bottom time on the first dive and the planned logistics of their second dive. But they'd been well within the decompression limits on the first dive and they wouldn't be going any deeper on the second one, and Ketch's computer and dive tables both verified they had nothing to worry about in that regard.

Len watched while the divers went about their business. "That there gaff you got's kinda short," he remarked. "How you gonna reach the gold with that?"

"It's longer than you think," Ketch said, taking it down. "There are two pieces, so it's twelve feet long altogether. I don't think that sub was more than twenty feet wide on the outside, and less inside, so it could work. It has a good sturdy hook on it, too."

"Man! What you need a gaff like that for on this lil' bitty boat?"

"I don't. I've never used it. It came with the boat."

Len again helped each of them to the gunwales when they were ready to go, then popped a beer and sat down with it on the padded pilot's bench behind the wheel. "Be careful, y'all!" he called to them. "Remember, if anythin's gonna happen, it'll happen out there!"

"*Captain Ron*!" Kari responded. Ketch knew it was almost impossible to stump her on quotes from old movies and TV shows. She didn't do as well with the newer ones, as neither of them spent much time in front of screens larger than a laptop's these days, but that particular film was a classic to them. And Len knew it, too, apparently.

They knew their way around now down below, and they were soon back at the open compartment. Ketch found he could reach several of the gold bars by gripping the gaff at its end and extending his arm into the compartment – but not any more of his body than that, as Kari had stipulated. They raised some more silt in the process, but they didn't really need to see the bars clearly since they knew where they were.

When they had ten bars piled up in front of them, Ketch called a halt. The lift bag he'd brought was rated for twenty-five pounds. If each gold bar was a kilogram, then ten of them equated to twenty-two pounds, so that was enough. He'd actually planned on taking fewer bars than that, but Kari had kept encouraging him to drag more out.

They stuffed the bars into the carry net attached to the lift bag, and then she wrote something on her slate. 'I GO U STAY', the message read. That meant she wanted to return for another load after guiding this one to the boat. He shook his head 'no', and she shook hers 'yes'. She tapped the slate with her finger to emphasize the message and started adding air to the lift bag with her octopus. He watched as she began to rise to the surface with the payload, angling herself toward where the anchor line should be.

It appeared a certain someone might have come down with a case of gold fever, he thought. He didn't think they should take any more, and anyway he doubted he could reach many more of the bars without entering the compartment. Rather than trying, he set the gaff down and decided to poke around the nearby bow of the sub while he waited for her to unload and return.

They hadn't actually gone right to the end of the bow on the first dive, after finding the compartment with the gold in it. He saw now that the cliff of sand backing the sub ended rather abruptly behind the bow, so he swam around the tip of the bow to have a look.

And almost bumped heads with what looked to

be a sandbar shark coming the other way around. Ketch knew they were the most common kind of shark found in these waters and they weren't known to be aggressive toward humans. But still, this one was probably about a six-footer. Remembering his training, Ketch folded his arms across his chest and hovered motionless. The shark warily eyed him, then altered its course to swim around him and continued on its way.

Though he'd kept his cool, that had still been somewhat of a surprise, so Ketch waited a moment for his heart to slow back to normal before moving on. Sharks and other kinds of fish often made homes in and around shipwrecks, so the animal's presence here wasn't unusual – and there was yet another reason to not blithely penetrate a wreck without taking precautions. If you trespassed on a potentially dangerous creature's territory, all bets were off.

It looked like an area had been dug out of the sand on the shark's side of the bow, forming another cliff that extended perpendicularly back from the end of the first cliff at least as far as he could see. And along the face of this cliff, there was some old wood showing.

A lot of wood, Ketch saw as he swam farther along, and now more wood along the bottom. He slowly came to the realization that, though the planking had long since rotted and collapsed in many places, the still largely intact framework indicated that this was part of the deck of a ship. A pirate ship? He turned his dive light on and panned it around, and that was when he noticed some more coins scattered about, like the ones he'd found on the beach.

He was flabbergasted. What were the odds of this happening, he wondered, of these two vessels from two different centuries ending up shipwrecked in virtually the same spot? It was incredible, and even more incredible that they were both treasure ships of some kind. Truth really could be stranger than fiction. Wait until Kari sees this, he thought.

He picked up several of the coins and pocketed them, then started finning back toward the bow of the sub along the cliff. He shouldn't dally here any longer, he decided. She should be back momentarily, if she wasn't back already. If she'd made it back to the compartment, she'd be alarmed by his absence and possibly starting to search for him. He'd never hear the end of *that*, he knew, but he was mostly concerned about upsetting and scaring her. She was the love of his life, and he had no desire to do either of those things to her.

Just as the bow came into view ahead of him, two distinct and rather loud booming sounds reached his ears, one almost immediately after the other. He looked quickly all around, but he didn't see anything out of the ordinary. Not that he expected to – the visibility still wasn't great and he knew sound traveled faster underwater than in air, making it difficult for human ears to determine its direction and distance.

But shortly after the initial booms, there was a dull *whumph* from directly in front of him as the other side of the sub's hull was impacted by something. So he knew where *that* sound had come from. Sand began cascading down the face of the cliff next to him then, so he kicked away from it and swam around the tip of the bow.

Those booms had sounded like explosions – and if that was what they'd been, then the hull of the sub had probably been hit by a pressure wave. With a sinking feeling in the pit of his stomach, he knew he had to find Kari as quickly as possible – if it wasn't already too late.

~ Eight ~

They were intoxicated by the romance of the unusual.

*A*nd now they were paying a price for that. He found her sitting on the bottom, slumped unconscious against the hull of the sub near the open compartment with her head lolling forward onto her chest. The pressure hull he'd been behind had shielded him from the force of the blasts, but she hadn't been as lucky. She'd lost her mask, her regulator wasn't in her mouth, and it looked like her BCD had ruptured.

It was obvious to Ketch that the situation was dire. Though his brain was screaming at him to panic, he knew time was of the essence and it wouldn't do her a bit of good if he gave in to that now. He needed to be detached and not think about who she was. So he buckled down and made himself concentrate on the procedures he'd learned during his rescue training for surfacing an unconscious diver.

The first thing he did after getting a good grip on her tank valve with one hand was to find the clip release for her integrated weights with the other and ditch the weights. He'd keep his own weights for added stability unless he found himself unable to float her adequately. He didn't waste valuable time trying to find a pulse or reinsert the regulator in her mouth. It was difficult to detect a pulse at depth, and she wouldn't aspirate any more water on the way up. Residual air in her lungs would expand as the ambient pressure decreased and that would automatically force her to exhale, if anything. He didn't know if there were any broken bones and he didn't take time to check. That was the least of their worries at the moment.

Her BCD was useless now, but he wouldn't have used it anyway as it would get in the way if he had to start the rescue breathing regimen in the water. His BCD would have enough lift capacity for both of them, and her exposure suit would help keep her buoyant since she was no longer carrying weights. He added a little air to his BCD and kept her upright from behind as they ascended.

He knew how to perform artificial respiration on the surface of the water, but he thought it would be best if he could get her back on the boat as quickly as possible. Full CPR wasn't an option in the water without specialized training and equipment, neither of which he had. He hoped Len would be able to help get her aboard – assuming he and the *TBD* were still there, that is. The boat at least should be, he thought, in some form or other. Even if it was in pieces, one of the selling points of the Whaler was that it was unsinkable by design. He brought Kari up as rapidly as he could without risking a pulmonary injury, and was relieved to see that the boat, and Len, were still in one piece.

"Hey, you guys!" Len called when he glimpsed

them breaking the surface near the stern of the *TBD*. "What happened down there? This other boat buzzed by here, and then – oh, man," he said, finally noticing that Ketch was towing a mask-less Kari, "did she get hurt?"

Ketch didn't answer until he'd reached the ladder. Then he removed his regulator long enough to say, "Get her aboard!" and put it back in his mouth. He unbuckled her mangled BCD and let it, the tank, and the rest of her gear sink back down to the bottom. He hated to have to do that, but she was dead weight and he needed to start working on her without further delay.

He held her as high out of the water as he could and Len grasped her wrists. While Len dragged her across the transom, Ketch yanked his fins off, tossed them into the boat, and climbed the ladder as quickly as he could with the remainder of his gear on. As soon as his feet hit the deck he unbuckled his BCD, dropped it and his mask on the spot, and knelt over Kari.

"What should I do now?" Len asked. He was all business, now that he knew he had to be.

She was already on her back. Ketch lifted her chin and tilted her head a little toward him, made sure there was nothing blocking her airway, and started mouth-to-mouth ventilation. Conveniently, her wetsuit had a front zipper. Pausing to unzip it enough to reach her neck and chest, he said, "Call the Coast Guard!" He pressed his index and middle fingers (not his thumb, which he knew had its own pulse) to the side of her neck over a carotid artery. Finding no pulse there, he began chest compressions.

Fortunately, Len knew his way around boats (despite his earlier *faux pas* with the anchor rode) and didn't need to be coached on using the marine radio. He issued a Mayday and waited for a response. Meanwhile, Ketch had ventilated Kari again and then resumed chest compressions. He'd alternate between the two for as long as it took.

"What should I say?" Len asked.

"Unconscious diver, underwater explosion, need EMS and medevac by chopper in Ocracoke!" Ketch barked.

Len had raised the Coast Guard. He repeated Ketch's instructions, then said, "They wanna know if they should send a chopper to us here."

"No, we'll make Ocracoke before they'd get here," Ketch responded as soon as he could.

He still hadn't checked for broken bones and they hadn't been very careful when moving her, he thought while he worked – but if he couldn't revive her soon, none of that would matter. And whether or not anything was broken, he knew there'd be other problems to be dealt with. He could see that she'd bled from both ears, she was undoubtedly concussed, and she probably had internal injuries – hence his decision to get professional medical intervention for her as soon as possible.

Len signed off with the Coast Guard. "Now what?" he asked.

"Take my knife, cut the anchor loose, and make a beeline for Jolly Roger's," Ketch spat. Len unsheathed the knife strapped to Ketch's leg, hustled to the bow, and began sawing vigorously at the anchor line.

During the next round of chest compressions, Ketch saw Kari expel some blood-tinged water from the side of her mouth. He stopped what he was doing and checked again to make sure there was nothing else in her mouth. This time when he checked for a pulse, he felt something. He listened to her chest and watched for a moment, then announced, "She's breathing!" She remained unconscious, but her heart and lungs were working – at least one lung, anyway.

He took a deep breath, his first one in a while. His arms and legs ached and he was tired, but he couldn't relax yet. What should he do next? He realized he didn't know how much time had elapsed since he'd found her, and he knew the EMTs would ask about that. He never wore a watch and the old-fashioned bottom timer he still wore on his wrist wouldn't give him what he needed, so he reached for his gauge console on the deck behind him. When he checked his dive computer, he saw that it had been six minutes and change since he'd begun to ascend with her.

Was that all? It seemed like it had been ages. But it might still be too much. It had been maybe as much as a minute since she'd started breathing again, but it had probably taken him at least that long to get to her after the explosions, so she could have gone six minutes or more without breathing. He knew that some brain cells started dying within five minutes of the onset of hypoxia. He didn't know when her heart had stopped, and thus how long blood flow to the brain had been interrupted.

And she was still unconscious. He tried to remain hopeful, but he knew her prognosis might not be good. He checked her pulse again, then tenderly smoothed her hair while he watched to make sure she continued to breathe.

Why had he pushed her to make that last dive? They could have been safely back in Ocracoke by now, having a beer at the Jolly Roger and laughing at themselves for letting some ghost stories spook them into forgoing a small fortune. Instead, she was lying here on the deck, unconscious and likely gravely wounded. There was a pile of gold bars in the locker, but that didn't matter a whit to him. He should have heeded the Sea Hag's warning... But wait, that had to have been all in his head, right? Well, then he should have listened to Pauline. His shoulders sagged as he wondered how he'd explain to her what he'd allowed to happen to her daughter, and what her reaction would be. He didn't want to think about it.

It looked like Pauline had probably been right when she'd raised the possibility that the convicts might have been murdered. He should have listened to her, damn it! Instead, he'd put her daughter in harm's way today, and Len, too – just as he had Pauline, Len, and the Captain last fall during that witch caper. Oh, and Suzanne last week. He ran his fingers through Kari's hair again, then rested his hand against the side of her face. His newfound love of a good mystery wasn't worth this. Nothing was. He was a rank amateur playing at dangerous games, and he needed to stop.

Before he could get further into beating himself up, Len broke his concentration. "Looks like they're comin' back!" he yelled over the now-idling engine. He pointed toward a boat coming up on them fast astern, then opened the backpack he'd brought with him. "Since she's breathin' now, how 'bout you take the wheel?" He pulled an impact-resistant case from the bag, opened it, and extracted a loaded handgun from it. Laying himself out on the deck behind the transom, he prepared to sight on their pursuer.

"When did you get that?" Ketch sputtered. "What are you doing?"

"I figured it might be good to keep one of these things handy after that business with that witch. It ain't safe bein' around y'all sometimes," Len explained, flashing Ketch a grim grin. "Don't worry, I got me a per-mit and I did some target shootin'. You drive and I'll put a couple holes in their hull, see if that changes their mind."

The other boat was now close enough for Ketch to make out three men on its deck. One was behind the wheel and the others were pulling cylindrical objects of some kind from a locker.

Taking Len's advice, he shut his mouth, went to the helm, and put the *TBD* in gear.

Len got one shot off just before Ketch floored it, and then fired two more as the *TBD* rapidly picked up speed. When Ketch glanced behind him a few moments later, he saw that the other boat was dropping back.

"They're veerin' away!" Len shouted over the noise of the engine. "Maybe they don't have guns."

Or they just hadn't wanted to get caught up in a gunfight, Ketch thought. Either way, it was a stroke of luck. When the other boat had sufficiently faded from view, he called Len to the helm.

"Take over, please. I want to check on Kari," he said.

"Sure thing," Len said. "Just lemme put this away."

Ketch watched him carefully stow the gun back in its case from the corner of his eye. He was also keeping an eye on the depth finder. "I thought you said you practiced," he called back to Len, "but it looked to me like maybe you got part of their windscreen instead of just their hull."

"Well yeah, I did say that, but I didn't say I was good at it. Besides, the boats were movin'. But hey, no harm done, they was all three standin' last I looked. Here, gimme the wheel."

Ketch dropped to his knees again beside Kari. She was still breathing and her mouth was clear, but gentle attempts to rouse her continued to prove fruitless. He decided to save the EMTs some time and got the scissors from their first-aid kit. That stylish wetsuit with the purple trim that looked so good on her would have to go at some point, and it might as well be now.

When he'd finished cutting it away from her, he tucked the space blanket from the kit around her to keep her warm. Hypothermia probably wouldn't help matters. He'd considered rolling her onto her side so she wouldn't aspirate fluid if more were to come up, but decided not to. Though there didn't seem to be any broken bones anywhere now that he'd had time to check, he knew the rescue manual advised against unnecessarily moving the victim.

The boat was bouncing some now, so he fashioned a cushion from part of the wetsuit and placed it under her head. To prevent her from sliding or rolling, he arranged the gear bags and backpacks on both sides of her torso. He again made sure she was breathing and her mouth was clear, then rejoined Len at the helm.

"Keep your eyes open and watch the depth finder," he said. "We have a shallow draft and I don't think we should have any problems, but we certainly don't want to run aground right now."

"Gotcha," Len said.

"I should thank you again, by the way, before I forget. I don't know what we would have done if you hadn't come along today – and if you hadn't been such a deadeye as well," he added with a sad smile.

"That's what friends are for," Len said, then let out a dour chuckle. "Though I gotta say, as far as friends go, you're kinda high-maintenance. But at least I don't get bored hangin' with y'all."

"Yes, well, I think I'm going to need to do something about that."

"How bad is she? Is she gonna make it?"

"I honestly don't know," Ketch answered with a hitch in his voice. "I've done everything for her that I know how to do. I think she was directly in the path of the blast. I was on the other side of the sub at the time, so I was safe."

"What were you doin' on the other side?"

Ketch scratched at the back of his neck. He should ditch his own wetsuit, too, before they made port. "Well, believe it or not, I found another shipwreck down there, near the bow of the sub. The remains of an old wooden ship. And I saw some more of those coins lying around there."

Len's eyes bulged. "Are you kiddin' me?"

"Absolutely not. I know it's unbelievable – but no, I'm not kidding."

"You think it's a pirate ship?"

"Maybe, but I don't know for sure."

"Man, ain't that somethin'! Just like that ole Sea Hag said... Say, you gonna tell the Coasties 'bout all this? Maybe not about that gold we took, but the rest of it?"

"I'm glad you brought that up. For now, I think our story should be that we found a wreck from the war and something exploded, maybe some old ordnance. You were topside and you don't know much. Keep it simple if anyone asks you."

"How come? Don't you want 'em to catch them bastards that bombed y'all?"

"Yes, but I want to talk to Dan at the SBI first." And give some more thought to an idea that was beginning to take shape in his mind. It might be that he'd have one more job to do before putting away the books he'd been reading on interrogation and profiling and such, and hanging up his spurs. "So what did you see up here?"

"Well, Kari come up with that bagful of gold. I emptied it into the locker and give it back to her, and she went back down. Next thing I know, this speedboat come zippin' by like a bat outta hell, and then I heard explosions, and *this* boat dang near left the water. They musta dropped somethin' in the water, dynamite or somethin', I don't know."

"I'm guessing it might have been Semtex, or something like it. I saw them fooling with some metallic-looking cylinders. But it could have been TNT, who knows?" Where would they have gotten either of those explosives, though? One couldn't just pick some up at the Ace Hardware. From some construction site, perhaps? Another thing to file away and think about later...

"Wonder why there were two explosions? Seems like one shoulda been enough."

Ketch raised an eyebrow at him. "The one that rocked this boat might have been meant to land *in* the boat. And I think they were going to throw some more at us back there."

"Man! Maybe I better get me a dang machine gun or somethin' for next time."

"There isn't going to be a next time." Ketch stood lost in thought for a moment. "We'll be there soon. I'd better go check on her again and get our things together."

She was breathing, but she still wouldn't wake up. Ketch stripped off his wetsuit and put his shirt, shorts, and shoes back on, then collected the dry bags he and Kari had brought. The dry bags held their phones, their keys, and most importantly their wallets. He'd be needing the medical insurance cards from hers. He didn't know if her regular insurance covered air ambulances, but he knew their DAN diver's insurance was supposed to. But if she wasn't covered for some reason, he'd pay the bill, steep though it might be. It was the least he could do.

He still had some time, so he packed up his gear and what was left of hers. Unlike what he'd done during his pre-dive preparations, he made no attempt to be organized about it this time. Everything would need to be rinsed, dried, and stowed later anyway, whenever he could get around to doing that. And if he never did, so what? He could buy new gear – or quit diving altogether, if he no longer had Kari to do it with.

They were approaching Ocracoke now, so he checked Kari's condition again and relieved Len at the helm. When they entered the harbor, he saw that the Ocracoke EMS ambulance was waiting near Jolly Roger's, along with a small group of onlookers. Although the island's ambulance service was administered by Hyde County, Ketch knew the county permitted the 'Ocracoke EMS' sign on the ambulance in deference to local pride.

It turned out that Kelsey, aka Nature Girl, was one of the onlookers. She trotted onto the Jolly Roger dock when she spotted the boat and waved the *TBD* to an empty slip. Two EMTs with a stretcher shortly followed. Len tossed her the bow and stern lines, and she tied them off.

"I was havin' lunch here after my tour and I heard what happened," she said. She sounded lackadaisical as usual, but there was a slight uptick in her cadence, which Ketch thought probably indicated concern. "How is she?"

"She's unconscious and cyanotic, but she's breathing," Ketch said, stepping up onto the dock and out of the way of the EMTs. Len followed suit. "Is the chopper here yet?"

"It was fifteen minutes out last I heard back there. They'll take her to the landin' site in the ambulance. You should go with them. I can help your friend with the boat. You should give him your keys."

"Yeah, and if you want to go in the chopper, I can drive your truck back," Len offered. "I'm Len, by the way," he said to Kelsey, who simply nodded back. "I'll lock your stuff in your galley and give the keys to Don if he's around. If he ain't, I'll call him."

"Thanks," Ketch said. "I'll still have Kari's keys, so just hang onto them otherwise and I'll catch up with you later."

"I'll stop by Suzanne's and let her know what's goin' on, too."

"Thank you. And please make sure Bean knows I'm okay, and that I miss him."

"Will do. You want me to call anybody else? Like Pauline, maybe?"

"No, I'd better do that myself. But thanks again. And thank *you*, Kelsey."

To Ketch's great surprise, she stepped smartly over to him and enveloped him in a big bear hug. Then she patted him on the back and pushed away. "You better get goin'," she said. "Don't worry, we've got things covered here."

Len headed off to where Ketch had left the truck, and Ketch caught up with the EMTs. They asked him some questions while they were getting Kari settled in the ambulance, as he'd known they would, and he gave them simple but informative answers. He couldn't use his cell phone in the ambulance and he wouldn't be able to in the helicopter, either, so he hoped he'd have time for a short call to Pauline in between – though he in fact was dreading that moment. But he had to do it.

He got his chance. When they reached the landing site, the EMTs were informed that the chopper was five minutes out. Ketch also learned they'd be flying to a hospital in Norfolk, because it had the closest Level 1 trauma center to Ocracoke.

The hospital provided regional air ambulance service and the Coast Guard had air ambulances as well, but the Coasties had arranged to send the Dare County EMS helicopter from Manteo, since it was the nearest one that was available.

He exited the ambulance and selected the number he had for Pauline from his phone's contact list. It was her cell phone, and it went straight to voice mail. He left a message briefly summarizing what had happened and where they were going, and said he'd be there. Though he was chagrined at not being able to reach her in person, he was also relieved. It would take her at least an hour and a half to drive from Manteo to Norfolk after she listened to the message, and he appreciated the stay of execution – and was ashamed that he did.

The chopper landed shortly after he'd put his phone away. Kari was transferred as expeditiously as possible while it idled, and then they took off.

He was told their flight time would be about forty-five minutes. That didn't sound like a lot of time to him, but it turned out to be time enough for the crew to thoroughly examine Kari, do an EKG, get her on oxygen, and begin ultrasound testing. They didn't volunteer much information along the way, and he wondered if their somber countenances might be a bad sign. They could just be focused and intent on their tasks, he supposed. But he didn't try to ask questions, as he didn't want to interfere with their work. It was too noisy to talk much anyway.

He simply sat in the back and tiredly watched them. The panoramic aerial views of his beloved Outer Banks unfolding outside his window, which he would ordinarily have found thrilling, went unnoticed by him. They were flying at low altitude to minimize expansion of any air embolisms, so the structures and natural features of Portsmouth across the inlet, the islands of Ocracoke and Hatteras, then the towns up the beach, and finally the beginnings of Tidewater Virginia, were clearly visible. But none of it registered. All he could think about was her.

She was immediately taken to the trauma center when they landed at the hospital. After some more questions from the staff and a blur of paperwork, he found himself consigned to a quiet and otherwise deserted waiting area.

Now that he suddenly had nothing to do, he felt an almost overwhelming urge to sleep. He hoped it was just due to his adrenalin level crashing rather than to his formerly habitual defense mechanism trying to kick in, wherein he'd sleep to avoid whatever unpleasantness he was experiencing. He'd resolved some time ago to stop doing that, and he resolved now to resist the temptation if that's what it was.

In any case, he'd be mortified if someone he knew found him snoring in his chair while Kari was fighting for her life, so he got up and started walking. He'd been told there was something called an 'atrium' nearby. Maybe he'd be able to find some caffeine there. And a rest room, so he could splash some cold water on his face.

His phone, which he'd silenced earlier, vibrated in his pocket and he stopped to see who it was. It turned out to be a terse text message from Pauline stating she was on her way – and that was literally all it said. Either she didn't want to talk to him or she hadn't yet configured the Bluetooth in her new car for hands-free calling. Probably the former, he thought, and if so he didn't blame her.

He continued on to the atrium, where he found rest rooms and a snack bar with fountain drinks. He bought a jumbo Diet Pepsi and sat down with it at an empty table. A large fountain sculpted from stone, or some material that looked like stone, dominated the center of this expansive space, and the water jets reached almost all the way up to the skylight in the cathedral ceiling. He had to admit the burbling of the water was therapeutic, which was probably its intended effect. In fact, everything in this room, from the bright mural that covered one whole wall to the comfortable settees beyond the tastefully appointed snack bar area, appeared to have been designed to convey the impression that all was well and there was no need to be alarmed.

But if one of your loved ones was in the ICU struggling to survive, that was a load of horse hockey. Ketch chuckled inwardly. Kari would know that expression and where it had originated, but he doubted most other people would nowadays. There were few women like her in numerous other ways as well, he knew, and certainly none that he'd ever met.

He wondered if she'd end up brain-damaged after all this, assuming of course that she survived at all. If so, and if all she lost was her extensive repository of film and TV quotes or some equally inconsequential capability, he'd gladly accept that. He wasn't a religious person and he doubted that praying to mythical deities of any persuasion, ancient or modern, would accomplish anything – but if there really is some kind of occasionally benevolent omniscience listening in from somewhere out there in the universe, he thought, please make a note of this wish.

He also wished he'd brought his underwater camera with him in his dry bag, but he'd left it in his gear bag back on the boat. He was thinking of the picture he'd taken of her posing at the stern of the U-boat. It might make him feel better if he could see it now. Or maybe not, since it could possibly be the last live photo of her. And for that same reason, Pauline might or might not appreciate seeing it today, so maybe it was just as well.

He rubbed at his tired eyes. This might well already be the longest day he'd ever experienced, and it wasn't over yet. As if to corroborate that sentiment, his phone began demanding his attention again.

"Hey, Ketch," Dan's voice greeted him when he answered it. "I thought you might like an update on what we talked about earlier. Is this a good time?"

Not really, Ketch thought. Besides being otherwise occupied, he realized he wasn't particularly curious about the vagaries of their little mysteries anymore, other than to figure out how to repay those scumbags from that other boat. Beyond that, everything else now seemed unimportant – including pretty much everything else that was going on in his life, too. Except for Bean, of course. But he didn't want to be rude.

"I have a few minutes," he said.

"Good! Well, you know that Coast Guard fellow the CGIS questioned? When they pushed him, he folded like a beach umbrella. First, he admitted to taking a bribe from the captain of that sand barge you gave me the name of, to keep their activities off of everyone's radar. Seems our man has a little gambling problem. So now we're going to start an investigation into that Cape Point development, since that's who the sand was for. That captain, or his boss, must also have been bribed by somebody."

"I see," Ketch said. He was listening, but he was also thinking he should get back to the ICU soon in case there'd been any new developments.

"It gets better. This guy really spilled his guts. Turns out he has a friend on the crew of that barge, who told him he'd found some old gold coins in some of the sand they dredged up at a certain location. Then our guy helped those convicts escape by smuggling tools to his brother-in-law and getting some help from a prison guard he paid. The brother-in-law was a certified diver, by the way. The idea was, the convicts would dive the wreck those coins must have come from, and they'd all split the take."

"Well, that certainly explains some things," Ketch said. "Thank you. Before we hang up, I should tell you –"

"Wait, you haven't heard the punchline yet. He said he thinks the convicts might have been killed by his friend from the barge, who may have decided to scare up his own diving crew. He hasn't been able to get in touch with his friend, so he's wondering if he might be next, which may be why he's being so cooperative. He's scared."

That finally piqued Ketch's interest. "Did he say why he thought his friend would do all that?" he asked.

"No – other than there being no honor among thieves, I guess, as the saying goes. The prison guard and the barge captain are being rounded up as we speak, but we haven't been able to locate that friend yet. When we do, maybe we'll learn more."

"Yes, maybe," Ketch absently replied. The friend might be at the dive site, he thought, or still out somewhere on that boat they'd battled with earlier. It seemed odd to him that someone would go to such lengths on the basis of a few old coins of uncertain value and marketability, even if they'd found a whole chestful of them. Since Dan hadn't said anything about a U-boat and hadn't mentioned gold bars, the explanation might be that neither Dan nor the Coastie knew about them, but the guy on the barge did.

Maybe that guy had a couple of other friends he'd decided to throw in with in place of the original gang for some reason, or maybe his new partners had heard him boasting in some watering hole one night and forced a new deal on him. Maybe the crew the *TBD* had run into today were all new and that Coastie's friend was out of the picture, too. The gold bars he and Kari had salvaged today were worth a total of about four hundred grand, according to Len. If there was significantly more gold on that sub than what they'd seen, that might be worth killing for in some quarters.

Whatever the truth of the matter was, he no longer cared. Dan could figure that out. All Ketch really needed to know now was how to find those bastards, and he thought he had a pretty good idea of how to go about doing that.

He decided to start walking back to the ICU. He'd originally intended to tell Dan about what had happened to him and Kari, but now he didn't think he would. He didn't want Dan interfering with what he had mind for the crew of that boat they'd encountered today. But on the other hand, it wouldn't be right to say nothing about her.

"Ketch, you still there?"

"Oh, I'm sorry, Dan. I have a lot on my mind right now."

"That's okay. What did you want to tell me before, when I interrupted you?"

"Well, I'm at a hospital in Norfolk. We had an accident when we were diving, and Kari got injured. They flew us here in an air ambulance."

"What? Oh, no! What happened? Does Pauline know?"

Ketch briefly explained while he walked. He didn't enjoy being duplicitous with Dan, when the man had never been anything but helpful and accommodating to him even when doing so had stretched the limits of legality. But he couldn't divulge everything to him just yet, so he gave him the simpler version of the story he'd instructed Len to stick with earlier. Maybe he'd be able to do better than that eventually, depending on whether he had the wherewithal and the fortitude to go through with what he was considering – but maybe not, again depending.

He graciously accepted Dan's condolences and best wishes, and finally hung up. Then he took a seat in the ICU waiting area and sipped at his drink. Before Pauline arrived, he'd have to give some more thought to what he was going to tell her.

It would be even more unconscionable to not tell her the whole truth, since she was Kari's mother. But would she be willing to keep Dan, a law enforcement officer who also happened to be her fiance now, in the dark for the time being – and was it fair to ask her to do that? It also wouldn't be fair to make her complicit in what he was planning. If he let her know what he was thinking of doing and she objected to it, would she rat him out to stop him?

He wondered if he had time to find the hospital's gift shop, where he might be able to buy something to blunt a burgeoning headache. Maybe he should ask one of the nurses if they could give him something first. As Kari might have said, there must be a *Nurse Jackie* type around here somewhere.

A middle-aged man in a white lab coat came into the waiting area and approached him. "Mister Ketchum?" he inquired. "I'm Doctor Compton." Ketch rose and shook the offered hand. "I have some news for you." He motioned for Ketch to sit back down and settled himself into an adjacent chair.

When the doctor had finished delivering his report, he reminded Ketch about the atrium and told him they'd look for him there if there were further updates, if he'd prefer to wait there. Then he shook Ketch's hand again and took his leave.

Ketch blew out a long breath. Kari would be in surgery for probably the next few hours and Pauline wasn't due yet, so he guessed he had time to hunt down something for his headache.

He hadn't gotten around to dealing with his dry bags yet, so he took care of that first. It was inconvenient to carry them with him everywhere as they were. His phone was already on his belt, and he found he had enough pockets in his cargo shorts for his wallet, Kari's wallet and keys, and the collapsed and folded dry bags themselves. Mission accomplished.

He tossed his empty drink cup in a trashcan and set off to find the gift shop. It didn't take long, as it turned out it wasn't too far from the atrium. Then he got himself another drink back at the atrium, claimed a vacant settee as far away as possible from the ever-present blatting TV, and took his pills. He decided he might as well stay there for a while, as the doctor had suggested.

Now what? He knew Len had said he'd talk to Suzanne, but he couldn't have made it back to Avon yet. There'd been the boat to trailer and then a good hour of driving overall, plus another hour on the ferry and who knows how long waiting in line for that. And Ketch didn't know how long he'd be here at the hospital, and he shouldn't just assume Suzanne would be willing or able to continue watching Bean for him. So he decided to call her.

It turned out Pauline had called Suzanne from the road, so she already knew the basics. In keeping with the story he'd been telling, Ketch didn't elaborate on the details. He learned Pauline had also called the Captain, who'd said he'd be hitting the road to Norfolk himself. He'd be at the very least an hour behind Pauline, and maybe more depending on when she'd called him and if he was coming from his Hatteras condo instead of Avon. He'd probably still have been in Avon, though, since he'd had that charter this morning. Ketch fleetingly wondered how Henry had made out with that, then decided that was one person he probably didn't need to worry about today.

So, Ketch thought, Pauline had made some calls from her car after all. She might be talking to Dan by now as well, and Kari's sister. He wouldn't be surprised if the only one in their world she wasn't calling was him. That might not bode well for him, but he couldn't fault her for it. He deserved whatever he was in for from her.

Suzanne offered to keep Bean for as long as necessary before Ketch could get around to asking, which he appreciated. When they were ready to end the call, he asked to speak to Bean.

"Are you okay, Papa?" Bean said when he came on the line.

"Yes, I'm fine. How are you?"

"I miss you," the diminutive voice plaintively answered. He sounded lonely, Ketch thought.

"I miss you, too. How are Jack and Chuck?"

"They're okay. We let them play with us before."

"That's good."

"Kari had a accident, huh? Is she dead?"

"No."

"Is she okay?"

"The doctors are working on her now. That's all I know so far." A little white lie there, but Ketch knew the boy wouldn't be able to comprehend the specifics without a great deal of explanation. He was thankful that Bean apparently hadn't heard that Kari had gotten 'blowed up', which might have put him in mind of the zombies he'd thought he'd seen in the water on Thursday.

"My mama had a accident," Bean said.

Ketch considered trying to reassure him that the outcome of today's accident would be different, but he didn't want to make a promise he might not be able to keep. "I know. That was sad," was all he said.

Bean was silent for a moment. Then he moved on to something else, as kids were wont to do. "Did you see the Sea Hag today?"

That took Ketch by surprise. He wasn't sure how he should answer. "Yes, I did," he finally said.

"What did she say?"

"She told me we should go home. We should have listened to her."

"Yeah," Bean simply said. Ketch could picture him nodding. "When *are* you comin' home?"

"I don't know yet. As soon as I can. I'm still at the hospital."

"Is the chopper gonna come here?"

Bean must have heard about his helicopter ride. "No, I won't be coming in the chopper." He imagined he'd be riding back with the Captain, since he had no other way to get home.

"Oh."

"I have to go now, Bean. You be good for Suzanne, and I'll come get you as soon as I can, okay?"

"Okay. I love you, Papa."

Ketch realized this was the first time Bean had ever said this to him. He almost couldn't answer, but he managed to. "I love you, too, buddy. See you soon."

After he hung up, he just sat for a while staring into space. There was one major flaw in his developing plan – what if he got caught, or ended up meeting the same fate as those convicts? What would happen to Bean then? Well, he decided, he'd just better find a way to ensure that neither of those things happened.

He was deathly tired again despite the caffeine he'd been ingesting, and he didn't feel like talking anymore. But he should tell Len not to bother trying to get hold of Suzanne and the Captain. He decided to compromise and send him a text.

Then, for lack of anything better and since he couldn't sleep, he got a copy of the local newspaper from a machine and sat down again with it and his drink. He wasn't really interested in whatever today's news was, but he needed something to do and he didn't want to run his phone battery down reading one of the Kindle books he had stored on it.

He'd gotten about halfway through the paper

when he felt someone sit down on the other end of his settee. He already knew who it must be before he lowered the paper to look.

~ **N i n e** ~

Now that he was the worst kind of unlucky, he wondered what the night would bring.

*I*t was Pauline, of course. She didn't say anything at all for a good little while, and neither did Ketch. She seemed to him to be regarding him as she might a strange new kind of bug that had landed on her sleeve. He cast his eyes downward and waited, and finally she spoke.

"Well, that's somethin' I hadn't seen yet on you," was the first thing she said.

"Oh? What's that?" he asked.

"That hangdog look you've got goin' on. Is that new?"

"No, not really." In fact, now that he thought about it, he'd probably worn that look during the majority of his waking hours for most of his life before moving to Avon.

"I had some time to think while I was drivin' up here," she said. "Lucky for you." A tight smile formed on her face when he glanced up at her. "You look surprised."

Ketch relaxed a little. "I am," he said. "Because you didn't slap me, I guess."

"Oh, I wanted to at first, believe me." The smile was gone now. "But then I realized it wasn't really your fault. My daughter's always been headstrong."

Just like Dan had said about Pauline, Ketch thought. Like mother, like daughter. "So I've heard," he said.

"It's true. She's been doin' what she wants when she wants for a long time now, and no matter what I might think about it. It didn't have to be her and you divin' for treasure today, it could just as easy been her and somebody else doin' somethin' on some other day. She just ran out of luck today, is all." She rested a hand on Ketch's knee. "I know you're blamin' yourself, but you really shouldn't."

"It's nice of you to say that – but I shouldn't have encouraged her. I feel terrible."

"I know you do. But I also know that if we could ask her, she wouldn't blame you either."

"Well, we won't be able to do that for a while. Even if she could regain consciousness, they're going to keep her in a medically induced coma until the swelling in her brain subsides and some of her other injuries start to heal. After she comes out of surgery, of course." 'After' as opposed to 'if', a word Ketch didn't want to use in this context. He wondered if Pauline had been told how risky anesthesia was in the first day or two after a blast injury. She probably had.

"I know. I heard all about it at the desk when I got here. Multiple barotraumas, they said. Her lungs, her heart, intestines, sinuses, and ears mostly. And the edema in her brain, of course.

They didn't mention other organs, so I don't know about that. Anyway, they're workin' on all that now."

"The other organs, like her liver and kidneys and pancreas and such, should be okay if there aren't too many damaged blood vessels and they're still getting blood," Ketch explained. "Internal injuries from an underwater explosion are caused by compression in the gas-filled spaces in the body due to the pressure wave from the blast, and those organs don't have air in them."

"I see. Well, at least she didn't get all cut up and nothin's broken. That's somethin', I suppose."

"Right, there are no external injuries from shrapnel or debris, like there could have been on land. But they'll have to watch for complications like hematomas, embolisms, hypotension, pneumonia, peritonitis, and internal bleeding. She might need more surgery later, and hyperbaric oxygen therapy."

After he'd said all that, he wished he hadn't. But they had to have told her most of that anyway, hadn't they? She didn't look surprised, he didn't think.

"And she might have brain damage," Pauline concluded. "Though I surely hope not. I guess that's the reason for the medical coma, right? But I don't see how that helps. I mean, she's already sort of in a coma, isn't she?"

"Well, if they let nature take its course, what would happen is her body would automatically perform a sort of triage on the affected parts of the brain by cutting off blood flow to those parts, to ensure that the rest of the brain gets what it needs. The induced coma shuts down everything but essential functions, which reduces the amount of energy all parts of the brain need, so hopefully it prevents the triage and gives the whole brain time to heal, instead of just some of it." Ketch's voice was getting hoarse, so he paused for a drink from his soda cup. "That's the idea, anyway, I think."

Pauline sagged back into her corner of the settee, sniffled once, and discreetly dabbed at her eyes with a handkerchief. "This is too much," she said. "I mean, it's a lot to take in, and I can't help but think none of it sounds good." She sniffled again and sat up straighter. "It's gettin' on toward dinnertime. When did you last eat?" she asked. "I bet you're hungry. I am, anyway, and from what I heard, I'm sure we have some time."

"I suppose I could eat something. I hadn't given it any thought."

"A drink is what I could *really* use, and maybe more'n one. But I'll settle for the cafeteria for now. I'll go tell the nurses, and you read that directory over there and figure out where it is, okay? Oh, wait!" she added when he started to get up. "I'm so sorry, I completely forgot to ask. Are you okay? Did you get hurt at all? Has anyone examined you?"

"I'm fine. I didn't get caught in the blast," he admitted, somewhat guiltily. "We weren't together at the time, and I was behind something when it happened."

"Oh, I see. Well, that's good."

"I'd trade places with her if I could."

"I know. Come on, let's go."

Ketch tried to make sense of the map on the directory, and when Pauline returned they wound their way through the inevitable labyrinth together. After only a couple of false turns, they eventually arrived at their destination. Ketch knew that most hospitals were difficult for visitors to navigate because they grew and changed over time, via another form of triage on a different, inanimate scale. But he thought they could at least make more of an effort with their signs and labeling. It seemed like none of them did, though, at least not the ones he'd been in.

There were some interesting options at the cafeteria. The hospital was at least making more of an effort in that area than they had in the old days. Ketch went for a grilled Cuban sandwich at the panini station, and Pauline hit the salad bar. Neither of them wanted a large, heavy meal. He picked up a bottle of water this time instead of what he'd grown used to calling 'pop', as everyone he now knew called soda, and she had a latte. They found a table away from the bulk of the crowd and sat down to eat.

They didn't talk much more until they'd gotten through most of their food. Pauline finished first, and when she had, she sat back and stretched and said, "So tell me, exactly what happened down there? All I know is, you two found a shipwreck and somethin' exploded. What blew up? Why were you separated when it happened?"

"Well..." Ketch began. He took the last mouthful of his sandwich so he could stall while he chewed. What should he say? If he told her the whole truth, what would happen then? But if he didn't, would she ever forgive him later?

"Ahoy there!" a familiar thundering voice echoed from across the cavernous dining area. When he looked up to locate the source of the disturbance, Ketch saw that an elderly woman nearby had almost dumped everything off of her tray. Other people moved aside as the Captain stomped his way to their table on as straight a line as possible.

He appropriated an empty chair from another table without asking its occupants and plopped down in it. "Whew! I got here quick as I could," he said. He extracted a can from a pocket of the light fishing jacket he was wearing, popped the top on it, and took a good long pull. "Ah, that hits the spot!" he exclaimed with a small, polite belch.

"Hey, Don," Pauline said.

"Captain, I don't think you're supposed to have that in here," Ketch said in as low a tone as he could manage. "And how did you get here so quickly? I wasn't expecting you for a while yet."

"Right! Well, you know how I feel 'bout speed limit signs, I like the whooshin' sound they make when they go by," he answered, ignoring Ketch's warning about the beer. "'Specially today. So what the hell happened? How's Kari doin'? I heard you saved her life."

Ketch grimaced. "Yes, after I endangered it." He proceeded to explain Kari's condition, with some help from Pauline. When he was finished, he considered asking the Captain if he had any more cans in his pockets, but he refrained.

The Captain turned solicitous then. "Well, I'm real sorry to hear all that," he said. "But she's a tough one, and I'd put money on her comin' through it all okay."

"I decided I'm gonna think positive," Pauline said. "A woman's like a tea bag, you know. You don't know how strong she is 'til she gets in hot water."

"I've heard something like that before," Ketch said. "Do you know who said that?"

"One of my personal heroes," Pauline answered, "Eleanor Roosevelt." She sat up and put her elbows on the table. "Okay, now that's enough of that. Ketch, you were gonna explain how this all happened before Don interrupted us, right?"

"Yes," Ketch said, and he began telling the unexpurgated version of the tale. The Captain deserved to know, too – and even if Pauline repeated the story to Dan, what could Dan really do about what Ketch was seeing as its logical conclusion? He couldn't arrest anyone until a crime had been committed, and even then he couldn't hold someone for more than forty-eight hours without sufficient evidence, and he couldn't watch everyone all the time. Pauline and the Captain listened intently without interrupting (which was unusual in the latter's case), even when Ketch confessed to his encounter with the Sea Hag or whatever that had been.

"I didn't tell Dan all this," Ketch concluded. "I just told him we found an old wreck and something on it exploded. And I asked Len to keep all this to himself – you know, in case."

"In case a what?" the Captain asked. He'd finished his beer, and now it turned out he did have another can squirreled away in a jacket pocket. But instead of opening this one, he put it back. "Guess I ought not to, if I might be drivin' again tonight. Gotta get you home sometime, right?" he said to Ketch. "Okay – so I'm tryin' to understand all this. There's a U-boat that the sand pirates uncovered, it has some Nazi gold in it, you got some of it, there's also some kinda old ship with some pirate gold in the same dang spot, somebody else knows about it, some folks probly got kilt over it, and the same thing almost happened to you today. That about cover it?"

"Pretty much," Ketch said.

"Oh, and you met up with some kinda ghost or somethin'," the Captain added. "Or you dreamt it. Almost forgot about that part. What's up with all that?"

"I honestly don't know what to think about it."

"Well, sounds like whatever it was, that ole Sea Hag knew what was she was talkin' about. Even if that was all in your head and it was just your subconscious or whatever, maybe you shoulda listened to her."

"Yes, I guess I should have. But unfortunately, I'm not superstitious. Or at least, I wasn't before," Ketch thoughtfully added.

"You never answered Don's first question," Pauline said. "You didn't tell Dan, in case of what?"

"Well, it occurred to me that it might be hard to prove those men on that other boat attacked us, not to mention what they may or may not have done to those convicts. Though I suspect they probably did pretty much the same thing to them as they tried to do today. Dan might not be able to make any charges stick, though."

"And?"

"And, well, that bothers me. I know there are reasons why I shouldn't be thinking like this, legal and otherwise, and I know it wouldn't change anything with Kari, but I'd like to find those guys and have a go at them myself. Maybe with a baseball bat or something. If their boat got trashed and they all ended up in traction, it might teach them a lesson. And maybe plant some kind of evidence to frame them for something."

"Now hang on a minute," the Captain said. "Not only do you got a whole lotta illegal goin' on there – you and what army? You got a death wish or somethin'? What if you end up in jail, or worse yet they finish the job they started today? What happens to Bean then, you thought 'bout that at all? And even if you got away with it, they'd probly just come after your ass again soon's they could."

"I know all that. I haven't worked it all out yet. I'm angry and I want to see justice done, that's all, and I'm just telling you how I feel. If you have a better idea…"

"I do," Pauline cut in. She had a cold look in her eyes Ketch hadn't seen before, and he could tell she was deadly serious. "Kill the bastards."

"What?" the Captain exclaimed.

"I mean it. Just kill them, and then we'll never have to worry about them again. It's what they deserve."

"Pauline, that's some serious shit you're talkin'. We can't do that!"

"Why not, Don? You've done it before."

"What do you mean, Pauline?" Ketch asked. "That thing with the witch at your place was an accident, and the Captain didn't kill Freddie."

"I'm not talkin' about that, I'm talkin' about Mick and you all dumpin' those drums way out to sea last summer with those bodies in them."

"Well, but that was really a accident too, and – hey, wait, how do you know 'bout that?" the Captain demanded.

"Kari told me all about it one time this past winter. I knew somethin' was botherin' her to the point it was worrisome to me, so I sat her down and we drank some wine and she told me. Turned out it had to do with Bob Ingram bein' on trial again for killin' his wife. So I know what Kari did, and I know what you two did. It's one reason why I'm so fond of y'all. What you did wasn't legal, but you did it anyway and it was the right thing to do, and I appreciate it and so did Kari. Does, I mean," she said, pulling out another tissue and dabbing at her eyes again. "And you didn't get caught."

"She never told me you knew," Ketch said. He found himself at a loss for anything to say beyond that.

"I'll be damned," the Captain said. "But still, you know..."

"I want them dead," Pauline flatly stated. "All of them. And if you two can't manage it on your own, I'll help."

"How would we find 'em?" the Captain pointed out. "We don't have no idea who the hell they even are."

"That's easy enough," Pauline said. "They want that gold, right? That's what it's all about, isn't it? And Ketch knows where it is and that's where they'll be, sooner or later."

The Captain shook his head. "I'm sorry, Pauline, but I don't know if I can be a party to that. I ain't never done nobody in, not in cold blood like that."

"Look, we're all pretty emotional right now," Ketch said, some sense finally working its way into him. "Let's not decide here. The Captain and I will give it some more thought and see if we can come up with some kind of plan that'll satisfy all of us. Maybe there's something else we could do that would be effective, and less extreme."

"Yeah," the Captain said. "If we don't think murder charges would stick – I mean, attempted murder – maybe we could frame 'em for somethin' like Ketch said."

"Okay," Pauline tiredly acquiesced. "Ketch, you're probably right. But don't think on it too long, or it might be too late. Once they get that gold, I imagine they'll be long gone."

"Agreed," Ketch said.

"Well, I'm gonna stay here at the hospital for the time bein'," she said, turning pragmatic. "Kari's sister will be comin' up later, and Dan's supposed to get us a place at the Residence Inn and bring me stuff from the house. Ketch, you've got Bean to take care of, and I'd appreciate it if you'd handle whatever needs to be done at the Sea Dog, so I think you and Don ought to get on back to Avon. I can call you if there's any news."

"I hate to leave you here," Ketch said, "and I feel like I should be here for Kari. But you're right, there's Bean, plus she had a class starting tomorrow afternoon, so I should inform those people and refund them their money. But then I think I'll just close the shop until further notice. After that, I can come back here and visit. Oh, and please allow me to reimburse you for the Residence Inn later."

"Whatever you think is best," Pauline said, rising from her chair and collecting her purse. "Okay then, I'm goin' back to the ICU. Let me know when y'all come up with your plan. And don't worry, I won't say a word to Dan about any of this."

Keeping secrets probably wasn't a good way to start a marriage, Ketch thought. But then, he supposed many people did in fact do just that in one way or another, with regard to past relationships, embarrassing moments, failed dreams, childhood traumas, things like that. This particular secret might turn out to be a little bigger than some, that's all. Like the one Kari had been sitting on until Pauline had plied it out of her.

Ketch gave Pauline a hug, and the Captain went to pick himself up a sandwich for the road. Ketch asked him to get him a bottle of Diet Pepsi as well, and then the two of them found their way out of the hospital and back to the Captain's truck.

"You must be tired after driving all the way up here," Ketch said. "Do you want me to drive back?"

"I doubt I'm anywhere near as tired as you," the Captain said. "You look plumb wore-out! I can drive." Ketch didn't repeat his offer. The Captain was right.

"It's a damn shame, what happened to Kari," the Captain said when they'd gotten underway. "I didn't want to say so to Pauline back there, but it sure don't sound good. You think she's gonna make it?"

"I hope so, of course," Ketch answered. "But I agree, it doesn't look good. I guess time will tell."

"Well, I'm real sorry. How you holdin' up?"

Ketch shrugged. "What can I say? I'm the one who got her into this mess, so I can tell you I feel terrible. And there's nothing I can do about it, other than try to get revenge." They rode in silence for a bit, and then he went on. "I know revenge doesn't usually accomplish anything, and I've never killed anyone, either. But I can't help but feel like I could make an exception for these guys, like Pauline said. It might be the simplest thing to do."

He did realize that what he'd said wasn't entirely true – the simplest, as well as probably the safest and most sensible, thing to do would be to step back, stay away from Portsmouth, and let Dan and the SBI handle things as best they could. He knew that logically speaking, vigilantism on his part wasn't going to do anything to help Kari. But he also knew he wasn't going to be able to just let this go. He was no longer built that way.

"I don't know 'bout that. It might not be that simple if you want to make sure you don't get caught," the Captain cautioned. "Say, you got any idea where that guy Doug got that boatload a pot he got busted with? Maybe we could get us a bale, stash it on their boat, and put the DEA onto 'em."

"No, I have no idea what he was up to."

"Think he'd tell you if you paid him a visit'n asked him?"

"Well, if he's trying for a plea bargain, he's

probably giving up his contact, so that wouldn't help us. And if he hasn't done that, I doubt he'd tell me. He'd probably think I was working with the police." Ketch thought for a moment. "I don't know if it's legal for those guys to have those explosives on their boat. Maybe they stole them. But even if it isn't legal, there's no way to prove they used them against us, and just being caught in possession of them wouldn't be good enough. They deserve more punishment than that for what they did."

"Yeah, they do. But I don't know 'bout offin' 'em. I'm pissed off about the whole thing too, but I don't know if I can go that far."

Ketch slumped in his seat. "I'm too tired to think about it right now. Maybe we'll be able to come up with something tomorrow."

"Yeah, okay." The Captain munched on his sandwich for a while. "So what you gonna do with that gold you guys got?" he asked.

"I haven't thought about that. I don't really care about it. Maybe I should just dump it back in the sea."

"Ha! What'd you say that haul's worth? Four hundred grand? You're probly the only guy I know who'd ever even think a doin' somethin' like that!"

"If I took the gold bars, and the coins too, back to where I found them and gave it all back, maybe the Sea Hag and the rest of the Portsmouth ghosts would forgive me and do something to help Kari," Ketch mused, staring out his window.

The Captain squinted at him. "You know that there's just crazy talk, right?"

"Is it? I'm not so sure anymore. But yes, I suppose it is." Ketch yawned. "Do you mind if I close my eyes for a little while?"

"Hell no, be my guest. Don't worry, I won't run us off the road."

"Thanks." Ketch snoozed until they reached the Bonner Bridge over Oregon Inlet. Somehow he could tell they were there, even though he'd been asleep. It was perhaps his favorite place in the world, so he was glad he'd awakened. And it might not be here much longer, at least in its present somewhat rickety form. The bridge replacement project was currently in limbo due to funding issues caused by political infighting, but that would hopefully change soon.

It had better, he thought. This bridge had been designed to last about thirty years, and it was over fifty years old now. Engineers had been warning for years that it was growing ever more unstable and unsafe, but still there were delays, mostly due to those damned environmentalists again. Now they were demanding yet another environmental impact study, and were suggesting a ferry service in place of the bridge, which was just downright stupid – but maybe not, if their goal was to discourage people from coming here so they could protect their precious birds.

The sun was on its way down now, and the views of the Atlantic and the Sound from the top of the elevated bridge in the fading light were simply stunning. The environmentalists couldn't take that away, and he put them out of his mind for now. He'd been too preoccupied to appreciate this transit during his earlier flyover, but now he again felt like new beginnings were imminent and anything was possible, which was how he'd invariably felt before when crossing this bridge onto Hatteras Island. While many things had changed since his first crossing years ago, this was one thing that never had, and he found it comforting that it still held true even now.

He half-listened to another harebrained idea from the Captain about how they might be able to frame their enemies while they cruised past Pea Island. It involved some riverfront dive the Captain had once frequented down in the Cape Fear area, where he knew one could score enough cocaine back in the day to put folks away for a long time. Ketch responded negatively but politely and then dozed off again.

He woke again, this time for good, when they were leaving the Tri-Village of Rodanthe, Waves, and Salvo. Avon would be next up, just a few more miles down Highway 12. He used the remaining time to make another call to Suzanne. He briefly updated her on Kari's condition and, since he'd have to spend some time at the dive shop in the morning, agreed to pick up Bean and the dogs after lunch. Suzanne said Bean was already upstairs in bed looking at a book. Ketch didn't want to get the boy stirred up, so he didn't ask to speak to him this time.

When the Captain pulled the truck into the parking lot at the boatyard, Ketch was surprised to see that the *TBD* was covered, in the water, and moored in its customary spot next to the *Port Starbird*. His truck was also parked where he usually left it, and there were lights on inside the houseboat.

"Looks like Len took care a your boat for you," the Captain remarked. "He's a good guy. Looks like he might still be hangin' around there, too." The Captain pulled into his traditional spot (which most folks knew better than to usurp) and killed the engine. "Hope you don't mind, but I'm not in much of a visitin' mood tonight. I'm pretty beat myself now, so I'm just gonna go crash on the *Minnow*. We can talk some more in the mornin' if you want."

"Sounds good to me," Ketch said. "I'm still tired, too. Thank you, Captain, for everything you did today. I appreciate you driving up there and bringing me back."

"Don't mention it! I woulda gone up anyways, for Kari, you know, and I'll likely be goin' again before too long. You go on and get some rest now." He slapped Ketch on the back and trotted off to his slip.

Ketch checked to make sure his truck was locked, then boarded the *Port Starbird*. He'd have to thank Len again for mooring the *TBD*, which he hadn't asked him to do. The cabin door was unlocked, and he went on in without a second thought – only to be shocked yet again.

"Hey there," a female voice called from somewhere farther back in the houseboat. "Ketch, is that you?" the woman asked, coming into the galley. "I was just hangin' up your gear in the bathroom. But I can move it if you want to use the shower. I didn't think of that."

"Kelsey? What are you doing here?" Ketch asked, incredulous. "I'm sorry, you surprised me," he quickly backtracked. "Thank you for doing, uh, whatever you were doing."

"You're welcome," she simply said. She pulled up a chair and sat down at the table.

Ketch went to the refrigerator for a beer. He figured he'd earned some today, his culpability in the day's events notwithstanding. He wondered how many times his adrenalin had spiked in the last twelve hours, and what he was going to do with this latest reason for that.

"Well, welcome aboard," he said, for lack of anything better. "I need a drink. Would you like a beer, or some wine or something?"

"Just some water, thanks. I don't drink. I got a pizza before, by the way. I got a large one, so there's a bunch left there in the fridge if you're hungry," she said, all in her usual unsmiling semi-monotone.

"Thanks. Maybe I'll have it tomorrow. I'm not that hungry right now."

"How's your girlfriend doin'? Is she gonna be okay?"

"We're not sure yet." He sat down at the table with a can of beer for him and a bottle of water for her. He took a swig, then tiredly summarized Kari's condition yet again.

"I'm sorry," Kelsey said.

"Thank you." Ketch was surprised that she wasn't asking how the accident had happened, but then he realized she'd probably already heard Len's cover story. "So, why did you come all the way up here?" he asked.

"Well, I wanted to know about your partner – Kari, right? – and I wanted to help, so I rode up with your friend. We got everything off of your boat, put her in the water, and tied her up. Then I cleaned her up and covered her. Then I got everything out of your truck except for the tanks, rinsed your gear, and hung it out to dry. I brought it inside when it started to get dark. I left your keys over there on the counter."

"Didn't Len help you?"

"He helped get the boat in the water, and then I told him he could go home. He seemed pretty tired."

"And you did everything else yourself? That was very good of you. You didn't have to do all that."

"I wanted to help," she repeated with a shrug. "I also took a shower, but I didn't use your towels. I got a new one from the closet."

"Oh, okay. Well, that's fine," Ketch said. He couldn't begrudge her a shower after everything she'd done for him.

"Oh, I almost forgot. In case you're lookin' for it, your friend has Kari's gear bag. He loaded some stuff in it from your boat locker. He said to tell you he'll keep it over at his place."

"Okay, thank you." Len had the gold, then. That was probably better than leaving it on the *TBD* – or here on the houseboat for that matter, since he had company. "So, you rode up with Len. Why didn't you drive your car instead?"

"I don't have one right now. I had an old one, but it died. I'm ridin' my bike around town for now."

"I see. Well then, you need a ride home." Ketch got up from the table and retrieved his keys from the counter. "It's getting late, so we should probably head out."

"You don't have to take me back, and you couldn't tonight anyway. You'd miss the last ferry back and get stuck on Ocracoke for the night. I've got a friend goin' down tomorrow I can ride with. I already called her."

"Okay... So do you have a place to stay tonight?"

"I thought I'd just stay here, if it's okay with you. I brought my toothbrush and a change of clothes."

What next, he thought. But again, he didn't want to seem ungrateful. "Yes, of course, no problem. I'm a little surprised Len didn't invite you to stay over with him, though."

"He did," she said with a rare, fleeting smile. "But he's not my type."

"Oh. Well, okay, you can take my bed and I'll use Bean's. Do you know about Bean?"

"Yeah, your friend told me. It was good of you to take him in. But you wouldn't be comfortable in that little bed." Kelsey finished off her water, then nonchalantly added, "We can both sleep in the big bed if you want."

Ketch was nonplussed. "I beg your pardon?" Was he hearing her right? "Do you mean – together?"

"Sure, if you're feelin' low and you need a body to keep you company. I don't mind. I've got a couple joints in my bag too, if you want to do that."

He didn't know how to respond at first. This was like a throwback to the 'free love' hippie subculture of the Sixties. And the communing with Nature, and the weed... All she was missing was the tie-dyed clothing. Perhaps there were some old hippies in her family tree, or some modern ones in her current family. All he knew about that was that her father had been a surfer and board maker until his melanoma. But another thing he thought he knew was that she wasn't being immoral or in any way devious, at least not to her way of thinking. He believed she was only trying to give comfort to someone who was feeling lost and adrift, in the best way she knew how.

"Uh, well..." he stammered. "Thank you, Kelsey, that's very thoughtful of you, really. But it won't be necessary."

"Okay," she dispassionately replied. "Well, I think I'll turn in. I'll take the small bed. Oh, do you want me to move that stuff out of the shower for you?"

"No, thank you, I can work around it."

"Okay. Goodnight, Ketch."

"Goodnight, Kelsey."

Ketch watched her head off to Bean's bedroom. She hadn't appeared to be disappointed that he'd declined her offers, which was good. He had a feeling she might be the most guileless person he knew, strange as that might seem, and he was glad he hadn't upset her.

He hadn't dissembled when he'd said he was tired. Although he'd slept some on the drive back to Avon, a quick rinse in the shower failed to stimulate him and he passed out as soon as his head hit the pillow. He didn't wake until the first rays of sunlight started to peek through the blinds on his window. The first thing he did was check his phone, which he'd fortunately remembered to charge overnight. There were no messages or missed calls. Then he pulled on his robe and went off to shower again, more thoroughly this time.

The gear that had been hanging in the bathroom was gone. He checked and found it all dry and put away in its designated closet – not exactly the way he would have done it, but close enough. The arrangement didn't much matter today, since the closet was half-empty without Kari's gear. As was his life now.

The smell of bacon greeted him when he got out of the shower. His stomach rumbled, and he realized he was starving. He dressed quickly and went to the galley, where he found Kelsey working diligently at the stove. He saw that there'd be bacon and scrambled eggs and toast for breakfast. Nothing fancy, but a more than welcome alternative to whatever he would have scraped together, if anything, on his own this morning.

"Good morning, Kelsey. You're up early. Thanks for putting away my gear, and for doing all this."

"Good mornin', Ketch. I figured you'd be hungry when you got up, and it's the least I could do after you let me sleep over."

"Well, it's a pleasant surprise. I thought you might be a vegetarian, or maybe a vegan. I forget what the difference is."

"Nope, not me, unless bacon and seafood start growin' on trees. Sit down. What do you want to drink?"

"Oh, some orange juice, I guess." He'd already had a healthy drink of water and what he really wanted now was something with some caffeine in it, but he was reluctant to expose his morning pop habit to her for some reason.

When she went to the fridge, she pulled out a can of Diet Pepsi along with the juice. "I don't drink coffee," she said.

Ketch had to chuckle. "Neither do I. Forget the juice and give me one of those, too, please," he said.

"What's so funny?" she asked with a slight smile.

"I thought you'd think I was peculiar if I drank one of those at breakfast."

"Oh. Well, you heard about that new ad campaign, right? 'Coke – it's not just for breakfast anymore.' Course, this isn't Coke, but you know what I mean."

"Yes, I do. Thank you."

She served him his drink and a plateful of food, then sat down with her own plate. "I can make more if you want," she said. They ate quickly, and mostly in silence from then on.

When they were finished, Kelsey insisted on cleaning up in the galley, so Ketch went outside to check on the *TBD*. He imagined she and Len had secured everything properly, but still... He wondered if he was starting to develop OCD, like an elderly neighbor he remembered trying to help as a kid. He'd noticed the man was having some trouble getting around, but when he'd offered his assistance with a particularly difficult chore the man had drily replied, 'Thanks, but you probably wouldn't do it to my satisfaction'.

When he was done looking the boat over, he sat down in one of the deck chairs and began mentally planning out his day. His first order of business would be to get things shipshape at the Sea Dog. He'd look up the records for today's students and call them, mail out refund checks, and post a note on the door saying the shop would be closed until further notice due to illness. Kari hadn't mentioned any other upcoming classes, but he should check on that, too, and call those people if there were any. He should also call Stuart, who'd be out of a job now. He'd give him a month's pay to help tide him over until he could find another second job. And he'd call Pauline, of course, at a reasonable hour, maybe around nine. And then after lunch, or maybe sooner if possible, he'd pick up Bean and the dogs from Suzanne's...

The Captain suddenly dropped into another deck chair, startling him. "Oh! I'm sorry," Ketch said. "I didn't notice you boarding." That was odd – usually he heard his boisterous partner in crime coming from a mile away. But also oddly, the old salt wasn't being boisterous today. "Good morning, Captain."

"I wish," the Captain said. "I swear, I was tossin' and turnin' half the night thinkin' on what to do 'bout them pirates that run you off yesterday." And that was another thing that would have to be resolved sometime today, one way or another.

"Oh. Well, what did you come up with?"

"Nothin' good," the Captain sighed. He threw up his hands. "I got nothin'."

"Well, we'll figure something out."

"You heard anythin' more from Norfolk?"

"No. I'll call Pauline from the shop around nine, if she hasn't called by then."

"Good," the Captain nodded in approval. Knowing Ketch was down in the dumps, he added, "Hey, no news is good news, right?"

"If you say so," Ketch said.

Kelsey came out on deck. "Ketch, I'm done cleanin' up from breakfast," she said. "Is there anything else I should do before we go? Oh, hello," she said to the Captain.

"Well, hello to you, too!" the Captain replied. Ketch thought he looked dumbfounded, another thing that didn't happen very often. "I'm Cap'n Don, who are you?"

"I'm Kelsey. Nice to meet you. Oh, I know – I'll go change the sheets on the bed, Ketch, so you won't have to do it later." With that, she ducked back inside.

The Captain stared after her for a moment and then blurted, "What the hell, Ketch?" No ribbing this time, no 'you ole dawg', no talk of 'tapping'. If anything could be laughable today, the expression on the Captain's face would qualify. But Ketch didn't laugh.

"It's not what you think. She's a Portsmouth tour guide I know. She helped us in Ocracoke yesterday, and then she rode up with Len to help out here. I didn't know she was coming, and I didn't sleep with her." But he could have. He decided not to tell the Captain about the offer she'd made him.

The Captain relaxed. "A tour guide, you say? How the hell old is she? She looks 'bout eighteen."

"She's older than Joette was."

"Huh," the Captain grunted. "*Touché*! So what's she still doin' here?"

"It was too late to take her back last night and she needed a place to crash. A friend of hers will drive her home later."

"Well, all right then." The Captain grinned. "You had me goin' there for a minute. I thought maybe you was bein' a dumb yankee again and turnin' into some kinda lowlife!"

"No, not yet. But give me time, especially if it's time with crackers like you," Ketch retorted with a straight face. They hadn't done their usual yankee-cracker routine lately, and this morning Ketch found it comforting.

"Ha! Seriously, though, I gotta hand it to ya," the Captain said. "You're a better man than me. Kelsey, was that her name? Well, if I had me somebody like that just across the hall all night long, there'd be no tellin' what could happen. She reminds me a that mermaid in that ole movie, what was it? *Splash*." He got a dreamy look on his face. "That one was half girl, half fish, and half hairdo. What a woman!"

That finally made Ketch smile for a moment. "I have to take care of some things for Kari at the shop this morning," he said, "and then I'm picking up Bean and the dogs. If you're going to be around this afternoon, we can do some brainstorming then."

"Yeah, I'll be here. I'll get my errands done this mornin'.

Ketch still felt guilty about not being in Norfolk. Yes, there were things here that needed doing, but he'd have to figure a way to get back up there before too long. Maybe he, Bean, and the dogs could stay someplace nearby for a while, like Pauline was doing. But then what would he do with the dogs when he was at the hospital? Maybe Suzanne would be willing to keep them for a while. He didn't know about Chuck, but Jack had never been boarded and he didn't want to do that to him now.

"Well, I'm off," the Captain said. "Lemme know if you get some news."

"I will," Ketch promised. He was sure there'd be some before too long, be it good or bad. As he'd soon find out, he was more right about that than he knew, and it wouldn't be the former.

~ T e n ~

Sometimes there's no sense in being anything but practical.

Nine o'clock came and went. Although he and Kelsey were in the middle of their dive shop chores now, Ketch decided to take a break and give Pauline a call since he hadn't heard from her yet.

Kelsey was still hanging around, but Ketch wasn't bothered by that. She was bright and versatile, and with her assistance the two of them were making quick work of the to-do list he'd assembled for this morning. She wouldn't be able to go back to Ocracoke until the afternoon and she'd wanted to continue to help, so he'd brought her here with him.

They'd already unloaded and stowed yesterday's tanks, called Stuart, reprogrammed the climate control system and the store lighting, made sure the air compressor and related items were shut down and disconnected, and emptied the cash register and Kari's emergency petty cash box. It turned out there was just enough altogether to cover the severance pay he'd wanted to give Stuart, plus the pay he was due for the previous week, so he decided he'd just give him the cash. And he'd keep it off the books so Stuart wouldn't have to pay income tax on it. Stuart would stop by soon to pick up the envelope.

Ketch knew it was illegal to pay employees under the table, but no one would know and it'd be a nice little bonus for a loyal employee who was always cheerful and had never once balked at being called in whenever he'd been needed. The government already bled the middle class enough, he figured, and at least partly in order to pick up the slack for the inversion gambits of big corporations that had moved their headquarters to foreign countries via strategic mergers to avoid paying U.S. taxes, something he'd read about recently. Until the IRS closed that loophole, among others, he'd never feel guilty about stiffing them whenever he got the chance. And after the porcine cut they'd taken from his bitcoin windfall, he imagined he'd remain unapologetic about this attitude for quite some time.

Kelsey was on the shop's landline at Kari's desk in a back room, talking to the students and writing out refund checks for him to sign later. Ketch tapped the icon for Pauline on his smartphone and made his call out in the showroom.

Pauline answered on the first ring. "Good mornin', Ketch," she said. "I was just about to call you. I didn't want to wake you up before."

"Hello, Pauline. Same with me, I didn't want to call too early. How's Kari making out?"

"Well..." she began. "I probably should have called you durin' the night, but I didn't want to bother you. I never left the hospital last night, and

I'm still there now."

"Why? Pauline, what happened?" Ketch went to a chair behind one of the display cases and sat down hard.

"Oh, she's alive! I'm so sorry, I should have told you that right off. Well, she was in surgery 'til around midnight. They had to put her on one of those heart-lung machines durin' the surgery, and then afterward they decided to keep her on it for a while. Excuse me," she said, and though she'd probably put her phone down Ketch could hear her blowing her nose. "Sorry. Ketch, I don't know how to say this..."

"It's okay, Pauline, just say it." He was trying to remain calm and he hoped that was how he'd sounded to her, but he had to make himself loosen his grip on his phone. He didn't know how hard it could be squeezed without breaking.

"Well," she sniffled, "they told me they're afraid she might be brain-dead. They can't tell for sure yet, so they're gonna keep her on that machine – and Ketch, they said I might have to decide whether or not to pull the plug on her! I'm sorry..." She excused herself again, and Dan came on the line.

"Hey, Ketch," he said. "Dan here. Sorry about that. I think Pauline needs to sit down for a while. And I'm real sorry about Kari."

Ketch was thinking again about that picture he'd taken of her posing at the stern of the U-boat. She was one of the smartest people he knew, but she could be such a goofball sometimes. And that acerbic wit of hers... But that was one reason he loved her. If she died – well, whether or not the Captain was willing to play along, those bastards who did this to her might well have to follow suit, even if he had to do it by himself somehow.

"Ketch, you still there?" Dan said.

"Yes, sorry."

"Thought the call might have gotten dropped. Listen, Pauline wants you to know you don't have to run right back up here. I'm gonna take her back to the hotel to get cleaned up, and then I'll stay with her when we get back to the hospital. No one's gonna be deciding anything today."

Ketch cleared his throat. "Okay. Thank you, Dan, for doing that. I'm at the shop now, tying up loose ends. When I figure out what to do with Bean and the dogs, I'll come back up there." He considered asking Dan to tell Pauline he was sorry. But he'd already said that himself, and he doubted it would make her feel any better right now.

"All right, Ketch. You take care now, and we'll see you later."

Ketch ended the call. He hadn't asked Dan anything about 'the case', as he was thinking of it, and Dan hadn't offered anything. That was just as well. Other things were more important now.

"Hey Ketch," Kelsey called from the back. "You off the phone now?" He was, so he went back to her. "I got everybody on the list," she said. "There were only five of 'em." She pointed to a stack of stamped, addressed envelopes. "The checks are in there. You just have to sign 'em and seal the envelopes. I also checked the calendar, and there's no other classes comin' up that anybody's signed up for yet." She stopped talking and looked him over. "You okay, Ketch?"

"Not really," he admitted. "Pauline said Kari made it through the surgery, but she's on a CPB pump now. That's cardiopulmonary bypass, a heart-lung machine," he clarified. "They're saying she might be brain-dead, but they won't know for a while."

"Oh. I'm sorry, Ketch."

"Thanks," he said. He rubbed his eyes. "And thanks for helping out again. I should be paying you a wage for everything you're doing."

"I don't need to be paid," she said. "What should we do next?"

"Well," he said, looking around. "I think we're probably done here, except for Stuart." He picked up the pile of envelopes and started signing the checks. One legal thing he and Kari had done that would come in handy now was to grant each other power of attorney. When he was sealing the last envelope, he heard the bell on the front door. "That's probably Stuart now," he said.

It was. Ketch spent a little more time explaining things to Stuart and commiserating with him. Then he gave him his envelope.

"Thanks, Ketch," Stuart said. "This is real generous of you."

"It's the least I can do, and you deserve it."

"Well, I appreciate it. I always liked you guys, you're good people." He shook his head. "Man! It's just awful what happened to her. I hope she'll be okay."

"Me too. Thanks again, Stuart. I'll call you if we reopen, in case you want to come back." They shook hands, and Stuart went on his way.

He'd said 'if' this time instead of 'when', Ketch suddenly realized. That wasn't good. He wanted to stay positive, but he guessed maybe he should also start preparing himself for the worst.

Kelsey came out into the showroom, silently put her arms around him, and rested her head on his chest. Ketch tensed at first, but it was just another innocent hug, nothing lascivious about it. Afterward, she stepped back and said, "I don't know how to set the alarm."

When Ketch had found his voice again, he said, "I'll take care of that. Then we should drop those envelopes off at the post office, and I'll pick up the mail for the shop. From here on, I'll just do that now and then and pay the bills for a while, I guess, and see to the training pool maintenance." And do the quarterly taxes before the end of the month, he remembered. He'd delegate that to Kari's accountant, though.

"Okay. I know it's earlier than you planned, but then should we get Bean? I wouldn't mind meetin' him."

Ketch checked his phone. It wasn't quite ten-thirty yet. She'd easily shaved off probably half the time he'd thought he'd have to spend here this morning. "Yes, we could do that," he said. "And then, after we take the dogs back to the houseboat, how about if I take you both out for a nice lunch?"

"I'd like that," she said. "Could we go to Dirty Dick's? I like their hushpuppies."

"Dirty Dick's it is, then," he said. "Bean likes that place, too."

They locked up and headed down Highway 12 to the south end of town. Kelsey stayed in the truck while Ketch went into the post office. When he came back, he passed the mail to her to put in the glove box. Before he could start the truck again, the opening riff of *Enter Sandman* started playing on his phone.

"Is that your ringtone?" Kelsey asked. "I love that song."

It was Suzanne calling. "Hello, Suzanne," he said.

"Ketch, where are you? Is Bean with you?" she demanded without preamble.

"No, he isn't. Why would he be? I'm at the post office."

"Sally just came in from outside. She and Bean were playing with the dogs out in the yard, and he didn't come in with them. Sally said Bean told her he was going home to see you."

"By himself? Well, he should know the way, since we've walked it often enough. But I guess I'd better get back there right now." He started the truck and put it in gear. The nav system picked up the call then, so he slid the phone back into his belt holster.

"I'll send Henry over, too," Suzanne said. "He can get there quicker than you can, and quicker than I could drive. Henry!" she called. "Ketch, I'm so sorry! I had no idea he'd do something like this."

"It's okay, Suzanne. It's not your fault. He's impulsive sometimes. We're working on that."

"Still, I should have been watching them more closely. What?" Ketch heard Sally saying something in the background. "Ketch? Chuck's here, but Sally says Jack went with Bean."

"Okay. That's good, actually. Jack definitely knows the way, and he'll look out for Bean."

"I hope so. Please call me when you have him, okay?"

"I will." Ketch hung up and focused on the road.

"Where did Bean go?" Kelsey asked.

"He decided to take off and walk back to the boatyard. Suzanne must have told him I was back, and he didn't want to wait for me to pick him up later."

"But he has one of your dogs with him, right?"

"Yes. But I don't know what he'll do or where he'll go if I'm not there."

Avon was a small town, but they were at its south end. They'd have to go back up Route 12 to the north end of town, turn off on Harbor Road, and then travel the length of North End Road. He drove as fast as he could without hitting anyone or anything. He didn't hear any 'whooshing' sounds from the speed limit signs along the way, but as the Captain would do, he paid them no attention.

When he finally pulled into the parking lot at the boatyard, Henry was waiting for them. "Mister Ketchum," he called when Ketch and Kelsey stepped down from the truck. "He's not here. I hadn't seen him anywhere."

"Who y'all lookin' for?" the Captain hollered from the deck of the *Minnow*. "Wait a minute, I'll come to you." He hopped up onto the dock and hustled down to Ketch's group.

"Bean's missing," Ketch said. "He decided to walk home on his own before I could pick him up."

"Suzanne let him do that?" the Captain asked.

"No, he took off on his own. Henry, have you seen Jack? Jack went with Bean," Ketch added for the Captain's benefit.

"No, sir. And I was lookin' for him, too."

"Since I wasn't here, maybe Bean wandered off. Or maybe he's on his way back to your place, Henry. Though if he is, you should have run into him... But maybe he decided to go a different way."

"Dang! I'm gonna go get my keys quick," the Captain said. "I'll drive around and look for him. I swear, sometimes it seems like if it wasn't for bad luck we wouldn't have no luck at all, just like that song says..." he muttered as he turned to go back to his boat.

Ketch nodded. "Kelsey and I will do that, too, after we take another look around the boatyard. Maybe he made friends with someone here, who knows? Henry, please go back home and see if he's there. And tell your mother what's going on. Call me if he turns up."

"Yes, sir! I'm on my way," Henry said, and took off running.

Ketch and Kelsey split up and covered the boatyard, calling Bean's name and asking the few people they saw out and about if they'd seen the boy anywhere. The Captain waved to them and took off in his truck while they were doing that. After they'd searched the boatyard in vain, they went back to Ketch's truck and prepared to do the same as the Captain.

The Captain had turned right out of the lot, so Ketch turned left. After they'd driven down a couple of the back streets calling the boy's name out of their open windows, Ketch was surprised to see Suzanne's car approaching from the opposite direction.

"I left Henry and Sally at the house in case he shows up there," she said when they pulled up to each other. "I've been all around this neighborhood, and I haven't seen him anywhere."

"We're not having any luck, either," Ketch said. "And I didn't think to leave someone at the boatyard in case he turns up there after all. Kelsey, do you mind if I take you back there and drop you off? Then I can keep looking."

"I don't mind," Kelsey said. "Whatever you think is best."

"Ketch, I'm so sorry!" Suzanne said.

"I know." Ketch gave her a rueful smile. "The Captain's out looking, too, so maybe one of us will get lucky."

"I hate to bring this up," Kelsey broke in, "but does he know how to swim?"

Ketch shook his head. "Not that well yet," he said. "I didn't think of that. That's another thing we're working on."

"I can't imagine why he'd go in the water," Suzanne said. "He wanted to see you. But I'll drive by the canals. Maybe he's puddling around somewhere."

"And I'll walk along the soundfront after I drop Kelsey off," Ketch said. "Though the Captain might already have that covered, since he went that way."

Suzanne continued on, and Ketch turned around and drove back to the boatyard. He parked the truck and he and Kelsey got out.

"You might want to go up on the party deck on the houseboat," he told her. "You'll be able to see farther from there."

"Okay," she said.

While she did that, Ketch tried to think of where he might go if he were a meandering seven-year-old. The cabins, which were near a stretch of shoreline that could pass for a beach in a pinch, were off to his right, so he started walking in that direction. He'd almost made it to the cabins when he heard Kelsey call out to him.

"Ketch!" she shouted. He stopped and saw that she was waving him back. He trotted back toward the houseboat, and she descended from the party deck to meet him.

"Is that Jack over there?" Kelsey said, pointing across the lot. "I saw him one time when you had him with you in your truck. That's him, right?"

Ketch looked. It was indeed Jack, emerging now from the brush and slowly making his way into the parking lot. He was panting and limping, and he had something hanging from the side of his mouth. Ketch ran to meet him, and Kelsey followed. Jack sat down when Ketch reached him.

"Jack," he said, kneeling in front of the dog and petting him. "Are you okay? Where's Bean?" Jack hung his head in shame. "It's okay, buddy. What have you got here?" A piece of fabric, perhaps from a shirt, had snagged on one of his canines. It didn't look like it was from any of Bean's shirts. When Ketch carefully removed it, he saw that there was blood on it.

"What's that?" Kelsey asked.

"I think maybe he bit someone," Ketch said. He passed the cloth to her, then checked in and around Jack's mouth. There was blood on some of the teeth but none at the gum line, and none anywhere else other than some spatter on the fur on one side of his neck. No teeth were broken or missing.

"This is blood," Kelsey said.

"Yes, and it's not his." Ketch gently palpated Jack's head, neck, torso, and legs. The dog whined when Ketch touched the shoulder joint of the leg he was limping on, and the nearby ribs as well. "I don't think anything's broken, but he may have a bruised shoulder and a bruised rib or two. Maybe he got kicked."

"If he bit somebody and got kicked, it might be because somebody was tryin' to take Bean," Kelsey calmly stated. "Jack could've been tryin' to protect him."

The same thought had occurred to Ketch, and now his heart was pounding. "That could be," he said, "but who'd want to take him? I've never heard of that happening here in Avon. Who'd do that?"

"I don't know, but maybe we should call in an Amber Alert."

"An Amber Alert?" The ramifications of that, and the likely reasons a boy Bean's age might be abducted, hit him hard. Steady, he told himself, fighting back a growing nausea. As with Kari yesterday, giving in to panic now wouldn't help anyone. "Yes, maybe," he said, breathing deeply, "but I don't know if they'd actually issue one. They have criteria that have to be met for those alerts. All I can give the police is his description. We have no vehicle information, no witnesses, and no evidence of an abduction."

"Jack and this bloody cloth could be evidence enough. I think you should try it."

"You do? Yes, you're probably right." Ketch fumbled his phone from its holster. Though his hands were shaking some, he managed to dial 9-1-1 and report the problem.

"They said they'd send a patrol car right over," he said after he'd hung up – which he then wasn't sure he should have done. He didn't recall being asked to keep the line open, though. He carefully hugged and petted Jack and periodically rubbed around his loyal friend's sore shoulder.

"Good boy," he occasionally murmured, still kneeling before the dog on the dirt surface of the lot. He wasn't sure if he was helping, but Jack wasn't objecting to his attentions and he was breathing more evenly now. Kelsey stood behind Ketch and silently massaged his neck and shoulders while they waited.

A Dare County Sheriff's cruiser pulled into the lot a few minutes later. Ketch could see two occupants inside the vehicle, a male and a female. Kelsey flagged the deputies down and they parked nearby. Jack growled when they got out of the car, but Ketch told him it was okay and he stopped. He kept a hand on his collar, though, just in case.

Ketch introduced himself from his kneeling position, then briefly explained the situation and answered their questions. Kelsey passed the bloody cloth to them and they examined it. The woman was apparently the senior of the two, and she did most of the talking.

"Do you have any photos of him?" she asked

Ketch.

"Yes, on my phone. Kelsey, could you hold Jack's collar?" Ketch stood up, and Kelsey knelt and took his place. He got his phone out, navigated to a series of pictures of Bean engaged in various activities, and started showing them to the officer.

"Okay," she said. "Text me this one, and this one." She gave him her contact information and he got to work on that.

"Well, we don't have much to go on here," she said. "He's probably too young to be a runaway, so he might just be wanderin' around somewhere. Maybe he got lost, even though you said he knew his way. But I agree, what happened to your dog might indicate otherwise, and it sounds like you and your friends have searched the area pretty thoroughly."

"Yes, and two of them are still out driving around," Ketch said.

"Right. Okay, please excuse us for a moment. We'll be back shortly." The deputies returned to their cruiser and got in. Ketch heard their radio crackle, but he couldn't make out what they were saying. He knelt again to relieve Kelsey and went back to comforting Jack while continuing to maintain a firm but gentle grip on his collar. She resumed kneading Ketch's shoulders in the meantime.

"Captain Don's back," she said. Ketch looked up as the Captain's truck rolled to a stop near the cruiser. The Captain reached Ketch and Kelsey before the deputies, who were now exiting the cruiser. Jack didn't growl this time.

"You found Jack?" he asked. "Was Bean with him?"

"No," Ketch answered.

"Dang!" The Captain removed his cap and scratched his head. "So what's goin' on here with the Dudley Do-Rights?"

"I take it you're a member of the search party?" the female deputy asked from behind him, bristling a little. He turned and sheepishly nodded. "Well, what's goin' on is we're activatin' an Amber Alert. Like I said, he might just be lost or wanderin', but the business with the dog makes us suspect an abduction. It's a judgement call, and that's our judgement."

"What happened to Jack?" the Captain asked. Kelsey dropped her hands from Ketch's shoulders and took him aside to fill him in.

"Thank you," Ketch said to the deputy. "So what happens now?"

"Well, a lot of things. The alert will go out to TV on the Emergency Alert System, and radio stations, marine radio, electronic highway signs and billboards, social media on the Internet, text messages to cell subscribers — the works. The FBI will be informed, and the NCDOT Ferry System is bein' notified in case they try to leave the island that way. We're also dispatchin' a cruiser to watch the Bonner Bridge traffic."

If Bean was just potting around somewhere,

Ketch thought, this would turn out to be one epic wolf cry. But that was better than the alternative. Embarrassment and inconvenience be damned.

"Thank you, Officer," he said. Had she introduced herself as a sergeant? He didn't remember. "I hope you don't get in trouble over this."

"Oh, I might catch some flak," she said, "especially if it turns out to be a false alarm. But better safe than sorry, in my book. Just make sure you call our office immediately if he turns up."

"I will."

"There's another cruiser in the area. I'll coordinate with them and send them your photos, and we'll both drive around here some more and keep an eye out for him. We'll also drop our partners off at the harbor so they can walk the shoreline, since you hadn't got to that yet. We'll all talk to any neighbors we come across, too, includin' here at the boatyard. I know you said you've got somebody checkin' the canals, but we'll do that, too, and we'll bring in more personnel if we need to. So you folks can take a break for a while if you want."

"Thank you," Ketch said again.

"Yeah, thanks," the Captain said. "We appreciate everythin' y'all are doin', ma'am," he politely added, perhaps trying to make up for the insulting remark he'd made before.

The deputy gave him a curt nod. "Mister Ketchum, we'll do everything we can. Meanwhile, you be sure and call if there are any new developments," she said, and she went back to the cruiser.

Suzanne's car pulled in as the cruiser was leaving. It had barely stopped when her door flew open and her feet hit the dirt. She left the door open and strode briskly to where Ketch, the Captain, and Kelsey were gathered around Jack.

"I didn't see any sign of him anywhere. Why were the police here? What happened?" she implored. Ketch and the Captain explained the situation to her while Kelsey left the group to make some phone calls.

"Poor Jack!" Suzanne exclaimed. "And poor Bean. I can't believe this is happening! And it's all my fault, I should have been watching them..."

"It's not your fault," Ketch said. "He should have known better than to take off on his own without telling you."

Not that he'd punish the boy when he found him. Kids should be able to roam their neighborhoods as they pleased without fear, as he himself had done in his small hometown when he was young. But Avon, though small, wasn't a rural backwater anymore and that wasn't the kind of world they lived in now, so of course he'd have a talk with him. All he really cared about right now, though, was finding him before any harm came to him.

Kelsey returned to the group. "I'm Kelsey," she said to Suzanne.

"So I heard. I'm Suzanne." She flashed Ketch a questioning look, but he didn't notice.

"Ketch, I canceled my ride for this afternoon," Kelsey said, "and I'm not goin' in to work tomorrow. So I can stay and help."

"Thank you, Kelsey, I appreciate that." Ketch started to rise stiffly to his feet and Kelsey stepped in to help him up. He thanked her again and swiped at his sandy knees. "Well," he said, "we've searched as much as we probably can for now – and thank you all for doing that – and the police are searching now, so I'd like to get Jack to the vet. He should be examined and X-rayed. He'll have to be anesthetized for that, so I'll just drop him off. Then we can decide what to do next. Kelsey, would you mind –"

"I'll drive you and Jack there," Suzanne interrupted. "It'll be easier to get him in and out of my back seat than your truck, and then they'll know who I am in case I have to be the one to pick him up later."

"That's good thinking, Suzanne. Thank you. I'll get his blanket from the truck."

"Oh, don't worry about that, just put him right on the seat. It's leather, it'll clean up."

"All right. I'll call on the way over so they'll know we're coming." And in case they weren't open, since he didn't remember what their hours were offhand. If they were closed, he'd offer to pay extra for emergency treatment.

He bent and coaxed Jack to his feet, then

guided him to Suzanne's car. The dog wasn't limping as badly as he'd been before, but Ketch carefully lifted him onto the seat so he wouldn't have to jump up.

"I don't have his leash, but they'll have one there," he said. "Oh, does anyone want anything for lunch? I forgot about that." He didn't care about himself, but he thought he should be considerate of the others.

"I can't set down an' eat," the Captain growled. "I got some junk food on the *Minnow*."

"I'm okay," Kelsey called.

"Me too," Suzanne said. "And Henry will feed Sally."

"Okay. We'll be right back," he called to Kelsey and the Captain.

The local branch of the Animal Hospital of Nags Head was just a few blocks up Highway 12 at the north end of Avon, and fortunately it was open. They were on Harbor Road when he completed the call. Suzanne didn't speak until then.

"So," she said, "where did this Kelsey person come from again?"

"Kelsey? Oh, she lives in Ocracoke. She's a Portsmouth tour guide, among other things. I've known her for a few years, but not that well. She helped Len with the boat yesterday when I went in the helicopter, and then she rode up here with him."

"She seems nice. She also seems eager to help you, even though you don't know her that well."

"Yes, and she has indeed been a help. She's something of a 'free spirit', I guess you could say, and she's basically just a caring and giving person." Exactly how 'giving' didn't need to be specified, he didn't think, especially since he hadn't taken advantage of that offer.

"I guess so. And she stayed over at your place last night?"

"Yes, because she had nowhere else to go." The cartoon light bulb over Ketch's head finally lit up then. "She slept in Bean's room," he casually added.

"Oh. Well, that's good. I mean, I didn't mean to imply..."

"The animal hospital is coming up on your left," he said. And none too soon, he thought. Was Suzanne grilling him about Kelsey because she was looking out for Kari, he wondered, or was there some jealousy developing there? When they'd parked and gotten out of the car, he went to Suzanne and drew her into a hug before fetching Jack.

"What's this for?" she said, surprise evident in her voice.

"I probably haven't thanked you enough for everything *you've* been doing for me lately," he said, holding her in his arms, "and I just want you to know that I appreciate all your help, that's all." He kissed her on the forehead, released her, and opened Jack's door. "I'll just carry him in, if you'll get the doors for me," he said.

Though she looked a little stunned, Ketch thought she also looked a little happier now. "Oh, of course!" she said. She closed the car door and hustled over to the hospital entrance. Once inside, Ketch got Jack checked in and squared away, hugged him as well one last time, and reassured his faithful friend that he'd be back to get him later.

He and Suzanne briefly discussed what to do next about Bean on the way back to the boatyard, then rode the rest of the way in silence. Ketch thought they should leave one person at the boatyard, and then the others could start canvassing retail shops along Route 12 that might be of interest to a boy like Bean, such as the Wings beachwear and souvenir outlet, Kitty Hawk Kites, and so on. Ketch would be very surprised if he'd somehow gotten all the way out to the main road on his own — but if he was simply lost, then like anything that was lost he must logically be somewhere he wasn't supposed to be, so he thought they should investigate that possibility.

And if the boy wasn't lost and had indeed been abducted? And if he furthermore had been harmed in any way? Well then, when Ketch got hold of the perpetrator or perpetrators, the result wouldn't be pretty.

There was probably no way anyone could prove beyond a 'reasonable doubt' that he and Kari, and then he and Len, had been attacked, nor by whom, and he knew those Amber Alerts were far from a lock. Thousands of people go missing every year in this country, many of them children, and a too-high percentage of them are never heard from again. Call him a vigilante if you must, he thought, but his patience with the system was wearing perilously thin and he no longer felt one iota of disquiet about that. What the hell, as he'd said before, he was already an outlaw. He'd figure a way to cover his tracks with both the pirates and the abductor, for Bean's sake – but it was becoming ever more likely that this would turn out to be his sole concern in the legal sense.

Something occurred to him then that he hadn't thought of when he'd agreed to the Amber Alert – what if this new crisis jeopardized Bean's adoption? And what if Kari was suddenly out of the picture, too? Would the authorities still judge him a suitable parent? Well, he'd just have to wait and see about that. Only worry about things you can change, he thought, reminding himself again of a piece of sage advice he'd incorporated into his personal philosophy a while back.

When Ketch and Suzanne got back to the boatyard, they saw Kelsey and the Captain sitting under the awning, as Ketch thought of it, that he and Henry had installed on the party deck of Ketch's houseboat a while back. The Captain waved them on up when they boarded the boat.

"I got some beers an' waters here in the bucket," he said when Ketch and Suzanne had climbed up. "This one here don't drink, did you know that?" he added, jerking a thumb in Kelsey's direction. "Grab yourself somethin' and set on down, and point your chair out thataway like we did in case Bean shows up somewhere."

They did as they were told, and then Suzanne began telling Kelsey and the Captain about Ketch's idea of checking at pertinent shops along the highway. As she was doing that, Ketch's phone dinged, indicating an incoming message.

"Maybe that's the Amber Alert," he said. "Though I don't remember if I opted to receive those when I got this phone." When he brought the text up and read it, his face turned deathly pale at first, and then rapidly began to redden.

"Are you all right, Ketch?" Kelsey asked him.

"No," he said. "No, I'm not."

"What is it?" the Captain said. "What's the matter?"

A multitude of conflicting thoughts were suddenly competing for Ketch's attention. He tried to set aside the vengeful ones for now and focus instead on the rational ones. Now he was angrier than he was scared, which was a welcome reversal. It was still a dangerous situation, of course, but this was a less nightmarish scenario for him than the previously assumed one had been. He could deal on this one. The first thing he had to do was call Len and get him over here, since he had the gold. And then he'd have to solidify the plan he was already starting to formulate and marshal his troops.

"Ketch?" Suzanne tentatively prompted.

He sat up straight in his chair, looked around at the others, and took command. "Forget about the shops," he said. "We have a new mission. Bean isn't lost, and he wasn't abducted by some nut job."

"What? Then what happened to him? What's goin' on?" the Captain demanded. "Spill it, man!"

Ketch took a deep breath. "He's been kidnapped," he said.

~ E l e v e n ~

Life isn't hard to manage when you have nothing left to lose.

A stunned silence initially greeted Ketch's announcement, but it was short-lived. Soon the others all began talking at once, firing questions at both Ketch and one another. Ketch stood up without responding to any of them and walked to the other end of the party deck.

"Where are *you* goin'?" the Captain demanded.

"I have to make a phone call," Ketch called back. "Please keep your voices down."

"A phone call? Who to?"

Ketch ignored him and brought up Len's number on his cell phone. It rang a few times and then went to voice mail. He left a terse, urgent message and put the phone away. He briefly wondered if Len could have betrayed him and absconded with the gold bars, then dismissed the thought. Len already had plenty of money of his own, and he was a trusted friend – wasn't he? Yes, he decided, he was.

"Did you call the police?" Suzanne asked when he returned to his chair.

"No," he sighed, "and I'm not going to."

That statement precipitated another hullabaloo. Ketch waited for it to subside before he spoke again.

"So who'd you call?" the Captain said.

"I asked Len to come over," Ketch said. "I know who the kidnappers are. Not by name, but they're the people we encountered yesterday at the dive site off Portsmouth Island."

The Captain nodded, and Ketch nodded back. To his credit, the normally loquacious mariner had said nothing so far about what he knew of the previous day's events, undoubtedly because Suzanne and Kelsey weren't in the know. That didn't really surprise him – from the adventures they'd shared in the past year, he knew the Captain could keep a secret. But he could use all the help he could get if they were willing, so he decided to bring Suzanne and Kelsey on board.

"Captain, I think you know what this is all about," he continued. "Bean's kidnappers want the gold Kari and I salvaged from the shipwreck we found yesterday. Ladies, I haven't told either of you the whole story of what happened to Kari. I'm going to do that now, and then you can decide whether or not you want to be involved in what I'm planning."

"You guys found a shipwreck with gold on it?" Kelsey asked in her usual detached manner. "Is it pirate treasure?"

"No, the gold we took was Nazi bullion we found on a U-boat. Gold bars. Almost half a million dollars' worth, according to Len," Ketch said. "And there was more there that we didn't take."

"Oh, my God," Suzanne breathed. "And these other people know about it, and they know what you did, and they want it all." She shook her head. "Ketch, this is serious. You have to call the police!"

"No. Those people tried to kill us yesterday, and they might be succeeding with Kari, and now they've taken Bean," Ketch said with a hitch in his voice. "And they said no police or he dies." He paused and angrily swiped at his eyes. He couldn't break down in front of these people now, not if he wanted to lead them. He took a drink of water and managed to settle himself down.

"And they'll pay dearly for all of that," he continued, "but it'll be done my way. I don't trust the police to handle this. You've heard how these things turn out sometimes when they get involved, haven't you? They're constrained by the law. I don't give a damn about the gold, but I don't want to risk these people getting away with this and then just disposing of... well, you know... because it's the easiest thing for them to do, and..."

This time he couldn't prevent it. He stopped talking and covered his face with his hands. The others waited patiently for him to collect himself. When he lowered his hands a minute later, his face was damp, but he was stronger.

"I'm going to rescue him myself," he insisted with growing vehemence, "and when I do, those people are going to die." Suzanne looked shocked by this bald declaration, but the Captain didn't – and, to his surprise, neither did Kelsey. "Whether or not you agree with me, mark my words, today is their last full day on Earth. And since I'll be rescuing a hostage, whatever I do will be considered reasonable force or self-defense as far as the law is concerned. I'll make sure of that."

Now that it would be a hostage situation and not just revenge, all bets were off, and he no longer had any qualms whatsoever about granting the wish Pauline had expressed at the hospital cafeteria. He'd never killed anyone before, but there was a first time for everything, wasn't there? Sometimes a man just had to do what needed doing – and after the shaky start he'd made of it for most of his life, he knew he was finally a man now.

In his present frame of mind, as far as he was concerned this situation was analogous to what soldiers were called upon to do in wartime. He was protecting his loved ones and preserving their way of life, that's all. Wasn't that what soldiers fought for, and weren't those things worth fighting for? In fact, weren't those really the *only* things worth fighting for? Well, they were to him, and though he'd never served in the military (nor ever even punched anyone, come to think of it) he was ready to fight now.

He saw that Suzanne was wide-eyed and unabashedly staring at him. Did she think he was crazy? Well, if he was, he didn't care. Crazy would get the job done, and if that's what it took, then so be it. Kelsey, on the other hand, simply looked intrigued, and the Captain looked thoughtful.

Ignoring Ketch's vengeful outburst for now, the Captain said, "What I'm not gettin' is, how did them guys figger out who you are'n where you live so fast, and how did they know about Bean? How did they even know what he looked like?"

"I don't know," Ketch said. "I suppose they could have seen the name on my boat and found me by looking up the registration, but yesterday was Sunday and it does seem like it should have taken them longer to do that. As for them knowing about Bean, I haven't got a clue."

"Ketch, I still think you should call the police," Suzanne said, "or at least your friend Dan. Maybe he could help somehow. People who take the law into their own hands can go to jail just like the criminals, you know. And I know the FBI handles cases like this, even when the kidnappers say 'no police'. Won't you at least think about it? They *are* professionals, after all."

"No," Ketch repeated. "I'm not going to risk it. I'm not calling Pauline, either, because I don't want to risk her saying something to Dan. And I won't be going to prison, as long as you all keep this conversation to yourselves. What you heard me say is evidence of premeditation, which could indeed land me in jail. It could also get you charged as accessories, so it's in your best interest, too, to keep quiet." Suzanne started to say something else then, but Ketch cut her off. "You don't know the whole story yet, Suzanne. Just please hear me out, okay?" he said, and then he launched into the tale one more time.

The Captain was able to help him out with some of it now and then, which was fortunate as Ketch wasn't a born storyteller like his salty friend and he had to pause several times for water. No beer for him from here on out – he'd need to stay on top of his game to pull this one off. As he'd ended up doing before on the boat, he again left nothing out, and he added what he'd learned from Dan since then and included key events from the previous days for Kelsey's benefit.

"Well," Kelsey said when he'd finished. "That's quite a story."

"It certainly is," Suzanne nervously replied.

"So there's some kind of pirate treasure down there, too, at the same location, just like the Sea Hag said," Kelsey went on. "That's interesting."

"Look, Ketch," Suzanne broke in, "I don't blame you for feeling the way you're feeling right now. What those people did yesterday was horrible, just horrible, and now they have Bean. But everything else aside, you could get hurt if you go after them yourself. And are you sure you're healthy enough to try? What about that business with that Sea Hag woman? That's worrisome. What if you hallucinate or black out again like you did in that house?" Then she gently and diplomatically added, "What if you have a serious medical problem that you don't know about yet?"

What if he had a brain tumor or aneurism, or

he was coming down with a case of early dementia, or some other disorder was affecting his mind, was what she meant. Ketch supposed any of those things might be possible, though he felt fine.

"There's nothin' wrong with him, and I know he's not goin' crazy," Kelsey quietly interjected. The others all turned to look at her. "Ketch, I didn't tell you the whole truth yesterday. I know about the Sea Hag. I've seen her."

"You have? When?" Ketch asked. "And who is she, really?"

Kelsey shrugged. "I think she's a ghost. I've spent a lot of time in Portsmouth. I don't just do the tours, I also volunteer for the Park Service sometimes, and I've seen her a few times over the years when I happened to be there around dusk. I tried to talk to her one time, and when I asked her who she was, she said she was the Sea Hag."

"Did she say anything else?"

"She thanked me for takin' care of the village, but I didn't understand what she said after that. And I couldn't talk anymore because bein' close to her made me feel weak and dizzy, like what you said happened to you." She looked up at Ketch apologetically. "I'm sorry I didn't tell you before."

"Why didn't you?"

She shrugged again. "I know people think I'm strange. I didn't want you to think I was crazy, too."

Before Ketch could respond to that, his phone rang. He didn't recognize the caller's number, but he took the call while the others muttered among themselves, mostly about Kelsey's revelation.

After listening to the caller's question, he said, "No, thank you, but I can't do that today. Maybe tomorrow." He listened again for a moment, then abruptly said, "Call me tomorrow. I have to go now. Goodbye."

"Who the hell was that?" the Captain inquired.

Ketch's phone rang again before he could answer. "No, I have no comment," he eventually said, "and I don't have time for that right now. Thanks anyway. Goodbye." He put his phone away. "That was a TV station offering to film me for the six o'clock news because of the Amber Alert," he explained to the others, "and then some reporter from the newspaper wanting to interview me for the same reason, and about me finding those dead convicts on the beach."

So that made three so far, counting that girl who'd come to the boatyard looking for him on Saturday. Cheryl, wasn't it? She hadn't bugged him since then, which was a point in her favor. If she continued to behave herself, then if and when he decided to talk with someone from the media he'd honor the promise he'd made her.

"Now that you done caught their attention, maybe you ought to mute your phone," the Captain remarked. "They're like dang telemarketers, they don't usually quit that easy."

"Ordinarily I'd agree, Captain. But what if the kidnappers call or send me more messages, or there's news about Kari? I'll just hang up from here on if it's anyone else."

"Right, I weren't thinkin', sorry 'bout that. Hey, speakin' a messages, what did that message you got say exactly?"

"Wait," Suzanne said. "Ketch, since there's an Amber Alert, won't people think it's odd if you don't take advantage of that extra publicity?" she asked. "And what about that alert? Do you think you should call that off now that we know what's really going on?"

"No," Ketch said. "If I do that, the police will want to know why, and I imagine they'd want to verify that Bean was back. Besides, though it's unlikely, we still don't know where he is and someone might see him somewhere."

Ketch saw Len's truck pulling into the boatyard lot. Well, that's a relief, he thought, though he'd never seriously doubted his eccentric but reliable friend. Len waved to him when he got out of the truck.

"So what's the plan, Stan?" the Captain asked. "And by the way, whatever it is, I'm in. What those sons a bitches did to Kari was bad enough, but takin' Bean on top a that, well that's the straw that broke the camel's back. You recall them old Slinky toys? Well, some folks is like them. They ain't good for nothin', but they do put a smile on your face when you toss 'em down the stairs."

Ketch couldn't help but smile a little at that himself. "Thank you, Captain. But let's wait for Len before we work on my plan."

"Hey, y'all," Len said when he'd boarded and climbed up to the party deck. "Ketch, I got your message. The bag's in my truck. What's up?"

Ketch and the others quickly filled him in. It didn't take too long, since he already knew about everything up until this morning.

"Damn!" Len said. "I got to set on down!" He pulled up another chair and dropped into it. "So now what? If we ain't gonna call the cops, then what *are* we gonna do?"

"We're going to give them what they want," Ketch began, "and follow them after they get it. I have an app that uses GPS to track down a missing smartphone. I have Kari's phone, so I'll hide it in the lining of her gear bag with the gold in case we lose sight of them. When they get to wherever they're going, we'll rescue Bean."

"They ain't said how they're gonna give him back to you?"

"Not so far. That's why I'm thinking I'll have to rescue him."

"And then he'll kill the kidnappers," Kelsey matter-of-factly added. "Ketch says it'll be legal because it'll be a case of reasonable force and self-defense in the course of a hostage rescue."

"No shit? You really wanna take it that far?" Len asked, and Ketch solemnly nodded. "Well, I can't say as I blame you." He fidgeted a bit, then concluded, "Okay, I got no problem with that. The bastards deserve it."

"Why don't we just jump whoever comes to pick up the gold, right there on the spot?" the Captain suggested. "And make 'em tell us where Bean's at? I got some fun ideas on how to go about doin' that."

Ketch shook his head. "That won't work. The message said we're to make sure the gold is in a bag on the end of the public dock in Portsmouth at eleven o'clock. We're also supposed to be long gone by then, of course. I imagine they'll swing by and snatch the bag from a moving boat, and there's no place there to hide that would be close enough for us to grab them."

"Portsmouth? We got to go all the way down there for this? How come?"

"Well, it's a ghost town, so there shouldn't be anyone else around. There won't even be any tourists that late, and fishing and ORVs aren't allowed in the village. It'll be easy for them to make sure there's no one lying in wait for them. I wouldn't be surprised if they were watching the area already as we speak, in case FBI agents try to come ashore at some point or a Coast Guard cutter or some strange boat starts hanging around."

"Dang!" the Captain exclaimed. "So what are we gonna do?"

"That depends," Ketch said, "on how many people we have to work with. Ladies?"

"I'll be happy to help," Kelsey said. "Just tell me what you need me to do."

Suzanne looked uncomfortable, Ketch thought.

"Well," she finally said, "I still don't agree with what you're planning on doing, and I'm still afraid you might get hurt. But I want to help you get Bean back." She sighed. "I'll do what I can, but I have Henry and Sally to take care of too, you know – and your dogs! So I don't know what I can do."

Ketch had figured as much, and he was a step ahead of her. "I know, Suzanne, and thank you. Here's what I think you should do. First, you could help us run some errands, if you don't mind. Then find out when Jack can be picked up, and if it's tonight then do that and keep him at your house. And then later, if it turns out that Len needs to pick Bean up somewhere here on the island, maybe you could go with him. He may or may not remember Len, but he knows you."

Suzanne nodded. "Okay, that all sounds reasonable – except what do you mean about picking Bean up? Mightn't there be a kidnapper guarding him, wherever he is?"

"Yes, there might be – and in that case, you'll stay in the car until Len brings him out. Len, you could call the sheriff at that point if you decide you need to."

"I'll have my heater with me," Len said. "That's what they call it on them crime shows, right? But yeah, if there's somebody else there and I don't think I can handle it on my own, I'll call the cops."

"Oh, my," Suzanne said, but then she steeled herself. "Okay," she finally said.

"Where are you'n me gonna be while all this is

goin' down?" the Captain said.

Ketch laid out the rest of his plan then. They discussed it and tweaked it here and there, and then they made a list of the supplies they'd need. When they'd finished, Ketch sent Suzanne, Len, and the Captain off on their assigned errands. Len still had the gold in his truck, but Ketch figured that was better than leaving it unattended at the houseboat.

"Kelsey, we might as well go get what we need from the Sea Dog before we do anything else," he said. "Are you sure you don't mind doing this?"

"I'm happy to help," she repeated. "Don't worry, I'm an excellent swimmer and I'm not afraid of the dark. Come on, let's go."

When they arrived at the shop, Ketch sent her to a back room with a couple of high-end wetsuits to try on. While she was doing that, he topped off two tanks and then started piling equipment near the front door. The two basic DPVs Kari had purchased for teaching the PADI Diver Propulsion Vehicle specialty course (yet another way for her, and more importantly that mercenary certification agency, to make money) only weighed about twenty pounds each, so he was able to handle them on his own. Their batteries were charged, and they'd each be able to run for about two hours.

"I like this one," Kelsey said, coming out into the showroom carrying the wetsuit she'd chosen. Ketch wasn't surprised, as it was the one with the paisley accents. "But are you sure you don't want me to try a less expensive one? This one's way better than mine."

"This one *is* yours," he said. When she tilted her head at him questioningly, he clarified. "You can keep it."

"Really?"

"Yes. Once you use it, it has to go to rental anyway, and then it becomes just another operating expense for tax purposes. Now you should find a mask, snorkel, and some fins to go with it. You can keep those, too. Do you have a BCD at home?" She wouldn't be using scuba gear tonight, but he knew she was a certified diver.

"Yeah, but it's pretty old."

"Well then, next time you're in town you can stop by and pick out a new one of those, too."

"You don't have to give me all this stuff, Ketch," she demurred.

"I know I don't, and I know you said you didn't expect to be paid for helping me. But this is something I can do for you that doesn't actually cost me very much, and it pleases me to do it."

"Are you sure? Well then, thank you." She set the wetsuit down on the pile and stood lost in thought for a moment. "Ketch, what do you think of me?" she asked him. He wasn't quite sure how to answer that, but then she bailed him out. "What I mean is, do you think I'm strange?"

So she still had that on her mind... Strange? No, not really. Different, yes, but not in a bad way. "No, Kelsey," he said, "I don't think you're strange.

I think you're beautiful." As in the way the kind, peaceful, communal hippies of the Sixties had been called 'beautiful people', was his intended meaning. Maybe he should elaborate on that?

She gazed wonderingly at him for a long second, then said, "That might be the nicest thing anybody's ever said to me."

Well, he guessed she'd 'gotten' it. Then she went to him and hugged him again, more tightly than before. This time, to his chagrin, he immediately became aroused. She looked up at him, gave him an innocent little smile, and then released him.

"Well, I'll get the rest of my gear, and then I guess we better get goin'," she said, wiping at one of her eyes.

Ketch started carrying items out to the truck while she selected the mask, fins, and snorkel she wanted. She helped him finish when she was ready, and then he set the alarm and locked up.

When they got back to the boatyard, they unloaded the contents of the truck to the houseboat. Ketch went inside and carefully packed his dive gear one more time, and of course his trusty backpack, while she attended to the other supplies they were responsible for. As they completed their tasks, they deposited their items neatly out on the deck for later transfer to the *Minnow* and the *TBD*. They'd both be sailing with the Captain when the time came.

Ketch had noticed while packing that the gold

coins he'd picked up yesterday at the wooden shipwreck (Peter Painter's ship?) were still in the pocket of his BCD. Kelsey must have overlooked them when she rinsed his gear. Though he wasn't sure why he felt compelled to do so, he went back into the cabin, gathered the coins Bean had started cleaning, and stuck them in the pocket of his BCD with the others.

He was setting up the tracking app for his and Kari's phones when the Captain rolled in with the new anchor for the *TBD* and a new handheld marine radio. Len and Suzanne followed soon after, Len with the fuel containers and coolers full of ice and Suzanne with what the Captain dubbed 'a dang boatload' of food, both hot takeout for now and cold staples for later. They stowed the cold food and some drinks in the coolers, and then Suzanne drove off again to pick up Henry and Sally.

Ketch tested the new radio while she was gone. When she returned a few minutes later, they all retired to the party deck where a folding table had been set by the others for an early dinner. Ketch had insisted they eat before departing, since they'd skipped lunch, and now everyone, even and especially the previously recalcitrant Captain, was digging in with gusto.

"Ain't nothin' better'n fresh fried srimp'n hushpuppies'n a cold beer," the Captain declared with a mouthful of food.

"'Shrimp', you mean," Ketch said.

"Righ', srimp, s'what I said." The Captain swallowed his food. "Awright, knock it off," he admonished the smiling Ketch. "You talk funny, too, you know, like a dang yankee matter a fact!"

"Ketch, ain't you been 'round here long enough now to know there ain't no 'H' in 'srimp'?" Len grinned.

"Yes, but I still can't get used to it. I guess I need some more time in cracker land. But at least I'm from upstate New York and not New York City, or worse yet South Boston. Even I can't understand what some of those people are saying sometimes, except for the 'F' word, which is just about every other word in some form or other."

Suzanne laughed. "We had some cheeschcads in the part of Michigan I came from. They were entertaining, too."

Ketch was glad to see that she was a little more relaxed now – and that they were all finding it possible to temper their emotions here in what was probably the calm before the storm. He hoped the dinner conversation wouldn't turn to anything that might upset Henry or Sally, but he figured the adults must all know better than that.

"We have a dialect in Ocracoke, too," Kelsey contributed, "that Hoi Toide one Ketch talked about before. I don't know very many of those people, though, and I'm not up on their vocabulary."

"The Sea Hag is a Hoi Toider," Sally stated.

"You remember that? That's pretty good,"

Henry said to her, tousling her hair.

Ketch looked at Suzanne and cleared his throat, and she took that as her cue. "Ketch, I called the vet," she said, changing the subject. "They don't think there's anything wrong with Jack besides some bruising, like you thought. They close at six, and they said he could be picked up around five. I'll go get him after we're done here."

"Thank you, Suzanne," he said. "I have another bag of food you can take with you, and some bones. Oh, and I should give you some money. In fact, I owe all of you money now, don't I?"

"Don't you go worryin' 'bout that now," the Captain said. "We kin square up later on." The others concurred, so Ketch dropped that subject.

"Chuck will be happy to see Jack," he said. "I miss both of them myself, but I'm glad you didn't bring Chuck over with you. It would probably have upset him to be brought home and then yanked away again."

"He's comfortable at my place," Suzanne said. "But I'm sure they both miss you, too. But they'll see you tomorrow." Though she didn't add any qualifications to that last statement, Ketch thought she was starting to look worried again.

Nonetheless, they all managed to get through the rest of the dinner in a benign manner. The Captain inquired about Kari's condition, and Ketch told them what he'd heard from Pauline, about her staying on the heart-lung machine after her surgery. Though they spoke encouraging words to him, Ketch could tell they didn't really believe what they were saying, either.

Kelsey insisted on cleaning up, so Len and the Captain went below to start loading the *Minnow* and the *TBD*. Ketch walked Suzanne and the kids out to their car.

"Okay," she said, standing next to Ketch, "you two get in. Henry, please take this bag and make sure Sally's seatbelt clicks. I have to talk to Ketch for a minute." As soon as the kids were out of sight, she reached up, pulled Ketch's face down to hers, and ardently kissed him. "That's for luck," she said when she came up for air.

"Uh, excuse me, sir?" Henry said. He was back out of the car and he had something in his hand.

"Yes, Henry?" Had the boy seen that? Ketch hoped his face wasn't too noticeably red.

"Sally wants you to take this, Mister Ketchum," Henry said, holding out the rag doll the Sea Hag had given Bean and Sally on Thursday. "She knows where you're goin', somehow or other, and she said it's so you'll be safe from the ghosts."

As far as Ketch knew, no one had told Sally much of anything. But had she overheard enough to know or infer that he was going back to Portsmouth tonight? She'd mentioned the Sea Hag at dinner, so maybe so. Regardless, he was moved by her thoughtfulness.

"Thank you, Henry. Is her window down?" He went to it and saw that it was. "Sally, thank you very much," he said to the diminutive figure in the car seat. "This is very nice of you. I'll keep her with me and I'll give her back to you tomorrow, okay?"

"Okay," she just said. "See you tomorrow."

"I wish I could do somethin' more to help," Henry said from behind him. "But Mama says I can't go with you."

"Thank you, Henry, but she's right to keep you home. I don't know exactly what will happen later, and we want you to be safe, too. You'll be helping me by helping your mother."

"Yes, sir. Good luck, sir," Henry said, extending his right hand. Ketch shook it, then started back to the boats.

"You be careful!" Suzanne called after him.

"I will," he called back. "Don't worry, I'll be fine now that I have this," he added, waving the doll at her as he walked.

"Well, we got both a the boats loaded," the Captain said when Ketch boarded the *Port Starbird*. "And like usual, we did all the work while you were lollygaggin' with a woman. Now I guess it's time to get your boat tied up. You take care a Kelsey and get ready to cast off, and I'll back around and throw you a line."

"Thank you, Captain," Ketch said. Len followed the Captain onto the *Minnow* and Kelsey stayed behind with Ketch. The *Minnow* would tow the *TBD* to Hatteras to save fuel, and then Len would take off for Ocracoke in the *TBD* while the *Minnow* gassed up. The *TBD* would thus bypass the Hatteras-Ocracoke ferry, which was always a potential bottleneck. Aside from delays caused by waiting in long lines of tourists, it had occasionally happened that one of the ferries broke down, and there had been two instances that Ketch knew of when a ferry had run aground in the shoaling inlet and had required a Coast Guard rescue. He didn't want to think about what could happen if they were late delivering the gold, so he'd decided to remove the ferry from the equation.

Kelsey would still have to deal with it, though, as someone needed to drive a vehicle to Ocracoke in case they needed it later to pick up Bean. The kidnappers hadn't sent Ketch any instructions yet in that regard, and he had no way to reach them to ask about it. He'd tried replying to their text message earlier, but it hadn't gone through. Maybe they'd used what the thriller writers called a 'burner phone' and then chucked it. So Bean could be almost anywhere, on one of the islands or even the mainland. Maybe they'd drop him off when they picked up the gold, but Ketch wasn't counting on that.

Kelsey's part in this was less vital than the roles of himself, the Captain, and most of all Len, but Ketch still hoped she'd be able to reach Ocracoke in time to hitch a ride with Len on the *TBD* as planned. If she didn't for some reason, they'd still be able to track the phone Ketch had secreted in the lining of Kari's gear bag along with the gold – but if the kidnappers found the phone or ditched the bag and Kelsey wasn't in position, they might be out of luck. Though even then, Len, who was supposed to be back in Ocracoke at that time, could follow them in the car if the kidnappers docked there, or in the *TBD* if they didn't.

It was too bad Suzanne couldn't have been the one to make the drive to Ocracoke, but he'd decided it was too much to ask her to leave Henry and Sally home alone, possibly all night. Ah, plans... like rules, even the best of them were made to be broken more often than not. He'd just have to do his best and hope for the same.

"You can take Kari's car," he said to Kelsey. "We'll definitely miss the last ferry back to Hatteras tonight, so we won't be towing the *TBD* on the road. And I won't be needing the car anytime soon, in case you don't want to drive it back here right away." He handed her the key, which he'd removed from Kari's key ring. "Just be sure and leave the key in it in case Len needs it, and don't lock the doors. In fact, leave a window open in case you forget."

"I won't forget," she said, pocketing the key. "I'll check in on the radio when I get to the lifesavin' station." She gave him another hug and said, "You better not lose that doll." Then she gave him a quick kiss on the cheek. "Good luck," she said and headed off to the parking lot.

Ketch stuffed the doll into one of the oversized pockets of his cargo shorts. Then he boarded the *TBD* and started loosening her lines. When the *Minnow* came around and Len threw him his line, he quickly tied it off. He used a bowline instead of his customary half hitch knot, which would be impossible to undo once the bigger boat pulled it taut. Then he undid the final line holding the *TBD* in place, signaled 'okay' to Len, and they were underway.

He'd decided to stay with the *TBD* on the way to Hatteras, and now that he was alone and he had a little free time he thought he'd give Pauline a call to see how Kari was doing. But first, he decided to do a quick inventory, though everything the others had stowed had looked good at first glance.

There were the fuel containers, check... And the bag with all of Kelsey's gear in it, check... And one of the DPVs, with two dry bags clipped to it containing between them the new handheld marine radio, a pair of binoculars, a couple of large water bottles, a towel, one of Ketch's heavy sweatshirts, a flashlight, bug spray, and some granola bars, check... A cooler with some drinks and snacks for Len (he already had Ketch's other handheld radio with him), check... And last but certainly not least, the gear bag with the gold. He double-checked that Kari's phone was still in that bag, verified again that his phone was able to track her phone, and finally settled down.

He sat on the stern deck with his back against the transom to get as far away as possible from the noise of the *Minnow*'s inboards and called Pauline's phone. Oddly, it went directly to voicemail. He disconnected without leaving a message and tried again, and then tried two more times.

Why wasn't she picking up? Was she in a part of the hospital where she'd had to turn off her phone? Had she simply forgotten to charge it? Or was there something further wrong with Kari? He didn't know what else could possibly go wrong with her, unless... He considered trying Dan's phone, but he didn't want to talk to him right now. But maybe he should? He needed to know about Kari.

Calm down, he told himself. If something bad had happened, Pauline would surely have called him. He decided to leave her a message. He hadn't told her about Bean yet and he wouldn't now, but he should let her know what he was up to, just in case.

"Pauline," he said, "it's me, Ketch." But she'd know that from his caller ID. "I'm sorry I haven't been in touch, but I've been very busy. I hope Kari's still..." What, 'doing okay'? She wasn't doing okay. "Anyway, I wanted you to know that I'm taking care of business tonight, like we talked about at the cafeteria. If all goes well, I'll see you either tomorrow night or the next day." Then he disconnected. He knew it wasn't a great message, but he guessed it'd have to do for now.

Meanwhile, his pieces were all in play now and there was nothing else he could do at the moment, so he leaned his head back, closed his eyes, and let the pleasantly cool salt breeze caress his face and neck. How had all this craziness happened, he thought again, and why did it have to happen to him? Well, he guessed he knew the answers to those questions.

He remembered that Hemingway had written something to the effect that when life breaks you, in the end you're stronger in the broken places. He hoped that would turn out to be true tonight, and that nothing more would break.

~ T w e l v e ~

Everything kills everything else in some way or other.

*T*he Captain's radio crackled. "Lookout to Captain, Lookout to Captain, over," Ketch heard Kelsey's voice say.

Good, she was remembering to use the nicknames they'd agreed on to maintain anonymity. They were communicating on one of the lesser-used noncommercial VHF channels tonight and eschewing the ubiquitous channel 16. It was a quiet night and they didn't need weather reports, and that channel was monitored by the Coast Guard. There shouldn't be much chatter, if any, around here at this time of night, but Ketch didn't want to take any chances. It seemed they'd chosen the right channel, he thought. The only transmissions they'd picked up on it so far were this one from Kelsey and some earlier ones from Len.

Ketch hustled over to the *My Minnow*'s radio. "Captain to Lookout, over," he said.

"Lookout to Captain, I'm in position and the bait is in place, over."

"Captain to Lookout, roger, out." They weren't following all of the recommended marine radio protocols to the letter, but he thought they were at least using the prowords correctly – 'roger', for example, meaning 'transmission received', and by implication understood. As it appeared they were the only ones on this channel, it didn't much matter as long as they understood one another.

"So she made it, huh?" the Captain said. "That girl is somethin' else, ain't she? I know she had the DPV, but still, swimmin' in from that boat on her own through the breakers in the dark like that... And now she's up in that tower or whatever all by her lonesome, and in a dang ghost town to boot. Better her than me, that's all I got to say, 'specially with that Sea Hag bidness. You really believe that was a ghost?"

"I don't know what to think about that," Ketch said. "But I guess I have to believe what I see, don't I?"

Though he didn't consider himself a superstitious person, he'd have to be plain stupid, or perhaps a politician (but as Mark Twain had said, was he repeating himself?), to deny something that was staring him right in the face. And intellectually, he knew there was indeed more going on in this world than meets the eye, as Len had asserted last week. The human race still had a very long way to go before it knew absolutely everything, if that was even possible.

The Captain started to speak again, but Ketch raised a hand for silence. "Do you hear that?" he said.

"Yeah... Sounds like another boat." The Captain picked up the binoculars and began panning the area north of them. The *Minnow* was anchored south of yesterday's accursed dive site off Portsmouth Island with its engines shut down and its running lights extinguished, and though it was highly unlikely they'd have a problem in this particular location, it still behooved them to watch for other marine traffic.

"Her lights are off too, but I think I got her," the Captain said. It might have been better if there'd been a new moon tonight, but though no one could have seen the *Minnow* then, he and Ketch would have also been unable to see much of anything. Since Portsmouth was uninhabited, there wasn't even any light pollution from the island. So the crescent moon was probably more of a help than a hindrance, and Ketch thought they should be far enough from the dive site to avoid detection.

"Looks like she's stoppin' at the dive site, or near enough," the Captain said. "And since she ain't showin' lights, it's gotta be our guys, right? Must be they're gonna go divin'."

"I guess — but then, who's picking up the gold? Kelsey said it was still there on the dock."

Zero hour was rapidly approaching, and Ketch's adrenalin was starting to ramp up. Could he be wrong about who'd kidnapped Bean? Could it be that someone else entirely had somehow learned of the gold he'd found? If the people who'd attacked them at the dive site yesterday weren't the ones who'd taken Bean, then who had?

Sunset had occurred a little before eight-thirty tonight. The *Minnow* had sailed past the lighthouse and through Ocracoke inlet right about then. Len had held back in Ocracoke until full dark, dropped Kelsey off on the Atlantic side of Portsmouth, doubled back to deposit the ransom (the 'bait') at the soundside dock a little before ten, and then returned to Ocracoke. He'd radioed the *Minnow* upon each mini-milestone as instructed, beginning with Kelsey's arrival in Ocracoke, which was good. The *TBD* had a shallow draft, but it could still be dangerous boating in the inlet at night when the shoals were harder to see.

Kelsey had fortunately completed her drive to Ocracoke in time – so Ketch now had eyes not only on the gold, but also on the sound, the inlet, and the ocean around the village. She was camped in the lookout cupola atop the preserved Portsmouth lifesaving station, where the surfmen of old had kept vigil over these waters in anticipation of ships foundering due to storms or navigational errors. Ketch thought this was a breathtakingly beautiful place, even tonight. But in the days before satellite navigation and modern meteorology, maritime disasters had occurred with sometimes depressing regularity in these parts.

And now Len was an amphibious asset, able to deploy by land via the car Kelsey had driven down or by water via the *TBD*. And the *Minnow* was where she was in case Ketch had to confront the divers to find out where Bean was being held, if they showed up at the dive site – which it appeared they now had.

So between Len and the *Minnow*, they were capable of going wherever they'd need to go to pick Bean up. There'd still been no word from the kidnappers on that, though, and it was ten-thirty now and Ketch was getting anxious. He checked his phone again to make sure it could still track the phone in the gear bag.

"Well, they're stayin' put," the Captain said. "Here, you wanna have a look-see?"

Ketch took the binoculars and trained them on the dive site. He couldn't make out what kind of boat it was, but it was definitely bigger than the one that had chased the *TBD*.

"That isn't the same boat we saw yesterday," he said.

"Well, maybe they got two boats," the Captain suggested.

"I hope so. Otherwise I don't know what to think."

But there must soon be another one picking up the gold, regardless of whose boat it might be. Even if the kidnappers were foolish enough to send someone to retrieve the gold by land, there was no way off the island other than by boat. But what if their boat was docked at the south end of the island where the cabins were, and they sent someone up the shoreline by ATV? He hadn't thought of that, but again that seemed like an unnecessarily risky way to go about things. The less they exposed themselves, and the less time they spent executing the retrieval, the better, right?

Well, he'd just have to wait and see. That was the hardest part, the waiting. Waiting until all their preparations had been complete earlier today, then waiting for dark, and now waiting for the eleven o'clock deadline to finally roll around.

Ketch passed the binoculars back to the Captain and asked him to continue watching the boat at the dive site. Then, to keep himself occupied, he began preparing his diving gear. He harnessed his BCD to the racked tank he'd brought, donned his wetsuit, and then mounted the speargun he'd appropriated from the Sea Dog onto the DPV. The Captain didn't know about that particular part of his plan yet.

"Lookout to Captain, Lookout to Captain, over," the radio squawked. Ketch dropped what he was doing and ran to the radio.

"Captain to Lookout, over," he said.

"Lookout to Captain, the bait's bein' taken, one man on a boat, no runnin' lights... He's slowin' down and gaffin' it... Okay, now he's takin' off into the inlet, and... Now he's headin' straight out to sea." Ketch wanted to respond, but she hadn't said 'over' yet. "Oh, over," she said.

She must be excited, Ketch thought, as evidenced by her forgetting to say 'over' and release the button. But he couldn't have discerned that otherwise, as her tone of voice was pretty much the same as it usually was.

"Captain to Lookout, roger, what is the boat's direction, over?"

"Lookout to Captain, wait... Okay, he's past the village now... He's turnin' south, I say again, south toward your position, over."

That was good, as it appeared his original theory about who the kidnappers were might be panning out. But she hadn't said what he'd most longed to hear.

"Captain to Lookout, roger, do you see the prize anywhere, over?"

This time there was a pause before the reply. "Lookout to Captain, no prize in sight, I say again, no prize... I'm sorry, over."

Ketch swore under his breath. So they hadn't dropped Bean off at the dock when they'd picked up the gold. "Captain to Lookout, roger... Good job, take a break, out."

That boat would soon pass out of her view, if it hadn't already, so her work was done. Now all she had to do was stay put and wait to be picked up. And now he had one more call to make, and then he'd have to decide what to do next.

"Captain to Tibbid, Captain to Tibbid, over." That was Len's handle for tonight, since he was on the *TBD*.

"Tibbid to Captain, over," Len answered over some gradually fading background noise. Had Len been over at the Jolly Roger? Maybe he'd had to use the facilities.

"Captain to Tibbid, did you hear what Lookout said, over?"

"Tibbid to Captain, yes, over."

"Captain to Tibbid, stay put and stand by, over."

"Tibbid to Captain, roger, wilco, out."

Well, if Len had gone over to the waterfront bar, he hadn't sounded like he'd had anything to drink. And he'd said 'will comply', so Ketch guessed he had nothing to worry about on that end.

The Captain had climbed up to the flying bridge to get a better view of the dive site, so Ketch joined him there. "Did you catch all that?" he said.

"Yep, sure did. I'm watchin' for that other boat now. Should be along any minute if she's comin' this way."

Things would be a lot simpler if she was, Ketch thought. If that boat was instead going to rendezvous with yet another boat out there, or was going somewhere else entirely, they'd have to try to follow it by tracking Kari's phone.

"Here she comes," the Captain announced.

Ketch could hear it now. It was initially hard to tell because the first boat's engine was still running, but the pitch of the second boat's engine was different and it was getting louder.

"She's slowin' down and pullin' up alongside the other boat," the Captain said.

Okay then, that settled it. The divers were the kidnappers. "Well, I guess I'm up, then," Ketch said. He went back to where his tank was racked, sat down in front of it, and slipped into his BCD.

"I still ain't seein' why you gotta go over there and scout 'em out," the Captain said, joining him. "Why can't we just pull the *Minnow* up'n go at 'em? I got my gun."

"Well, we know there are three of them. What if they all have guns? And don't forget, they have explosives. They'd have time to prepare when they heard us coming – and then maybe they'd just toss a bomb at us, who knows? We'd have a better chance if we waited until we knew they were diving, but even then there's bound to be someone topside."

"Yeah? So what's gonna change if you go over there first? How're things gonna be any different?" Ketch saw the Captain's eyes widen as he finally noticed what was mounted on the DPV. "Are you thinkin' you're gonna take out the topside guy your own self? With *that* thing? I swear, you gotta be the craziest dang yankee I ever saw!" The Captain's face darkened. "You been plannin' on doin' this all along, right? Ain't you learned nothin' from all the stuff we been through?"

The answer to that was, yes, he had been planning this all along. Even though the Captain had come fully on board with Ketch's murderous intentions, he'd wanted to spare his good friend from direct culpability. But now there was another factor that definitely sealed the deal, and there was no way he'd allow himself to be dissuaded.

"Captain," Ketch said as calmly as he could, "there's something else we have to think about now. We still don't know where Bean is. What if he's on that boat?"

"What? Well..." The Captain thought for a moment. "Yeah, I guess we wouldn't want to be startin' no gunfight then. If a stray bullet didn't get him, they might do somethin' to him. But what if there's more'n one guy topside? You're only gonna get one shot with that speargun. Maybe you should take my gun. You got another one a them dry bags?"

"Yes. So okay, I'll take it just in case." He'd been about to insist again that he was going no matter what, but it seemed the Captain had already accepted that. He must be getting soft, Ketch thought.

When Ketch was done suiting up, the Captain helped get him and the DPV out to the swim platform. The gun was now in a dry bag clipped to the DPV.

"The safety's off, so all you gotta do is pull the trigger," the Captain said. "Don't forget about that and shoot yourself by accident."

"I won't. Thanks, Captain." Ketch, now seated on the edge of the platform, spit in his mask and rinsed it in the water.

"Say, you think maybe we should wait a while longer and see if those guys contact you? Maybe they got Bean somewhere else, or maybe they'll drop him off somewhere so we can just go get him later."

"They don't seem to be too motivated to contact me. That's why I'm going to them." They might just dump poor Bean's body somewhere if he waited too long, he didn't want to say – nor even think about right now. "And besides, then they wouldn't get to die," he did gruffly add. "Though the one topside will have to stay alive long enough to tell me where he is."

It looked like the Captain was about to say something, so Ketch said, "That's enough talking. I'll radio you when it's safe to bring the *Minnow* over." He put his mask and fins on, inflated his BCD, and slipped into the water, then pulled the DPV in after him. "Thank you again, Captain," he said. "You're –"

"Yeah, I know, a good friend and all that. I've heard it all before. But hey – you too, buddy. Good luck, and stay safe." Ketch nodded to him, put his regulator in his mouth, and clipped the DPV's lanyard to his BCD. Then he started up the DPV and headed out.

He advanced slowly at first to adjust his buoyancy so he could travel with the DPV and most of his body just below the again fairly calm surface of the water. It wasn't quite 'slick cam' this time, he thought, but it was close enough. When he'd gotten that straightened out, he sped up.

Since they were south of the dive site, he'd figured the current would probably be with him. He was right. The DPV didn't have to strain too hard and he was soon approaching the kidnappers' boats. He'd originally intended to turn the DPV off some distance short of the goal and fin the rest of the way – but though both boat engines were silent now, he could hear a motor of some kind running somewhere on the larger boat. Since it was louder than his DPV, he continued on. When he'd gotten close enough to make out the decks of the now conjoined boats, he saw that there was no one out and about on either of them.

And when he'd gotten that close, he could also see why the larger boat had begun to look naggingly familiar to him over the past few minutes. It was a weathered old wooden trawler, a twenty-five footer if he recalled correctly, that hadn't been used for fishing in a long time and was missing most of the rigging that would ordinarily be associated with that activity – and yes, there was still a small winch bolted to the aft deck. He knew whose boat this was, and now he was even angrier than he'd been before.

There was still no one on deck and that motor was still running, so he drove the DPV almost up to the stern ladder before cutting it off. The boat's transom was riding high enough out of the water that he shouldn't be immediately visible if someone did come out on deck. The boat was anchored at the stern as well as the bow, so he let go of the DPV (which was neutrally buoyant), removed his regulator and BCD, fully inflated the BCD, and clipped it and the attached tank and

DPV to the anchor line.

He kept his mask and fins on. His wetsuit wasn't providing quite enough buoyancy to keep his mouth completely out of the water without finning, so he decided to use his snorkel. As he was unclipping the dry bag from the DPV, a lazy swell quietly washed over the exposed end of the snorkel from behind him and he aspirated some seawater. Not much, as he reacted quickly, but enough to make him gag momentarily and lose his grip on the dry bag. He grabbed for it and missed, then helplessly watched as the Captain's gun sank slowly into the deep.

Great, now what? Well, damn it, he'd planned on doing this with just the speargun in the first place, so that was what he'd do. He'd never handled a firearm in his life anyway, but he had learned how to use a speargun. Though he'd never actually fished with one, he'd done some underwater target shooting back in the day and he was comfortable with it.

He carefully removed the loaded but uncocked speargun from the DPV, this time without using that damned snorkel. With his gun arm hooked around a rung of the ladder, he removed his fins with his other hand and let them dangle from his wrist by their straps. Then he climbed the ladder and quickly swung himself onto the deck.

There was still no one else in sight. He set his fins down and cocked the gun. First things first... Then he pulled his mask off, dropped it on top of the fins, and took a look around.

The running motor turned out to be a hookah compressor. A gasoline-powered one, he noted. He further noted that there were two hoses, or umbilicals, running from it up over the port gunwale and then down into the water. That meant there were two divers below, which in turn meant there should be one guy topside – assuming that the three men they'd seen on the smaller boat yesterday were the only ones involved in this little conspiracy.

A hookah... Now that was interesting. Why would they choose a surface-supplied air rig over scuba? He'd have thought dragging air hoses behind them would be disadvantageous when penetrating the interior of a shipwreck. They could get snagged on something, and if they were breached while the divers were inside the wreck they'd be S.O.L. Maybe they were carrying pony bottles to cover that eventuality.

The advantage, of course, was an unlimited air supply versus scuba tanks, and perhaps more saliently an inexperienced or untrained diver could quickly learn how to function with a hookah – which Ketch knew was one of the biggest knocks against it. Aside from the safety issues, which were admittedly valid, you didn't have to show anyone a certification card to use a hookah like you would if you wanted to fill or rent scuba tanks. And if you didn't have to earn a C-card, the certification agencies didn't make money.

So maybe these guys weren't certified divers. Ketch recalled that Dan had said only one of the dead convicts who'd washed up on the beach had been certified. If the convicts had also used a hookah, then that would explain why they hadn't had tanks and regulators when they'd washed up on the beach. Maybe this current crew had stolen this hookah rig from the convicts.

Okay, so now what? Should he tap on one of the cabin windows? Knock on the door? He'd been extremely fortunate so far that he hadn't been challenged, and he appreciated that, if anyone up there was listening – but now it was time to get down to business.

There was a small pile of diving weights nearby, he saw. He was thinking about tossing one at the cabin door when it opened and a stocky black-haired Hispanic man stepped onto the deck.

Or more accurately, half-Hispanic. Ketch hadn't seen him since last June, but he remembered that his mother was Mexican and his father wasn't. He was a little shorter than Ketch and about thirty years younger. Ketch knew him to be a jocular and generous sort of outlaw – or rather, criminal now, in his book. He was the kind of guy who'd give you the shirt off his back if you were down on your luck – but then he'd stab you in the back through that very same shirt if he needed to in order to get by.

Ketch had learned that final bit last summer during their confrontation on the Captain's boat.

He leaned back against the transom, raised the speargun, and held it steady with both hands.

Incredibly, the man hadn't noticed him yet. Granted, it was dark, but still... Maybe the music from his earbuds was distracting him, and maybe he'd been smoking some of what he'd been selling back at the boatyard last summer before the storm. Ketch had sampled his product with Kari on a couple of occasions back then. Those had been some fun times... But now, fun time was over.

"Hello, Mario," Ketch enunciated, loudly and clearly.

Mario, who'd been turned away from Ketch, did a double take and spun to face him. He ripped the earbuds from his ears and let them dangle from the device on his belt.

"What the hell! Well, hey Ketch! Holy shit, you about gave me a heart attack! What the hell are *you* doin' here, man?" Mario ran a hand through his hair. "Long time no see, huh?" Ketch noticed that he seemed twitchy. Maybe he was just nervous – or maybe he was a meth head now, who knew?

"Stand still and keep your hands where I can see them," Ketch commanded.

"Okay, okay. Hey man, come on now, you don't have to be pointin' that thing at me. We used to be buds, right? We had us some good times back at that old boatyard, didn't we? Man, those were the days..."

"Cut the crap. Where's Bean?"

Mario's eyes anxiously flitted between Ketch's stony visage and the speargun. "Hey, no worries man. He's right inside there, down in the berth, safe and sound. How about I go get him for you?" He took a step toward the open door of the cabin.

"Stay put!" Ketch said, aiming the speargun directly at Mario's chest. "I mean it, don't test me."

"Okay, no problem, man. Hey, you know, it wasn't my idea to take him, but those other guys..."

"Shut up," Ketch said. "Bean!" he shouted. "Bean, are you in there?" He was answered by what sounded like a couple of muffled yells from the interior of the cabin. "Why can't he talk? And why can't he come out here on his own?" he demanded.

"Well, he's tied up, and he's got some tape over his mouth," Mario admitted. "But seriously, man, he's okay. None of us did nothin' to him but that, I swear! He's your grandson, right? I wouldn't let nothin' happen to him."

"Oh, really?" Ketch replied. "When were you going to return him to me, then? Why haven't I heard anything about that?"

"We were gonna do it later, man, I swear, just a little later on! We just wanted to finish gettin' the rest of that gold first, before you or the cops tried to come after us. You understand, right? It's just business, that's all."

"Bean, it's Papa!" Ketch shouted again. "Don't worry, I'm coming to get you!" He returned his attention to Mario. Although he ached to drop everything else (after first incapacitating Mario, of course) and run to the boy right now, he also needed to take care of some other matters. And the way it looked like things would likely end up going here, he supposed he'd better do that first.

"How did you know I had a grandson?" he demanded. "And what he looked like, and where I live now? You've been back to Avon, haven't you? And you spied on me, didn't you?"

"Yeah, I stopped by there now and then, but not to spy, really. I just wanted to touch base with some old friends and see how y'all were makin' out after that hurricane and all. Hey, I'm sorry about your house, man. But the boatyard looks great, and you got a great boat!"

"The Captain thought maybe you'd gone to Mexico after what happened on his boat last June."

"Well, I did go on down to Florida for a while, but then I never heard nothin' about what happened with Mick and all, so I figured it was okay to come back. Now I'm mostly up in Manns Harbor, got some friends there, and – say, what went down with Mick, anyway? What'd you guys do with him? You can tell me, I sure as hell won't tell nobody. I'm technically the guy that shot him, right? Even though it was an accident, really, I didn't mean to –"

"We took care of it. It was just business, like you say. Speaking of business, was trying to kill me and Kari and Len yesterday just business, too?"

"Hey man, I'm sorry about that, really! I didn't know it was you at first. Once I saw it was your boat, I made those guys back off, I swear!"

"Do you mean when Len was shooting at you?"

Mario chuckled. "Oh yeah, well... But we got guns too, you know, we could have shot back."

"You must have seen that it was my boat when you bombed us before that." Mario had nothing to say to that. "Kari's in the hospital, you know. She's in a coma and she might be brain-dead, they're not sure yet."

"Aw man, I'm sorry to hear that. She was a cool lady."

"She *is* a cool lady, you lying piece of shit. She's not dead yet. So what happened with those escaped convicts? Did you kill them?"

"Yeah, but we had to, man. That dude from the barge, the one that found the coins, he told me what he was up to. I was workin' at that condo project in Buxton. So then I told these other guys, and they wanted in, and that dude went after us, man! It was self-defense."

"Really? So you killed that guy, too? Where's he at now?"

"I don't know, man, those other guys took care of that."

Ketch fell silent. He guessed he'd gotten all the answers he needed for now. If he was missing something, so be it. It was time to finish up here and see to taking care of poor Bean.

"So what happens now, man?" Mario asked.

"You gonna call the cops? Look, you don't have to do that. We can just do some business here, right? There's ten gold bars in that bag over there. Well, I guess you know that," he nervously chuckled. "How about if you just take that and the kid, and then we all go our separate ways? And you'll never see me again, I swear, and I'll make sure those guys don't bother you no more."

Ketch could see part of a crate back in a corner of the cabin, and it looked like it had some kind of canisters in it. It was probably the explosives Mario and his friends had used to try to dispose of him and Kari yesterday. After he took care of Mario, he could drop a couple, maybe more than a couple, of those in the water, like they'd done to him. But what if he mishandled them? Bean was on the boat, too.

Since Ketch wasn't answering right away, Mario added, "I can give you a little more gold too, if that's not enough."

"Maybe," Ketch said then, playing along. "But I'm not satisfied with one thing you said, so first you're going to do me a favor."

"Sure, anything man! What do you need?"

"Do you see that tarp there? Spread it out over top of that compressor, and make sure the edges are tucked in all around it."

"Huh? How come?" Mario's face clouded. "Oh, that's cold, man." He'd apparently realized what Ketch was thinking, and he was hesitating.

"Do it now!" Ketch barked. "If I have to do it

myself, it'll be over your dead body. What's your problem? It's just business, right?"

"Yeah man, I guess so." Mario stopped talking and began doing as Ketch had instructed.

It was critical to the safety of the divers that the hookah air compressor take in clean and uncontaminated air. That was undoubtedly one reason the boat's engine had been shut down, so that no engine exhaust would enter the compressor intake. Carbon monoxide was even deadlier at depth than it was at the surface, because increasing the partial pressure of a component of a breathing gas also dramatically increased its toxicity. Even pressurized oxygen was toxic at depth at high concentrations. In fact pure oxygen, beneficial as it was at the surface, could kill you twenty-five feet under the water if that's all you were breathing. People liked to say they'd never use most of what they were made to learn in school, but here was an example of the Ideal Gas Laws of physical chemistry in action, Ketch thought.

The four-stroke gasoline engine that was powering this compressor also created exhaust, which was currently being routed downwind away from the intake. But with the tarp over the unit, that would no longer be an effective system. Carbon monoxide poisoning was insidious enough on land, and at depth those divers breathing their pressurized air would never know what had hit them. The bastards would be goners before they even had a clue that something was wrong, and that was just fine with him.

"So who did Jack bite?" Ketch asked while Mario worked.

"Oh, one of those other guys. He's got it taped up." Mario was finishing up now. "Hey," he said, "that tarp's plastic. What if it gets hot and starts meltin'?" When Ketch looked unconcerned about that, he said, "Oh, right, the fumes will get 'em, too. But what if it catches fire?"

"Don't worry, I won't burn down your boat," Ketch promised.

"Okay, if you say so." Mario's restlessness looked to be increasing now. "Well then, I guess we're done here, right? I'll put that bag on the other boat for you, and you can get the kid and take off in that. Oh, but you want a little more, right? I forgot. I'll get you some more from the hold."

Yes, we're done here, Ketch thought, more done than you realize. "Sorry, but that's not good enough. Don't move," he said.

"What? Aw, come on, man, what else do you want?" Ketch didn't answer. "You want *all* of it? Hey, come on, you're gonna get me in big trouble if you take it all!"

Well, wait now, this could be interesting... "Oh? Those two down below won't be giving you any trouble. So who will you be in trouble with?" Ketch asked. Mario appeared reluctant to say more. "Answer me!" Ketch growled, making a show of sighting along the barrel of the speargun.

"Hey man, chill!" Ketch lowered the gun a little. "Okay, look, I got a boss, the foreman at that condo development. And he's connected, know what I mean? And if I don't bring him somethin', man, I could end up in some swamp somewhere, you know?"

So there was a mobster involved with the Cape Point condominium project? Ketch was glad now that he hadn't shot Mario yet. He heard another muted shout from the interior of the boat. It was killing him that he hadn't gotten to Bean yet, but he had to hear the rest of this story.

"Keep talking," he said. "And make it quick."

"Okay, well, I was runnin' some square grouper for this guy on the side, you know, like I do, and the Coast Guard got onto me and I had to ditch a load. So now I owe him for that, and he said if I got this gold for him, he'd forgive my debt plus give me twenty percent. See, he's out the cost of that load, and the environmentalists he had to pay off to get his permits cost more than he thought they would, so he needs some cash. He doesn't want to look bad to *his* boss either, you know?"

And who might *that* be, Ketch wondered? Well, Dan could figure that part out. He was more interested in the environmentalists.

"Who did he pay off?" he asked. "And why? Was it the Audubons?"

"I don't know who they were, one of those environmental outfits. It was somethin' about buildin' on nestin' grounds for some birds."

Wait until Bob and RAM and the CSFCP members hear about *this*, Ketch thought. It was well-known that the environmentalists, primarily the Audubon Society, had been driving the actions of the NPS since the beginning of the beach access controversy. When they'd first started dictating beach and ramp closures back in '07, they'd sent the rangers out to guard the protected areas with guns, so there'd be no doubt they meant business. The CSFCP, and the OBPA, could make good use of this tidbit of information.

But now he needed to wrap this up. "How did your boss find out about the gold?"

"I don't know, I guess he heard about it somehow."

Ketch thought for a moment. "Yes, I'm guessing he did, somehow— and then you heard about it from him, not from the guy who found the coins. Since you're in debt to your boss and you're a known scumbag, he drafted you to do his dirty work. And getting rid of that guy and his convict friends was part of the job, wasn't it? Am I warm?" Mario looked down and shifted uncomfortably on his feet. "And you hired those two divers down below to help you, and you have to pay them out of your share. *Had* to, I mean. Am I hot now?"

"Well yeah, man, pretty much, but –"

"So that makes *you* the boss of this little operation, doesn't it? And that means everything is your fault."

"Okay, okay," Mario said, throwing his hands up. "But you gotta leave me *somethin'*, man," he whined, "or I'm up the creek! Hey, tell you what, I'll just take that bag with me in the other boat, and you can keep everything else, how 'bout that? You can keep the boat, too. There's at least thirty more gold bars in the hold, maybe more than that, I forget. So how about it?"

"You have a lot of nerve expecting anything at all from me, after what you've done," Ketch said. "You tried to kill us, and then you took my grandson. *You took my grandson!*"

"Hey, I know how you feel, man, really I do. But like I said, it was just business, you know?" Then Mario noticed that Ketch's face was even stonier now than it had been before. "Okay, so what are you gonna do now, shoot me? You can't do that! Come on, man, we're buddies, remember?"

"Shut the fuck up, Donny. You're not my buddy. All you are to me now is a loose end," Ketch said.

"Huh? Why you callin' me 'Donny'? What's goin' on, man?"

He was sounding panicky now, Ketch thought. The bravado was just about gone, and the false camaraderie along with it. And was that a wet spot on his shorts? Good.

"That's a line from *The Big Lebowski*," Ketch said. "Have you seen it? No? It's what they call a 'cult classic'. Kari's quite the film buff, you know, and she's chock full of movie quotes. She might say something like that if she were here – and if she could talk, you bastard! So that was for her."

He thought about what Suzanne had said to him back on Thursday, that she wasn't always as good a person as she should be. Well, neither was he. He leveled the speargun, aimed it, and held it steady. His hands weren't shaking at all.

"And so is this," he said.

Mario tried to charge him then, but he didn't make it. Ketch pulled the trigger and the spear found its mark, dead center of Mario's chest. Mario collapsed to his knees and ineffectually flailed at the embedded shaft with an astonished look on his face, then toppled over on his side.

Ketch went to Mario and knelt beside him. He calmly set the speargun down next to Mario's prone body. A line ran from the gun to the spear, so he couldn't do much else with the gun unless he wanted to try to disconnect it or pull the spear out. Maybe he'd just leave it here.

The compressor was still chugging away nearby. But despite that, Ketch thought he could hear some wheezing coming from the body. Mario's eyes were open, but that didn't necessarily mean anything. Ketch found a faint pulse when he checked, though, so he took hold of the barbed shaft, pushed it in a little more, and twisted it around some. When he checked again, Mario was silent and there was no longer a pulse.

There was another tarp nearby, so he draped it

over the body. Then he dropped a couple of the lead weights he'd seen onto the tarp and went into the cabin. He heard another muffled shout and followed the sound down into the berth.

Bean was sitting on the floor with his hands bound behind his back around a post. A swath of duct tape covered his mouth. Ketch knelt before the boy and started peeling the tape away as gently as he could.

"Papa!" Bean blurted, and then he start sobbing.

"It's okay, son, I've got you, you're safe now," Ketch said, hugging him. Tears were streaming down his own cheeks now as well, but he paid them no mind. "It's okay now, you're okay," he said. He finished pulling the tape off, then reached around behind Bean and began untying his hands.

"I was scared, Papa!" Bean wailed. "I was scared!"

"I know, but you're okay now, it's okay..." Ketch stayed with him and kept hugging him and murmuring to him until he'd calmed down some.

"Are the bad guys gone?" Bean was finally able to ask between sniffles and hiccups.

"Yes, they're all gone. It's just you and me now." He'd better let everyone know what had happened, Ketch thought. The Captain had probably told the others what he was up to and then worn a hole in his decking, fond of pacing as he was. "Bean," he said, "we have to tell the Captain to come and get us now. How would you like to call him on the radio? I'll show you how to do it." That might help take the boy's mind off of his ordeal, he hoped, or at least be a start in that direction. The sooner his world returned to normal the better it'd be for him, he figured.

They went up into the cabin, and Ketch taught Bean how to turn on the radio and tune it to their special channel. Then he gave the boy some more basic instructions and handed him the microphone.

"Goonies to Captain, Goonies to Captain, over," Bean said. They'd neglected to establish a nickname for either of the kidnappers' boats, and that was the best one Ketch could come up with on the spur of the moment. The boy had found that old *Goonies* movie enthralling when they'd watched it a while back – and after all, there was treasure and perhaps even a pirate ship right below them.

"Bean, is that you?" the Captain's voice blared over the speaker. He was apparently abandoning protocol now.

"This is Bean! And Papa!" the boy announced, also forgetting he wasn't supposed to use his real name. Ketch whispered a reminder to him. "Come and get us! Over!"

"Well, thank the Lord!" the Captain exclaimed. "I'll be right there, out."

"Thank you, Bean, good job," Ketch said. He took over at the radio then, but he kept an arm around the boy. There was still a box of bombs here in the cabin – and now he noticed there was a handgun resting on a nearby bench. It was a good thing he hadn't been fool enough to let Mario get out of his sight.

He figured Len and Kelsey were also listening in (they should be, anyway), and he no longer cared if anyone else was, so he dispensed with protocol as well.

"Ketch here," he said. "Bean and I are both safe and the site is secured. Tibbid, retrieve Lookout and meet us in Ocracoke, over."

"Roger that, good work Ketch, out!" came in then from Len, and "Headin' down to the dock, congratulations, out," from Kelsey.

"Bean," Ketch said, "do you want to sign off? Do you remember how to do that? Here..."

Bean took the mike and pressed the button. "Goonies – out!" he said, with a big smile on his tear-streaked face.

~ T h i r t e e n ~

Luck can come in many forms.

*K*etch and Bean went out on deck to wait for the *Minnow*. There was no life jacket that would fit Bean, so Ketch kept a close eye on him, as well as at least a hand most of the time. He also scanned the waters around the boat in the extremely unlikely event that one or both of the hookah divers surfaced. It didn't hurt to be cautious. If either of them did come up, he knew where Mario's handgun was.

"Is that your boat, Papa?" Bean asked, referring to the smaller boat tethered alongside them.

"No, Len has my boat right now. Do you remember Len? He's a friend of mine. He's picking up Kelsey, a lady who's another friend. We were all out looking for you tonight."

Bean looked puzzled. "How did you get here?" he said.

"I swam here from the Captain's boat. My diving gear is hanging on the anchor line. I'll have to get it before we leave."

"You swimmed all the way here, in the ocean?" Bean sounded impressed. Then he changed tack, as kids do. "What's that?" he asked, pointing to the machine still chugging under its tarp.

"There's a compressor under there. It gives air to divers. But that one isn't working right." Neither was the boy's grammar, as usual, but he'd come around in time. He didn't need to be corrected on this particular night.

"Are there divers? Where are they?" Bean demanded. He sounded alarmed.

"They're at the bottom of the ocean," Ketch said. "I don't think they're coming back, so don't worry."

"Did you kill them?" Bean asked.

Ketch considered before answering. He decided he wouldn't lie to the boy. "I think so, yes."

Bean just nodded. "What's under that one?" he then inquired, pointing to the other tarp. "Is that a speargun? Can I see it?"

Ketch saw that the tarp wasn't completely covering the speargun. He also saw a bare foot sticking out from under the tarp. "No, we'll leave that where it is," he said.

"Is there a bad guy under there?" So the boy must have seen the foot as well. He looked up at Ketch with wide eyes. "You shooted him? With a *spear*?"

"Yes," Ketch said. He wasn't proud of that fact, exactly, but he was pleased that he hadn't choked under pressure, as he might have years ago – and most of all that Bean was safe now, whatever the cost. He just hoped the boy wouldn't be irreparably damaged by all this. Maybe if he tried to explain a little more...

"Bean," he began, "I hope you understand that it's not right to hurt people. But these people were bad, and I had to do it so I could rescue you." Well, that might not be the whole truth – but it was enough truth for now. The boy didn't need to know all the sordid details. "Do you understand?"

"Yes, Papa," Bean answered, looking thoughtful. "Papa, are you a superhero, like Aquaman in the Justice League?" That was another cartoon Ketch had let him watch.

"What? No, son, I'm not a superhero." Well, the boy didn't seem to be too traumatized thus far. Was he already becoming desensitized to real-world violence by TV and video games? Something to think more about later... In any case, maybe that was enough explaining for now and keeping things light was a better strategy here in the moment.

"But I do have a superpower," Ketch said. "Do you want to see it?" The boy nodded eagerly. "Okay then, watch this." Ketch sat down on the deck. "I'm even shorter than you now, aren't I? But when I stand up," he said, rising dramatically to his feet again, "I get really, really tall. See?"

Bean looked confused for a moment, and then he grinned. "Silly Papa," he chided. Then he got serious again. "Papa, why did the bad guys take me?"

"Well, Kari and I found some gold yesterday when we went diving here, and they wanted me to give it to them."

That grabbed the boy's interest. "You found Peter Painter's treasure?"

"Maybe. There are two shipwrecks down there,

and one of them is an old wooden ship."

"Wow, now we have treasure! Can I have some?"

"No, I'm sorry, but I'm afraid not. We can't take it home."

"Why?" Bean asked, sounding disappointed.

"I'll tell you later. Here comes the Captain," Ketch said. He could finally hear the *Minnow*'s engines now, and he saw that her running lights were on. There weren't any fenders in plain sight on either of the kidnappers' boats, but then he saw that the Captain had already put some out on the *Minnow*. He'd had to haul anchor on his own, too, Ketch remembered. So that was why it had taken him as long to get here as it had.

When the *Minnow* got close enough, the Captain put her in neutral and threw Ketch a mooring line. Then the Captain nudged her forward a little more, and Ketch pulled her in close enough to bump the small boat that had picked up the ransom out of the way a bit. Then he cleated the line to Mario's boat.

Bean said he was starving, so Ketch passed him across the gunwales to the Captain. Had Mario not fed the boy in the time he'd had him? The Captain slipped a child-sized life jacket onto him, then took him into the cabin to show him where the snacks and drinks were. While he was doing that, Ketch pulled up the gear he'd tied to the stern anchor line of Mario's boat. He'd never known the actual name of this boat, and the lettering on the stern was upside-down to him and too faded to decipher in the semi-dark.

Then he went to the compressor and yanked on one of the hoses. It wouldn't come up, so he tugged harder. It finally went slack, and when he pulled it up he saw that it had been severed. It must have gotten snagged on something in or on the wreck. The second hose came easily, with the regulator still attached at the end of it. He watched out over the water for another minute or so, but nothing disturbed the surface as far as he could see in any direction. Well, that settled that then, he thought. Those two weren't coming back.

The Captain came out on deck. As quietly as possible, Ketch summarized what had happened here while he passed his gear over to him piece by piece.

"You lost my gun?" the Captain said. "Dang! I got that gun for my ex-wife, you know."

"Yes, I know, and it was the best trade you ever made," Ketch said, stealing the Captain's punchline. He'd heard that one before. "I could do a bounce dive and look around a little for it if you want me to."

"Nah, forget about it, it's too dark down there. I can get another one sometime. You done enough for one night." The Captain shook his head. "I can't believe you just went on ahead anyways after you dropped that gun. Lordy!"

When he was done transferring his gear to the Captain, Ketch took a good look around to see if he'd forgotten anything. He considered turning on the running lights on the kidnappers' boats, but decided against it. The moon would be waxing to full in the coming days and he doubted there'd be any nighttime boat traffic in this vicinity anyway, so there shouldn't be any accidental collisions. And he didn't want to draw attention to the boats until he'd spoken with Dan.

"All right, Captain," he said then. "There's just one more thing I have to do before we go."

"Now what?" the Captain said. "Good Christ, hadn't enough already happened today to gimme about five heart attacks?"

"Don't worry, it's not dangerous." Ketch went to where Kari's gear bag sat on the deck of Mario's boat. He opened it and counted ten gold bars. Good, they were all there. But wait, he *had* almost forgotten something.

"Captain," he called, "please pass me back that BCD."

"What the hell for?" the Captain asked, but then he popped the buckles, lifted the BCD away from the now-racked tank, and tossed it across to Ketch.

Without answering, Ketch toted the BCD over to the gear bag. He removed the gold coins that were still in the pocket of the BCD where he'd put them earlier and sprinkled them into the gear bag among the gold bars. Then he retrieved Kari's phone from its hiding place, zipped the bag shut, and dropped the bag over the port gunwale into the water.

He climbed across the starboard gunwale and joined the Captain on the deck of the *Minnow*. "Okay, now we can go," he said.

The Captain stared at him disbelievingly. "Did you just do what I think you did? Did you throw all that gold you brung up back in the ocean?"

"Yes."

"Well, why the hell did you go and do that?"

"It's caused me nothing but trouble," Ketch said. "Maybe the Sea Hag was right and the ghosts of Portsmouth need it more than I do for some reason."

"Are you serious? You ain't really buyin' into all that foolishness now, are you?"

Ketch shrugged. "I figured it couldn't hurt. I don't want to take any more chances. Everyone who's gone down there and tried to take that gold is dead now, you know, except for me and maybe Kari."

And last he'd heard, it had sounded like she'd probably be dead soon, too. He didn't definitively know what his 'port fee' would entail if he were to try to keep any of the gold, but based on what the Sea Hag had told him, he had a feeling that the price would be unacceptably steep and that he might already be on the verge of paying it. He had no clue what ghostly protocol he'd violated in the first place, but according to the Sea Hag that no longer mattered. 'Hain't but one way to pay naow', he remembered she'd warned – and if there was any chance of preventing that fee from being collected, he'd take it, even if he was just being silly.

"I thought you wasn't superstitious," the Captain quietly remarked, as if he'd been listening in on Ketch's thoughts.

Ketch just looked at him. He knew he didn't have to explain himself to the best friend he'd ever had, which was good since he didn't feel like trying to. "You wouldn't happen to have a spare beer on board this old tub, would you?" he said.

"Does a one-legged duck swim around in circles?" the Captain grinned. "A course I do! Untie us and I'll dig some out for you."

"Thanks. I need to get this wetsuit off, too."

"All right then. Hey, wait a minute, though – you forgot to shut that compressor down back there."

"I didn't forget. It's probably hot now, so I decided not to fool with it. It'll run out of gas after a while."

Ketch took in the line that connected the *Minnow* to Mario's boat and coiled and stowed it. Then he sat down on a locker to rest a bit and soak in the scene around him.

Two forlorn boats in the wan moonlight, soon to be abandoned in the middle of nowhere, one with its captain lying dead on the deck with a spear sticking out of his chest... The night ocean surrounding them all, relatively calm at the surface but undoubtedly teeming with unseen nocturnal activity below... The water almost indistinguishable from the sky above, out beyond the range of the *Minnow*'s lights... No land in sight...

It might have been possible to make out Portsmouth Island in the distance had there been any light there. He remembered reading an article about the island of Sark, in the Channel Islands south of England, which had recently been officially designated the world's first Dark Sky Island. There'd been dark sky zones and preserves here and there for a long time, usually to facilitate astronomical observation, but never an entire island. Like Sark, whose six hundred inhabitants had banned cars and public lighting at night, Portsmouth could perhaps qualify for this distinction. But there was no one there to submit an application.

Ketch got up to go into the cabin and change back into his clothes. When he went inside, he found a six-pack resting on one bench and Bean fast asleep on the other. It looked like the Captain had put a pillow from his berth under the boy's head and covered him with a blanket. Bean must have lain down and passed out right after he'd gotten some food in him. It was way past his normal bedtime – not to mention all he'd been through today – so Ketch wasn't surprised.

The *Minnow*'s engines, which had been idling, changed pitch and Ketch felt the boat start to move. The Captain must be up on the flying bridge. Ketch started peeling his wetsuit off. After he got dressed, he'd give Suzanne a call as soon as he could get a signal. But not the Coast Guard – that hoopla could wait until he'd had a chance to talk with Dan first.

What else did he need to do now, besides the obvious things like seeing to the dogs and his gear and so on? He started making one of his mental to-do lists.

He should call Pauline and see how Kari was doing, of course. He'd also need to tell her what had happened at his end today, but with any luck maybe he could talk to both her and Dan about that at the same time. And maybe he'd wait to do that when he drove up to Norfolk, which he wanted to do as soon as he'd caught a little shuteye. It wasn't really necessary for him to call Dan tonight, since those boats wouldn't be going anywhere and he didn't much care how badly Mario's body might rot in the meantime. Oh, and he should call off the Amber Alert at some point. Maybe Dan would take care of that for him.

And then later on when he had time, he should tell the CSFCP group, and especially Bob and RAM, what he'd learned about the corruption at the Cape Point condo site. The almighty environmentalists (well, some of them anyway) in league with organized crime? And not only breaking the law, but also subverting the self-righteous principles they publicly professed to believe in and were trying to force everyone else to follow, all to make a buck? They were going to love that.

And then he should call that reporter, Cheryl. He certainly had a tale to tell her now, though he figured he'd have to omit certain details. Dan would advise him on that. He wouldn't be surprised if the newspaper coverage and the certain outrage of the CSFCP, the OBPA, and the other access preservation organizations led to another lawsuit against the environmentalists. Maybe all that publicity would finally start eroding away some of the Teflon those environmental groups, in particular the Audubon Society, had seemed to be coated with thus far.

He should also think about finding ways to reward his friends for helping him so selflessly during this trying time. He wasn't sure exactly how to go about doing that, except maybe in Kelsey's case.

He knew her father had transferred ownership of their modest Ocracoke cottage to her before he'd died, and that she'd lived there since childhood. She didn't want to sell it, but she'd mentioned that keeping up with the payments was a burden. So there must still be a mortgage. That was probably why she'd been driving a clunker and hadn't bought another one. Well, she could keep the Outback a while longer if she wanted to – and if it was a thirty-year mortgage there shouldn't be that much principal left on it, especially given the lower property values back when it had started. So maybe he could pay that off for her, if she wasn't too proud to accept his help.

As for the others – well, he'd already bought them enough stuff, so he supposed he'd have to get creative there.

When Ketch put his shorts back on, he realized he still had Sally's rag doll, the one the Sea Hag had given to the kids, in one of his cargo pockets. Who knows, maybe that was why his luck hadn't run out tonight and he hadn't ended up like Mario and the divers. He removed it and tucked it under the blanket next to the unconscious boy. Maybe it would protect Bean from any further mishaps tonight, he thought, and thus guarantee them all safe passage home. Then he put the brakes on his superstitious daydreaming and carried two cans of beer up to the flying bridge.

"I talked to Len on the radio before," the Captain said when Ketch had joined him there. "He's nervous about drivin' your boat back up to Avon all alone in the dark, says he's afraid he might a used up all his luck rammin' around the inlet tonight. So he's gonna ron-day-voo with us just outside the harbor so's we can tow her back." He laughed. "I guess he ain't worried 'bout *my* boat runnin' aground!"

"Give him a break," Ketch said. "He's helped a lot. After that runaround we gave him with those witches last fall, I thought we might never see him again."

The Captain grunted. "You're right, seems like

he's grown a set since then."

"I assume he'll put Kelsey ashore before he joins us?" If so, that'd be a little disappointing. Ketch had hoped he'd have a chance to at least thank her again and tell her she could keep the car for a while. So that was another call he'd have to make... Strangely, though she'd only been with him since yesterday, he'd gotten used to having her around and he realized he was going to miss her. But Ocracoke wasn't that far away, and he had Bean – and Jack and Chuck, of course, and the Captain and Suzanne and Henry and his other Avon friends. So he'd only be alone at night.

"Yeah, he said that was what he'd do." The Captain took the beer Ketch proffered him and opened it. "I know you said there weren't nothin' goin' on between y'all – but you kinda like her, ain't that right?"

"Well... Yes, I do, but I'm not quite sure in what way. Not in the way you're thinking, though. She's too young."

"You think so? I don't much care 'bout that myself. Look at what's-his-name, that actor. Warren Beatty and his wife. He's twenty-some years older'n her and they been together a long time. And she's an actor, too, so she ain't no gold-digger. I know some regular folks like that too. And that girl sure seems to of latched on to you. Or does she cook and houseclean and give massages for everybody?"

"Maybe I remind her of her father."

"I don't know 'bout that, that ain't how it looked to me." The Captain chuckled. "Nor to Suzanne, I don't think. Seemed to me she didn't much like her hangin' around. I s'pose that one there might be a better match for you, though, and the kids all get along."

"Well, I like her, too – but why are you trying to play matchmaker all of a sudden? This is all pointless as long as Kari's still around, and I think it's morbid and disrespectful." And shameful on his part that he'd allowed the conversation to get this far, which was really what he was upset about.

"Awright, awright, I hear ya. Don't go gettin' testy on me, I was just jawin'."

"I know," Ketch apologized. "I'm sorry. I'm just worried about her."

"I know you are. And hey, I'm sorry too. I know I can be a tactless son of a bitch sometimes."

"Okay, so we're both sorry. Still friends?"

"A course!" the Captain acknowledged with a grin.

They sipped at their beers in companionable silence for a while, and then Ketch went back down to check on Bean and pack up his diving gear. The boy was still sound asleep, and he finished packing just as they pulled up outside Silver Lake in Ocracoke.

Len shortly joined them then, and they tied the *TBD* off behind the *Minnow* and headed north up the sound to Avon. The Captain regaled Len with Ketch's tale of derring-do up on the flying bridge while Ketch gave Suzanne a call below. Bean remained dead to the world throughout it all.

Suzanne was relieved and not at all concerned about the lateness of the hour. Ketch briefly summarized the night's events, promised to tell her more later, and then told her he'd like to take Bean to Norfolk with him the following day to visit Kari. When he started to ask her if she or Henry would mind taking care of the dogs yet again, she broke in.

"Ketch?" she said. "Excuse me for interrupting, but do you really want to drag him all the way up there, and do you really want him to see her like that? I think you should leave him with me. I'll have the dogs anyway, and I think he'd be better off just relaxing after his ordeal and playing with Sally, don't you?" She paused and then added, "If you still trust me to take care of him, that is."

"Of course I do," Ketch reassured her. "But I hate to keep asking you for favors. You have your work to keep up with, and I'm taking up too much of your time."

"Don't worry about that, I can manage. I have kids of my own, too, and I honestly don't mind. Bean will keep Sally occupied, and Henry can help." She paused again. "And Ketch? I'm here for you, in case you didn't already know that. If you need anything from me, all you have to do is ask."

He didn't know what he'd done to deserve the abundance of kindness and generosity his friends were showering him with these days, nor how he'd managed to find such good friends in the first place, and he was momentarily overcome. "Thank you, Suzanne," he finally said. "I'll bring him over tomorrow when I'm ready to leave."

After he'd hung up with her, he went back up to the flying bridge with another can of beer. He knew the other two already had some. It was too crowded up there now for him to stay long, but he wanted to thank Len again for his help.

"You're welcome, Ketch," Len said. "Man, sounds like that was some time you had over on that boat, even better'n the time I was havin'," he then commented with his trademark goofy grin. "It's like *déjà vu* all over again, ain't it? Like with them witches'n all, I mean. You sure know how to throw a party, that's all I got to say!"

"Well, I don't think there will be any more parties like that from now on," Ketch said. "But you're always welcome to come to any conventional ones I might throw."

Ketch went back below after that and dozed a bit in the cabin along with Bean, who continued to sleep soundly all the way back to Avon. When they arrived at the boatyard, Len and the Captain moored the *TBD* for him in her usual spot alongside the *Port Starbird* while he roused Bean enough to walk him down from the *Minnow* and into the houseboat. He changed the groggy child into pajamas, washed him up some in the bathroom, and then steered him to his bedroom – where he promptly went right back to sleep in the fresh bed Kelsey had made up for him.

When Ketch came back out on deck, he saw that his gear bag, backpack, and coolers were just outside the cabin door. He waved to Len and the Captain, who were now tiredly shuffling off to their own accommodations, then carried his bags inside. He'd deal with their contents, as well as the coolers, in the morning, he decided. Right now, all he wanted was a quick shower and his own bed.

He got about six hours of sleep in before his phone rang. That wasn't too bad. He could have used more, but he had a lot to do today. He rolled over, checked to see who was calling, and answered immediately.

"Kelsey?" he said. "Good morning."

"Good mornin', Ketch," she said. "Did I wake you up? I'm sorry."

"That's okay," he yawned. "I needed to get up anyway. What's up?"

As was typical with her, she came straight to the point. "There were some explosions and a big fireball out on the ocean durin' the night. I figured you probably hadn't heard about it yet, so that's why I called."

"Oh," Ketch said, suddenly more alert. "Where exactly did this happen?"

"From what I heard, it sounded like near where you were at, off Portsmouth Island. Did you do it?"

"Maybe," he said. Bean was still asleep, so Ketch took some time to tell her what had happened when he'd rescued the boy. "I suppose another boat could have run into them, but I think that's highly unlikely. I don't think there would have been explosions and a fireball in that case. I think the tarp on that compressor must have caught fire," he decided. "And then when the fire reached that crate of explosives, or the fuel tanks on the boats, or both..."

"Boom," Kelsey said, minus an exclamation point as usual. "Well, no harm done, I guess, since they were all dead anyway. When do you want your car back?"

He almost laughed. The Captain was right, this one was indeed 'something else'. He told her she could keep the car until further notice, but he didn't mention the business about paying off her house. He could discuss that with her the next time he saw her.

"You can still drive up here sometime when you get a chance, though," he said. "I'd like to see you, and you still haven't met Bean. Just call first, because I'm not sure what I'm doing yet about Norfolk. I might stay up there for a while, or maybe just drive up every so often, I don't know."

"You'd like to see me?" she said. "Okay. You can come here, too, sometime if you want. I'd like to meet Bean."

"Thanks, maybe I'll do that," Ketch said.

"There was somethin' else on the news. Did you hear about that barge?"

"No."

"Well, some barge got caught up in a freak

squall last night and ran aground off Cape Point. What was the name of that sand barge you saw?" Ketch told her. "Yep, that's the one. It got stuck real good, and it's still there. The Coast Guard had to rescue the crew."

"How about that? Serves them right." That had to be just a coincidence, he thought. The barge hadn't been anywhere near Portsmouth Island, not that its location should make a difference anyway. And they'd been stealing sand, not gold – well, except that there'd been some gold coins in some of that stolen sand.

After a short lull in the conversation, which other people might have filled with small talk, Ketch said, "Well, thanks for calling. And thank you again for all your help, Kelsey. I appreciate it."

"You're welcome. Bye," she said and hung up.

Well, this could cast a different light on things, Ketch thought. If those boats had been blown to smithereens, there might not be any evidence left that could end up biting him. Not that he was too worried about that anyway. He knew he could cover himself legally if he had to – a simple case of self-defense and/or reasonable force for Mario, and a not-uncommon accident on the part of the hookah divers, perhaps, after their air compressor had been left unattended. So should he just keep his mouth shut and leave well enough alone? He might not have to tell Dan, nor anyone else, anything at all if he so chose.

But no, he decided. Too many people already

knew what had happened. Plus, if he didn't come forward and the Coast Guard investigated the explosions (as they surely would) and found some potentially damning bit of evidence, that wouldn't look good for him. And finally, he wanted the Cape Point condo corruption he'd uncovered to be investigated, and he wanted the beach access preservation groups to be able to use that information. So yes, he would talk with Dan.

He wondered, too, if the explosions could have caused those shipwrecks to be covered over and buried again? If so, that wouldn't be a bad thing, either, from his point of view. It occurred to him then that if Mario's boat had exploded and sunk, then all of the gold that had come from the shipwrecks should now be back at the bottom of the ocean where it belonged – according to the Sea Hag, anyway. If there was anything to all that hoodoo, that should count for something.

Enough cogitating – he'd better get cracking. Bean would probably be up soon, and he had his gear and the coolers to take care of, and he should cover the *TBD*... And then later on he'd pay a visit to Suzanne and poor Jack and Chuck, who'd have to do without him for another day, and leave Bean there again... Though he agreed with Suzanne, it was probably best for him to stay there when he went back to Norfolk.

He wondered what he'd find when he got there... He'd have to give Pauline a call before he set out on the road. Even though he didn't want to tell her everything until he could talk to her and Dan together, he should let her know he was coming and see if anything had changed. Though what could have changed, for the better anyway, he didn't know.

But doctors didn't know everything either, so he could still hope. As Patricia had said near the end of *Joe Versus the Volcano*, one of his and Kari's favorite movies (despite what those party-pooper critics had thought of it), no one really knows anything for sure – you just take the leap and see what happens, and that's life. Well, he'd done all the leaping he could think of doing.

So now he'd just wait and see.

~ Fourteen ~

It's a sin not to hope.

*T*he beaches of Hatteras Island can sparkle at night. When you kick up sand as you shuffle along the shoreline, tiny marine plankton called dinoflagellates are disturbed and a chemical reaction causes them to become bioluminescent and emit a blueish-green light. It was just one of the small delights Ketch had come to appreciate here, and one that most non-natives were too oblivious to notice.

He called the kids over to him, told them to turn off their flashlights, and demonstrated the phenomenon for them. They were all out stalking the semi-translucent ghost crabs that came up from their burrows at night to forage on the beach – Ketch and Bean, Suzanne and her children, and of course Jack and Chuck, for whom this was great sport. Ketch had been wanting to do this with them again for a while now, and he was glad they'd finally found the time.

Jack seemed to be back to his old self now. And so far Bean, too, seemed none the worse for wear, which Ketch was grateful for. He hoped it would last. He thought he'd finally made peace with the fact that life was for the most part filled with annoyances, obligations, struggles, and outright misery at times, interspersed with fleeting oases of joy if you were lucky and open to them. Tonight was one of those ephemeral times.

But tomorrow morning he'd head back up to Norfolk again, for the last time. Kari's condition had marginally improved a few days after her surgeries, enough to be taken off the heart-lung machine, but she was still comatose and had been on a ventilator for the past six weeks. At Pauline's request, her meds were being withdrawn and tomorrow the ventilator would be switched off. He, Pauline, Kari's sister, and Dan would attend.

Ketch hadn't argued with Pauline over her decision – not that he had a legal leg to stand on in that regard anyway, since he and Kari weren't married. The brain scans hadn't been encouraging and Pauline didn't want her daughter to remain indefinitely in a vegetative state, and he couldn't disagree with that. That was no way to live. He certainly wouldn't want that for himself, and he knew Kari wouldn't want it for herself, either.

Dan wasn't officially 'family' yet, but he'd been there for Pauline every spare moment he could wrangle from his job. He'd been a big help to Ketch as well, guiding him through the inquiries that had followed after Bean's kidnapping and the boat disaster, calling off the Amber Alert, and discreetly smoothing the path from time to time where necessary. He didn't agree with everything Ketch had done, and there were certain aspects he'd wanted to know as little about as possible, but he'd still been invaluable. Ketch wouldn't be suffering any legal repercussions, and he had no problem with Dan being present on this solemn occasion.

He also wasn't suffering any emotional repercussions, he didn't think. The scales had been balanced, and he believed in what he'd done to help achieve that. His Banker friends, being of a similar mindset, supported him in that belief – and even Suzanne, herself only a recent émigré, seemed to have come to terms with it all. It was simply the kind of thing that was sometimes done hereabouts by those who still believed in old ways.

Not that he had any desire to go through anything like this again. He had Bean to consider now, and he'd resolved to try and temper the recklessly adventurous side of himself that had emerged over the past year. His virtual private eye shingle was coming down for good. If he wanted a new hobby, he'd have to find something else.

He already had plenty of other things to keep himself occupied, though. The ongoing beach access controversy wouldn't reach a final solution anytime soon, but it was gratifyingly beginning to blow up some in the Audubons' faces now. The thanks for that went largely to Dan's SBI investigations into the sand barge and building permit briberies at the Cape Point condo development, but Ketch's *Outer Banks Monitor* interview with Cheryl had also helped.

And then there was his new house, which was coming along nicely and should be finished soon (though an insurance settlement on the old house still hadn't materialized), and mating for the Captain on his fishing and diving charters, and raising Bean and teaching him the charms of the islands and the sea. There'd of course also be more mundane and unpleasant issues to be dealt with, such as the fate of the Sea Dog Scuba Center. But that was life. The point was, there'd be plenty for him to do without poking his nose into dark alleys from here on.

He supposed he could do some recreational diving, too, if he wanted to. That was still a fine hobby, though it held little appeal at the moment since he couldn't do it with Kari. But Kelsey was a certified diver... There was no way he'd return to Portsmouth for that purpose, though, even though he knew the location of some interesting shipwrecks. He'd reported that location to Dan and the Coast Guard, and he'd heard some underwater archaeologists from one of the colleges were taking an interest in the wrecks and petitioning to have that area marked off-limits to other divers. He hoped they'd remember to pay their port fee.

And after Kari was gone? Though Suzanne had been unfailingly virtuous since Bean's rescue, he knew she was available. Kelsey, too, had made it clear in her taciturn way during her last visit that she'd like to spend more time with him – but he still thought there couldn't be much future in that. The correct answer for him, at least for now, would be neither. And it was wrong to even think about such things at this time, so he'd stop.

And instead direct his attention to Bean, who was excitedly trying to show him a large whelk Sally had come upon in a pile of seaweed that had washed up from the surf. Sally had apparently decided to share it with Bean – but not the Sea Hag's doll, which she carried with her everywhere and was clutching even now.

Surprisingly for this locale, the shell appeared to be undamaged. "Well, kids," he said, "this one's a keeper, that's for sure. It's not even chipped." He knew low tide after a storm was the best time for shell hunting, and a storm had passed through just this afternoon, but this was still a lucky find.

"What kind is it?" Bean asked.

"This is a lightning whelk, I think... Yes, the opening is oriented to the left. If it was on the right, it'd be a knobbed whelk, and if it had grooved channels here instead of these spiky ones, it'd be a channel whelk." Ketch peeked inside the shell. "Uh-oh, it looks like your lightning whelk is occupied."

"Huh?" Bean said. "There's a animal in there?"

"Yes. The whelk is a kind of sea snail, and the snail makes the shell, and it's in there right now."

Sally wanted to see it, so Ketch pointed it out to her. "Ew!" she said when Bean dared her to touch it.

"Should I boil it up later, sir?" Henry asked, coming over to inspect Sally's find. "Is that the best way to clean it out?"

"Not in *my* kitchen," Suzanne said, laughing.

What Ketch really wanted to do was return the unfortunate creature to the sea, but he didn't want to take the shell away from Sally and Bean.

"I don't know," he said. "I've tried boiling them and freezing them in the past, and it was hard to get the shell clean either way. You know what works the best?" The others shook their heads. "Just leave it out in the back yard for a while. It'll be perfectly clean when the ants get done with it."

They agreed that was what they'd do. Ketch deposited the whelk in Suzanne's shell bag and they all continued on their way. When both they and the dogs had had enough beachcombing and crab-terrorizing for one night, they walked back to the Avon Pier, where they'd parked their vehicles.

Ketch declined Suzanne's invitation for a nightcap. He wanted to get an early start in the morning, he said. She just gave him a quiet hug, and then they went their separate ways.

When he and Bean got back to the boatyard, he dug out a couple of bones for Jack and Chuck, got the boy ready for bed, and read to him some more from his favorite book. He'd wondered at first if the boy would find *The Old Man and the Sea* boring, in which case Ketch would have been happy to revert back to the children's books – but he'd seemed interested then and still did now, so Ketch kept on with it.

After he'd tucked the boy in, Ketch went out on

deck with a beer and sat down in one of the chairs to enjoy a little more of the evening before turning in himself. There was a cooling sea breeze blowing in from across the island for a change, so the mosquitoes weren't much of a problem, and the marsh and the channel and the glistening sound beyond were mesmerizing in the moonlight. Still, he hadn't dissembled with Suzanne – he really would retire earlier than usual tonight.

But not quite as early as he'd anticipated. The Captain, who'd been puttering on the *Minnow*, saw that Ketch was out and ambled over to join him. Knowing it was Bean's bedtime, he refrained from announcing his presence beforehand this time and kept his voice down when he arrived. Will wonders never cease, Ketch thought.

"You got another one a them?" the Captain inquired, pointing at Ketch's bottle.

"You know where the fridge is," Ketch said. The Captain went silently into the galley and got himself a bottle.

"So tomorrow's the day, huh?" he said, dropping into the other deck chair.

"Yes. I'm leaving first thing in the morning, as soon as Bean gets up, and I'm turning in early tonight."

"You sure you don't want me to ride on up there with you?"

"No, that's okay," Ketch sighed. "There's no sense in making you go to two funerals."

"Aw now, don't be talkin' like that. You never

know what could happen. It ain't over 'til it's over, right? Ain't that what your hero, Yogi, used to say?"

"Yes. But as he also used to say, it's getting late early."

"That's the spirit! That's what I like best about you, you're always lookin' on the bright side a things." Ketch didn't smile. "Hey, I know, it don't look good. But speakin' a spirits, who knows, maybe that Sea Hag done put in a good word for you since you give back all that gold."

Ketch glanced sidelong at him. "You don't really believe that, and neither do I."

"Oh yeah? Why'd you go'n do it then?" Ketch didn't answer, so they just quietly drank for a while.

The Captain finished his first. "Well, I guess we'll see soon enough," he said. "I'm truly sorry, Ketch. Lemme know if you change your mind 'bout takin' me with you. I'm stayin' on the boat tonight." He stood up, clapped Ketch on the back, and headed off to the *Minnow*.

Ketch didn't change his mind. After getting a good night's sleep, he was up at the crack of dawn as usual. By the time Bean woke, he'd already taken the dogs out, fed them, and gotten dressed. He'd had a hard time deciding what to wear, as he'd never had to dress for this kind of occasion before and there was no one here who could help him with that. Finally acknowledging that he was probably the only one who really thought it was tasteful, he'd put his best Hawaiian shirt back in the closet and opted for a solid polo shirt and slacks.

Suzanne had told him to bring Bean over for breakfast, so he got the boy dressed and walked him and the dogs over to her place. It wasn't far, but he let Bean, who'd complained he was hungry, munch on a Pop Tart on the way. Now there was some good parenting, he thought, but he'd do better later.

The younger ones weren't fully aware of the significance of the day, but both Suzanne and Henry were appropriately somber when he let himself into their kitchen. Bean ran off with Sally and the dogs, either forgetting he hadn't really eaten or temporarily satisfied by the cold toaster pastry. Henry excused himself and went to keep an eye on the little ones, and Ketch and Suzanne were left alone in the kitchen.

"Well," Suzanne began. "I don't know what to say. 'Good luck' sounds cavalier, and 'I'm sorry' seems premature – and it might be *bad* luck as well."

"You don't have to say anything. You've said and done more than enough already." She nodded at that, and they settled for another silent hug.

"I'll call you when I'm ready to drive back," he said. "I don't know if it'll be tonight or tomorrow." Ketch hadn't packed an overnight bag for Bean, but he already had some clothes and a toothbrush here from previous stays and Suzanne had taken to keeping a store of dog food and treats.

"Okay," she said, and he took his leave.

Despite the reason for the trip – or perhaps because of it – Ketch found the drive up Highway 12 more soul-soothing than usual today, especially when he crossed the old Bonner Bridge over Oregon Inlet. Though it was taking him away from his island this morning, the stunning views of the sound and the ocean were as cathartic to him as always. The only thing that was better than crossing it in this direction, he reflected, was crossing it in the other.

When he got to the hospital, he parked and navigated his way to the ICU like a pro. He ought to know his way around, he thought, he'd been back and forth here enough times over the past few weeks. He was told Pauline and Dan had gone to the cafeteria, so he wended his way there next.

"Ketch! Thank you for comin'," Pauline said, getting up from their table to give him a quick hug and kiss. "I know Kari will appreciate you bein' there for her." She seemed to be remarkably composed, considering. But then, she'd had plenty of time to reconcile herself to the inevitable. "Kari's sister isn't here yet. When she gets here, we'll go up."

Dan and Pauline had coffees, so Ketch got himself a Diet Pepsi before sitting down with them. He'd thought he might be hungry, but he also thought eating something now might make him sick, so he'd passed on the apple fritter he'd been eyeing. He'd had this same kind of feeling before, he remembered, whenever he'd had to put down a beloved dog. Making an appointment with the vet to do something that final, and then keeping that appointment, had become exponentially more stressful to him as the time had approached – and he was starting to get that same panicky feeling now.

"So Ketch, what do you think?" Dan was saying. "Care to take a guess?"

"I'm sorry," Ketch apologized. "I'm afraid I wasn't listening." Pauline placed a hand over one of his, and that helped him calm down some and pay attention.

"I was just saying, you might be interested in who we found out has been pulling the strings with that Cape Point development and the shenanigans that have been going on there. The man behind the curtain, as it were."

"Yes?" Oh, he was supposed to make a guess. "Uh, someone from the Audubon Society?" he ventured.

Dan was amused by that. "You've really got it in for those people, haven't you? No, it's an old friend of yours. Well, not exactly a friend." When Ketch continued to stare blankly back at him, he said, "Bob Ingram!"

Well, that *was* interesting, Ketch thought in a detached way. The imprisoned developer who'd tried to take *Port Starbird* away from him last summer before the hurricane had... "Really, how about that?" he said, since he knew he was expected to say something.

"Yeah, that guy again! You know, between that business about killing his wife – plus his RICO racketeering convictions – and now this, that poor bastard might not ever get out of jail."

"Yes. Well, that's good," Ketch distractedly replied. It looked like Kari's sister had arrived, and Dan and Pauline were greeting her and pushing their chairs back. When they stood, he followed suit and trailed behind them in a fog as they made their way back to the ICU.

There was a doctor at Kari's bedside when they arrived there, and a nurse and a clergyman of some kind. No one seemed surprised to see him, so they must have solicited his services. Kari had never gone to church in the time he'd known her, and Ketch had forgotten which church her family belonged to. He guessed it didn't much matter.

The clergyman was saying something now, but the words weren't registering with Ketch. He was feeling flushed and a little wobbly on his feet. He looked around for a chair or something else he could sit on. But he didn't want to appear rude, so he found a bare patch of wall he could lean on instead.

First Dan, and then the sister (he couldn't remember her name), went to Kari and held one of her hands. They each spoke some words as well, though Ketch couldn't make them out through the blood that was now pounding in his ears like an angry surf.

It appeared it was his turn next after that, but his feet didn't want to move. Noticing that he was having trouble, Pauline went to him and gently guided him to Kari's bedside. He took one of Kari's hands in both of his and gazed down at her for he didn't know how long. He knew he should say something, but he couldn't. After what he supposed was a decent interval, Dan steered him back to his wall and Pauline took his place at Kari's side.

Before he knew what was happening, someone turned off the ventilator and it was over. Shortly after that alarms started going off in his head, but then he realized it was just the monitors sounding their death knell. He lowered himself to the floor beside the wall he'd been leaning on and sat there with his elbows on his knees and his face in his hands.

No one bothered him. After perhaps a minute or so, he became peripherally aware of people muttering over by Kari's bed. The voices started getting louder, and then Pauline spoke up above the others.

"I'm not imagining it! I swear, I saw her hand move!" she was saying. "Get that doctor back in here!" she commanded the nurse.

Ketch was on his feet and at Pauline's side in a flash. Dan and the sister stood nearby, looking confused and concerned.

"Pauline," Dan started to say, "I honestly don't

think —"

He was interrupted by a wheezing sound coming from the bed. They all turned toward the source of it and watched as Kari's eyelids fluttered. Then her eyes opened fully and rapidly widened as she tried unsuccessfully to say something.

The doctor came in, saw what was happening, and quickly examined Kari. "Her tracheostomy tube has a cuff, a balloon, on it, which is in her trachea," he explained while he worked. "It's filled with air, which makes her exhale into the tube and prevents air from reaching her vocal cords. Since she appears to be conscious now and breathing on her own," he said wonderingly, "I'm going to deflate the cuff. Then she should be able to make some sounds."

When he'd deflated it, he raised his voice and said, "Kari, can you hear me?" She nodded, then slowly raised a hand and pointed to her right ear. "Okay, one ear's working, that's a good start. Kari, if you want to talk, you'll have to take a deep breath and then exhale forcefully while you speak. Do you understand?" She nodded again, and inhaled deeply.

"Mama," she croaked on the first exhalation, faintly but discernably.

"Oh baby, I'm here!" Pauline said. She knelt and took one of Kari's hands and began tearfully kissing it. "Thank God!" she said.

"Sonuva... bitch... gimme... a drink," Kari managed to get out on subsequent exhalations.

"She's learning fast," the doctor said. "Nurse, a sippy cup please, stat."

"Ketch," Kari wheezed next, after she'd caught her breath.

He desperately wanted to crush her in an exuberant embrace, but he knew better than that. So instead he just ran a hand through her hair. He found he could speak now, despite the large lump in his throat.

"I'm here," he said into her good ear. "How are you feeling?"

The nurse returned with her water then, and she took a sip before replying. "You really... aren't... that bright... are you?" she eked out, and then smiled wanly up at him. "I feel... like crap," she then tacked on.

He almost laughed aloud at that, but settled for smiling back. "I missed you too, and I know," he said, kissing her forehead. "But you're back now." At least they'd done a tracheotomy on her, which he'd read was actually more comfortable for long-term ventilation than nasal or laryngeal intubation. If she'd had to deal with either of those right now, she'd have felt even worse.

"You saved... me," she said next, a tear trickling down one cheek. "You... know what."

"Yes, and me, too," he said. He kept on smiling at her and stroking her hair while he half-listened to the other conversations taking place elsewhere in the room.

"This is amazing," the doctor was saying. "I've

never personally seen anything like this before. All of the diagnostics were indicating severe brain damage. The functional MRI we just did showed no brain activity in response to external stimuli, and she flatlined when we turned off the ventilator."

"So what happens now, Doctor?" Ketch heard Pauline ask.

"Well, I'll remove her cannula, but I'm going to keep a nasal mask on her for a while to be safe. She's not completely out of the woods yet by any means, and she'll have to stay here a good while longer. But this is certainly a tremendous improvement." The doctor looked toward the clergyman standing in the corner. "In fact, I think it might qualify as a miracle. What do you think, Reverend?"

"It could be. The Lord works in mysterious ways," the clergyman solemnly intoned.

Kari must have been listening, too. "No... Sea Hag..." she whispered to Ketch, and then she winked at him and closed her eyes.

She was probably exhausted from the effort of trying to speak. The doctor noticed and sent the nurse off to fetch a nasal mask. Ketch imagined she'd have to wear that whenever there was a chance she might fall asleep. But it wasn't invasive, so that would be an improvement.

He wondered what she'd meant by that last remark... Had the Sea Hag paid Kari a visit in her dreams? Did she also work in mysterious ways?

What, if anything, had Kari seen when she'd flatlined?

She might have some interesting things to tell him, Ketch thought, and he certainly had a lot to tell her. Whether or not there had in fact been some brain damage, and what faculties she might have lost as a result, remained to be seen. She seemed all right so far, though. He knew she still had a long road ahead, there might be pitfalls along the way, and nothing was guaranteed.

But nothing ever was – and now, thanks to whomever, they at least had some more time.

~ ~ ~

Afterword

Save a Bird, Kill an Island?

Life has never been easy for the inhabitants of the Outer Banks. Over time, the challenging environment, the storms, and the isolation hardened them into a resourceful people who survived by salvaging shipwrecks, building boats, fishing, and doing whatever else they could think of to get by. But the natural beauty, peacefulness, and wild freedom of these islands made it all worthwhile, and most of the residents had no desire to live anywhere else. That still holds true today – just ask some long-time locals.

Times have of course changed, and today's islanders rely heavily on beach-related tourism and world-class recreational fishing to make their livings. Paradoxically, there's considerably less modern development on Hatteras and Ocracoke Islands than in many other coastal areas, due to the appropriation of much of their acreage for the Cape Hatteras National Seashore. But being able to experience the islands in a near-pristine state and fish the abundant waters are two big reasons why people visit and vacation there. So although it didn't seem so at first to many, being under the purview of the National Park Service turned out to be largely a blessing.

Until recently, that is. Today's islanders are

facing another crisis, an economic one brought on by some overzealous conservation efforts initially spurred by an endangered seabird called the piping plover. Beaches are being closed to pedestrians as well as vehicles, tourist dollars are evaporating, and local businesses are being severely impacted.

Ketch's involvement with the fictional organization Common Sense For Cape Point (CSFCP) in *The Port Fee* only scratches the surface of this important issue. If you'd like to learn more about how the human habitats on these islands are being threatened along with those of other creatures, please follow the links below when you have some spare time.

The first one is a short documentary film from the pro-beach access point of view, the second one is a brief summary of the history and goals of the Outer Banks Preservation Association (OBPA), and the third one leads to resources that provide a complete chronology of the issue from both sides.

http://bit.ly/1XQAppW

http://bit.ly/229dXON

http://bit.ly/1TcYpEJ

There are numerous other related resources out there online, including more videos, but the above links should be enough to get you started.

A final word – if you think this issue isn't pertinent to you because you live or vacation somewhere else, please keep in mind that these extreme conservation policies appear to be becoming a national trend. The Outer Banks isn't the first place in the country where something like this has happened, and it probably won't be the last.

Thanks for your attention!

Garrett

About the Author

Garrett lives in upstate New York, where he and his wife serve as the housekeeping staff for two rather spoiled dogs. He has degrees in biology and computer science. After a career that ranged from testing experimental drugs (not on himself!) to developing computer operating system software, he decided to retire from the real world and try his hand at writing fiction.

Garrett lived in coastal North Carolina for a while some years back, and the current focus of his writing is a place that's very special to him, the Outer Banks region of North Carolina. THE PORT FEE is his third novel.

In addition to being a writer, Garrett is a so-so tennis player and sometime scuba diver. He also plays guitar and writes songs from time to time. If you'd like to hear some bad recordings of original music that's untainted by success, visit his web site at:

www.GarrettDennis.com

While you're there, sign up for his reading list to receive updates and news of special offers.

You can also visit Garrett Dennis on **Facebook** at:
www.facebook.com/garrdenn

On Facebook, you can join his **PORT STARBIRD** fan group and LIKE his **Author Garrett Dennis** page.

You can also follow him on **Twitter:**
Garrett Dennis @PortStarbird

There's an Amazon author page for Garrett at:
www.amazon.com/author/garrettdennis

and you can follow him there as well.

You can reach Garrett via e-mail at:
GarrettDennis.Author@gmail.com

If you enjoyed this book, you might also enjoy Ketch's previous adventures:

And you can pick up this additional short tale FREE at Garrett's web site or wherever e-books are sold:

Keep a weather eye out for the next Storm Ketchum Adventure!

Thanks for reading this book. If you have time, please consider taking a few minutes to post a review at Amazon and/or Goodreads. Reviews help increase an independently published book's visibility, and the author would greatly appreciate it.

Made in the USA
Middletown, DE
16 September 2017